BLACK WATER

ROSEMARY McCRACKEN

Rosemary McCracken

BLACK WATER
A Pat Tierney Mystery - Book 2

http://www.rosemarymccracken.com

FIRST EDITION TRADE PAPERBACK

Imajin Books - http://www.imajinbooks.com

May 24, 2013

ISBN: 978-1-927792-02-5

Cover designed by Ryan Doan - www.ryandoan.com

In memory of my late mother-in-law, Helen Piwowarczyk. A true story she told is at the heart of *Black Water*.

Acknowledgements

Many people have made *Black Water* possible. My deepest thanks go to my husband, Ed Piwowarczyk, my first editor and biggest supporter. I am grateful for his editing skills as well as his patience and forbearance. It's not easy living with a writer.

Thank you, fellow members of my writers' circle—Catherine Dunphy, Madeleine Harris-Callway, Lynne Murphy, Joan O'Callaghan and Sylvia Warsh—who provided deadlines and valuable insights. And another round of applause to Catherine Dunphy, for addressing the "big picture."

The title, *Black Water*, was suggested by Gail and Ted Bowen. Over the past several years, Gail Bowen, author of the Joanne Kilbourn mystery series, has provided excellent advice.

Thanks to authors Rosemary Aubert, Maureen Jennings and Dorothy McIntosh for their encouragement and support.

Crime Writers of Canada and Sisters in Crime Toronto have provided years of nurturing. Organizations like these are instrumental in furthering writers' careers.

Members of Canada's financial services industry helped me understand the important work they do and shared their enthusiasm for it. *Investment Executive* and *Insurance & Investment Journal*, two industry trade publications, provided further opportunities to meet financial professionals and discuss the issues that matter to them.

Thanks to Rebecca Weeks of the Midwifery Services of Haliburton-Bancroft.

Special thanks go to Imajin Books' publisher Cheryl Tardif and her team for bringing the Pat Tierney books to readers.

And a warm thank-you to my wonderful readers who have told me how much they enjoyed *Safe Harbor* and want to read more about Pat Tierney. You are the people who make everything worthwhile!

Black Water is set is in an imaginary part of Ontario cottage country that bears a strong resemblance to the real Haliburton Highlands. None of the Haliburton Highlands' residents appear in this book.

PROLOGUE

I killed her sister. Can she forgive me?

Lyle gripped the wheel of the black minivan. Beside him, Ross was yakking about the AA meeting they'd just attended.

Will she help me?

A thaw earlier that week had left the highway clear, but the temperature had plummeted the night before. The minivan's heater was cranked up full blast.

"Crazy weather," Ross said. "One day, you figure it's time to dig out the summer clothes, next day it's colder than a witch's tit. Must be all that global warming crap."

Lyle sneezed and reached for a tissue in the box on his lap.

"Bless you," Ross said.

"Fine thing to come down with a cold today," Lyle grumbled.

"Yeah, like the missus was sayin'..."

Lyle tuned out Ross as they approached Braeloch. *Told the Collins girl I was sorry. But that weren't enough for her. Wouldn't let it be. Told her I'd sic the law on her. She backed off then.*

Lyle pulled up in front of Ross's bungalow. "Here you go."

"Thanks. Be seein' you next week, then." Ross stepped out the van and gave a wave. "Take care of that cold."

Lyle gave him a curt nod and drove back to the highway. He glanced at the dashboard clock. *Almost nine.* He'd made it back in good time from the six o'clock meeting.

Wish Ross wouldn't talk so much, but he's all right. Thank God for the AA fellas. Got me through the worst of it. Confession with Father Brisebois set me square with the Lord, but it wasn't the same as goin' over it with the guys. Father, he's a good man but he don't understand how the devil can live in a bottle. Pull you in and suck out your soul. The boys do, though. They been there.

Lyle slowed down as his headlights picked out the edge of his driveway.

She should've got the letter by now. She's gotta understand. She's gotta help me stop this thief from taking from good folks like Pearl. She's a big-shot lawyer now, so to catch a thief, that's her job.

He braked suddenly as he pulled into the driveway. He blinked and stared through the windshield.

The garage door was open.

No way. That sucker was down when I left. Gettin' old but I ain't senile.

He rolled down his window and stuck his head out. He squinted as he tried to see into the depths of the garage where the headlight beams didn't reach. Tools on the tool rack, snow blower, lawnmower. All in their proper places as far as he could tell.

"Anyone in there? Show yourself if you know what's good fer ya!"

He sneezed and reached for another tissue. *Just what I need. Damn punks!* He rolled up the window and pulled into the garage.

He heard a metallic clatter behind him as he got out of the minivan. He gasped as the wooden garage door slammed down with a thud. He made his way cautiously toward it in the pitch-black garage.

"Hey!" He pounded on the garage door. "Hey!"

He groped to find the chain for the overhead ceiling light and yanked it. In the bulb's dim glow, he saw a large stain on the floor.

What the...

He touched the walls. *Damp.*

He held his fingertips against his nose. *Gasoline. With my cold, I couldn't smell it. The place is soaked in it.*

He staggered as pain shot through him. He clutched his chest and bent over. Then he straightened, breathing deeply.

He heard a whoosh as he lurched toward the garage door. Flames licked its bottom and side edges. He fumbled for the metal handle then jerked his hand away when he found it. It was hot.

He groped in his jacket pockets, pulled out a pair of gloves and groaned. *Wool. No insulation. No leather palms.*

He slipped them on but he needed something more for protection. *A rag. If I get it around the glove, maybe I can grab the handle.*

He stumbled and reached out to the wall on his right. *Gotta be one around here. If I could just...*

He spilled the contents of a plastic storage box on the floor. Half-full paint and varnish cans clanked as they hit the concrete. *No rags.*

Flames danced on the door and surged up the walls. He groped for the van's door handle and pulled himself inside. *Get her started. Maybe I can crash through.*

He fumbled for his key and stuck it into the ignition. He was about to start the engine when he gagged, clutched his chest and gasped in pain.

He slumped against the steering wheel, unable to lift his hand to the ignition. He knew that when the flames hit the gas tank, the minivan would become a fireball.

Lord, please make it quick.

CHAPTER ONE

I was chilled to the bone when I got home that evening. An Arctic air mass from Nunavut had moved into central Ontario and held the city of Toronto in a deep freeze. Cars refused to start. Streetcars broke down all over the city. Pedestrians hurried along in down-filled coats with scarves over their faces.

If spring was on its way, there was no sign of it that Friday in March.

Maxie, our golden retriever, greeted me at the door with a rapturous dance. She wanted to play, but I was in no mood for games. A note on the kitchen counter told me Laura had taken her for a walk before she headed out to a party to celebrate the beginning of winter break.

I crumpled up the note. *Thank goodness for that!* The last thing I wanted to do was walk a dog in sub-zero weather. Or make dinner. Tommy, my youngest, was with his grandmother that night so I had the evening to myself.

On the way to the phone to check voicemail, the hall mirror told me I looked as bedraggled as I felt. Shoulders slumped, mouth a thin slash across my tense face, short blond hair stuck out like a scarecrow's. I looked every one of my forty-seven years. Maybe even a few more.

I pressed the button on the phone to activate unheard voicemail.

"Good afternoon. This is Detective Inspector Stewart Foster of the Ontario Provincial Police. I'm trying to reach Tracy Tierney."

I swallowed back the panic that was rising inside me. What did the police want with my daughter?

"Ms. Tierney, we need to speak with you as soon as possible," the message continued. "I'm in Toronto today. Please give me a call at..."

I jotted down the phone number on a notepad, pressed a button to save the message and hung up.

Is Tracy in trouble? I took a deep breath and tried to stay calm. The police wanted to speak to her, so she was alive and well. Nothing had

happened to her. The call had something to do with her work. The year
before, Tracy had finished law school and she was articling at a Bay
Street firm. She must have asked the police for information. I needed to
give her the message.

Tracy had moved out four weeks before, which was why I was
feeling down. She was twenty-four years old, and I was all for her setting
up a home of her own. It was how she'd left that bothered me.

The front door opened and a familiar voice called out, "Mom! You
home?"

My heart did a flip-flop and I hurried into the hall.

Tracy had on her good black coat and a red cloche hat, and her
cheeks were rosy from the cold. She held a casserole dish in her hands.
She gave me a tentative smile.

I blinked back tears and studied my firstborn. Pretty, heart-shaped
face. Serious brown eyes—my late husband Michael's eyes. I moved
toward her, my arms outstretched. "Tracy, honey…"

She set down the dish on the deacon's bench and gave me a hug. "I
missed you, Mom."

I wrapped my arms around her. Tracy is a petite girl. My younger
daughter, Laura, towers over her.

I didn't want to let her go, but she pulled back. She took off her hat
and shook her head. Wavy brown hair fell around her face. She picked
up the dish on the bench. "Cassoulet. Jamie made it the other night. Have
you eaten dinner?"

I moved away at the mention of Jamie—Jamie Collins, a lawyer at
the firm where Tracy was spending her articling year. The woman my
daughter had moved in with.

"Mom, we need to talk." She led the way into the kitchen.

I remembered the phone message from the police. "What's wrong?"
I asked as I followed her.

"It's Jamie. Something's happened to her."

I was relieved that Tracy was all right. But as I looked at her
troubled face, it hit me that this wasn't just a friend who was in trouble.
Jamie was the special person in my daughter's life. Her partner. "What's
happened?"

She sat down at the table and fixed her eyes on me. "On Wednesday,
Jamie got a letter from a guy called Lyle Critchley. Made her really
upset."

"Something to do with her work?"

"No. Jamie knew Critchley up north, where she grew up. Near
Braeloch, one of those towns in cottage country."

"I didn't know she's from up there."

"How would you?" Her voice rose in irritation. "You haven't spent
any time with her."

I looked up from my computer and saw Tracy and a striking woman with burgundy hair in the doorway to my office

"Mom, can we come in?"

"Of course." I got out of my chair as they came into the room.

Tracy took the woman's hand. "Mom, I want you to meet Jamie. Jamie Collins."

I took a step back. My daughter had been talking about Jamie for weeks. I'd assumed Jamie was a man.

Jamie held out a hand to me. "Tracy thought it was time we met."

I took her hand and looked at Tracy. She had a smile on her face.

My head was reeling. "Yes, well, I..." I struggled to find the right words.

Just then, Rose, my administrative assistant, came to the door. "Keith Kulas on the line, Pat."

My CEO. I dropped Jamie's hand and reached for the phone. Keith's call would give me time to adjust to this bombshell. "I have to take this."

The smile left Tracy's face and she stiffened. "We'll leave you to it, then." She took Jamie's arm. They walked out of the office without turning back.

My heart sank as I watched them leave.

I tried to make amends. Later that afternoon, I phoned Tracy, hoping to get a second chance. "Honey, please don't be mad. I had to take the call. It was important."

"More important than your daughter and her future?" she asked.

"Of course not. It's just..."

"Just what?"

Just too much to take in at the moment. I didn't say anything.

"Mom?" Tracy's voice rose in a mixture of anger and sorrow. "Say something."

The call had been a mistake. I should have waited, tried to get my mind—my emotions—around Tracy and Jamie.

"Mom? Are you still there?"

"Goodbye," I whispered.

"Wait! Mom—"

I placed the receiver in the cradle and began to cry.

I had no inkling of Tracy's orientation. I'd always considered myself a champion of diversity—religious, racial and sexual. My business partner and friend, Stéphane Pratt, is openly gay. I have gay and lesbian clients. But it's easy to be open-minded until your kid comes out.

Three days after their visit to my office, Tracy moved into Jamie's condo. I threw myself into my work. I didn't tell my friends about Tracy. I didn't tell Devon, the man in my life. I hoped my daughter would get over her infatuation. At night, I tossed and turned in bed, sometimes crying into my pillow.

What had I done wrong?

"Listen to me, Mom," Tracy said. "I'm talking to you."

I looked at her. She was right. I hadn't given Jamie a chance. Sure, I phoned my daughter every couple of days to see how she was, but I called her at the office. I either got her voicemail—my messages went unanswered—or a curt response that she had to run off to an "important meeting."

"Ten years ago, Lyle Critchley killed Jamie's younger sister."

That got my attention.

"Drunk driving. Her family never forgave him."

I stared at her. I'd have trouble forgiving someone who'd mowed down one of my girls.

"And then, out of nowhere, he writes Jamie this letter. He wanted her help."

"Legal help?"

"I'm not sure. She'd run the letter through the shredder by the time I got home. She was that mad at him."

"I don't blame her."

Tracy looked surprised, then pleased. She seemed to relax a little. "She spent the rest of the evening on the computer. Yesterday morning, she called me at work and asked to borrow my car."

"She was going to see Lyle?"

"I don't know. She said she'd tell me all about it that evening, but she never came home and she hasn't called. She doesn't answer her cell. She didn't take her laptop with her, but I've sent her emails because she's probably hit an Internet café. She hasn't answered them. And I found a voicemail at home tonight from someone at her office who wanted to know if she was feeling better. She must've called in sick."

Her eyes grew large. "Mom, I watched the news when I got home today. There was a fire near Braeloch last night. Lyle Critchley was killed in it. The police found traces of an accelerant. They're calling it a murder."

I gripped Tracy's hand—hard. That was why the police had called her. Jamie had taken the Honda Civic that was registered in Tracy's name.

"She has your car," I said.

She pulled her hand away. "So? She doesn't have a car. Jamie's a greenie. Walks and bikes wherever she can."

"There's a voicemail for you from the OPP. Maybe they found your car and traced it to this address and phone number."

She went over to the phone and listened to the message. "They want to talk to me."

She turned to face me. "What if they've arrested Jamie? She and her family hated Lyle. But, Mom, she didn't…Jamie wouldn't hurt a fly."

"You'd better call them."

Tracy went to the phone, and I let Maxie out on the back deck. When I returned to the kitchen, she was leaving a voicemail message giving the number at the condo and her cell phone number.

"I'll heat up Jamie's cassoulet," I said when she got off the phone. "Vegetarian?" I assumed the environmentally conscious Jamie wouldn't eat meat.

Tracy gave me a little smile. "Of course. Beans, carrots, tomatoes. It's good."

First I'd heard that she liked vegetarian fare. But then I hadn't done a very good job of keeping up with her life, had I?

She sat down at the kitchen table. "Look, I handled it badly. I shouldn't have sprung Jamie on you at your office. I should have sat down with you and told you about us."

I turned on the microwave and sat down across from her.

She reached over and took my hand. "For a long time, I was pretty confused. I didn't even come out to myself until my first year at law school. But I've come to terms with who I am." She smiled. "And now it's wonderful to have Jamie in my life."

She squeezed my hand. "The old Tracy was unhappy because she was keeping a secret from you."

And I'd thought we had no secrets. I love my girls and I don't want them to keep things from me.

Something inside me shifted. I had to show Tracy that I was worthy of her trust. I decided that I'd get to know Jamie. If she was the one for Tracy, I'd stand by her choice.

"You've talked to Laura?" I asked.

"She's cool. Thinks I'm crazy not to be hot for guys, but it's my life, she says."

I had to smile at that. Laura had been boy-crazy since she was twelve.

Tracy touched my cheek. "Mom, I'm out. It's official. Do you good to talk to a friend—or two."

My eyes started to tear up. Then the doorbell rang.

Through the front window I saw two men in overcoats on the porch. Both were tall and poised with apparent military bearing. A cold blast of air hit me when I opened the door. I pulled up the collar of my suit jacket. "Yes?"

"Ontario Provincial Police," the older of the two men said with a pronounced Scottish burr. He was in his late fifties, with a gray moustache and gray eyes sinking into the folds of skin around them. He showed me his badge. "I'm Detective Inspector Stewart Foster and this is

Detective Lew Anders. We're looking for Tracy Tierney."

"I'm Tracy Tierney," my daughter said behind me.

"We have some questions to ask you. May we come in?"

Tracy was the first to speak when we were seated in the family room. "What's this about?" she asked.

Foster fixed his eyes on her. "Your car was found in Braeloch this morning."

I studied his face for a sign of what was coming, but he kept it neutral.

"Can you account for your whereabouts around nine last night?" he asked.

Tracy paused. "I got home at seven-thirty. I ate dinner then I watched some television."

Anders, a big, fair-haired man with a ruddy complexion, wrote this down in his notebook.

"You were home, too?" Foster asked me.

"Yes," I replied.

"I wasn't here," Tracy said. "This is my mother's home. I was at my place downtown."

"Tracy moved in with a friend a few weeks ago," I said. "They have a condo on The Esplanade."

He frowned. "The address on your car registration is here."

Tracy made a face. "I haven't got around to changing it," she mumbled.

I flashed her my no-nonsense look. Tracy is a lawyer. She should have done the paperwork.

"Was anyone with you last night?" he asked her.

"No. I was alone all evening."

"A man died in a fire in his garage last night," he said. "Outside the town of Braeloch in Glencoe Highlands Township. A car similar to yours was seen on his property earlier in the day. Can someone confirm that you were in Toronto last night?"

Tracy was thinking hard. "I was at the office till seven with a couple of lawyers. How long would it take me to get to Braeloch? Three hours? And I'd be caught in traffic leaving the city. I couldn't be there by nine."

"Then how did your car get to the parking lot in Braeloch?" he asked.

She just looked at him. The foolish girl was trying to cover up for Jamie.

"You have no idea how your car found its way to Braeloch?" he asked.

She looked down at her hands.

I'd had enough. My daughter was being treated as a suspect in a murder investigation. "Tracy lent her car to a friend yesterday."

She shot daggers at me with her glare. Foster sat up straighter on the sofa.

"Who is this friend?" he wanted to know.

She didn't reply.

"Ms. Tierney, we can charge you with obstructing a murder investigation. I will repeat my question. Who did you lend your car to yesterday?"

"Jamie Collins," she said.

"And where can we reach Mr. Collins?"

"Ms. Collins." She looked at him defiantly. "Jamie's the woman I live with. My partner."

"Is Ms. Collins at home right now?" he asked without missing a beat.

"I haven't seen her since yesterday morning." Her voice broke in mid-sentence.

Foster paused for a few moments. "Describe Ms. Collins."

"Jamie has red hair," she said. "Burgundy, I guess you'd call it."

Foster nodded at Anders who scribbled in his notebook.

"Tell them about the letter," I said.

If Tracy's look could have killed, I would have been six feet under. Foster nodded at Anders again.

"What about this letter, Ms. Tierney?"

She didn't answer for a few moments. "Jamie got a letter from Lyle Critchley," she said slowly. "He wanted her help."

"What kind of help?"

"I don't know. She'd put the letter through the shredder before I got in, and she spent the rest of the night on her computer."

"What day did this letter arrive?" Foster asked.

"Wednesday."

"And she drove up north in your car on Thursday?"

"Jamie called me at work yesterday and asked if she could use my car. She didn't say where she was going."

"You don't know where she is?"

"I told you I haven't spoken to her since yesterday morning. But I'll try the condo now."

She picked up the cordless phone on the end table and hit some buttons. "No one's answering."

Anders took down the address of the condo, Tracy's phone numbers and the names of the colleagues she was with on Thursday afternoon. He told her that forensics would check out her car, and she could pick it up at police headquarters in Orillia in a few days.

"And we'll need to take a look at Ms. Collins's home computers," Foster said.

"Right now?" Tracy asked. "I was about to have dinner with my mother."

"The sooner the better," Anders said. "This is a murder investigation."

Foster looked at his watch. "We'll meet you in your condo lobby at nine."

At the door, he handed Tracy his card. "Don't leave Toronto without letting us know."

When the door closed behind them, Tracy turned to me. Anger flashed in her eyes. "Now you've done it!"

I opened my mouth to protest when she spat out, "You've had it in for Jamie since you met her. So you told them she took my car and you told them about Lyle's letter."

"Tracy—"

"They'll charge her with killing him."

She held her hands over her face. I tried to put my arms around her, but she pushed me away. "We should have gotten married, then I wouldn't have to testify against her. We've been talking about it. We thought maybe this summer."

Marriage? That was news to me, but I'd been completely out of the loop. I gripped her elbow and led her back to the kitchen where I sat her down at the table. I pulled up a chair beside her.

"We had to tell the officers who drove your car up there," I said. "You know that. And it will all work out. I'm sure it was a coincidence that Jamie went up there on the day Lyle was killed. She'll turn up, and she'll tell them where she was and who she was with."

But my brave words belied my thoughts. Anger and other strong emotions can provoke anyone into a violent act. Even someone who wouldn't hurt a fly.

"I'm going to Braeloch," Tracy said through her tears.

"Tracy, the officers told you not to leave city without telling them."

"I don't care."

"And even if they gave you the go-ahead, they'd follow every move you made. They'd think you'd lead them to Jamie."

She brushed away her tears with the back of her hand. "But they wouldn't follow you. Mom, will you go up there and look for her? Tomorrow's Saturday. You'd have the weekend to find out what's going on. I'll come over tomorrow morning and stay here with Tommy."

I was about to say that if I found Jamie, I had no idea what I could do to help her. But Tracy's pleading eyes were cutting me to my very soul. I had to let her know that she could count on me. Any time. Like right now. It was important that I restore my daughter's faith in me.

I nodded. "I'll see what I can do."

I gave Jamie's cassoulet a few more minutes in the microwave.

While the dish was spinning, Tracy phoned Jamie's mother in Braeloch and told her that I'd come by her home late the next morning. Veronica Collins said she hadn't heard from her daughter in more than a week.

When we sat down at the table, neither of us felt like eating. "Jamie went to see Lyle about something he told her in that letter," Tracy said, her eyes wide with concern. "So whoever killed him would want her out of the way, too."

I'd been thinking along those lines, but I didn't want to add to her worries. I told her the killer probably didn't know about the letter. "And whatever Lyle told Jamie might have nothing to do with why he was killed."

She didn't buy that. "She knows way too much."

"She's dropped out of sight to check up on what Lyle told her."

"Maybe. And thanks to you, the police are looking for her." She gave me a sidelong glance. "And when they find out about the feud between the Collins family and Lyle—"

"Feud?"

"There were a lot of bad feelings."

Of course there were. He killed the Collins girl.

"When they do, they won't look any farther for Lyle's killer."

We were going around in circles. "We don't know that," I said. "They may have several irons in the fire by now."

I pushed my chair back from the table. "I'll drive you over to the condo."

"What's Veronica like?" I asked Tracy when we were in the car.

"I've never met her. Tonight was the first time I spoke to her."

I couldn't believe my ears. Tracy had talked about marriage, but she'd never met her intended's family.

"Jamie doesn't go back to Braeloch much. Says it brings back memories of her sister...and Lyle. She took Veronica to New York this Christmas."

"At some point, you'll have to meet her."

"I guess. We'll probably drive up there this summer."

On your honeymoon?

CHAPTER TWO

Saturday was a beautiful day. The cold air mass had moved out overnight and the temperature in Toronto hovered just above freezing. That's balmy weather for central Canada in the winter. The sun shone down from a true-blue sky and "Spring" from *The Four Seasons* poured out of the stereo speakers as I drove north out of the city on the Don Valley Parkway. Maybe it was the sunshine, maybe it was Vivaldi, but my spirits lifted as I left Toronto behind.

Three hours later, I pulled into Braeloch. The little town on the shore of Serenity Lake was postcard-pretty that morning with a fresh dusting of snow sparkling in the sunlight. Its main street hugged the lake, which was frozen over and dotted with ice-fishing huts. A small public parking lot was tucked behind Main Street's old brick buildings, and behind that a grid of residential streets climbed the hill behind the town. On top of the hill, two huge granite outcroppings embraced Braeloch like a pair of protective arms.

I cruised down Main Street past a bakery, two banks, a library, Stedman's Department Store, a couple of eateries, the Dominion Hotel and a police station. I saw that Norris Cassidy, the investment firm I work for, had a branch in a handsome Victorian house on the corner of Main and Queen, and I recalled reading about that new venture in the company's newsletter. Morrison's Funeral Home was housed in an even grander old home across the street. I smiled, thinking that Braeloch was a one-stop-shopping mecca.

I found Prince Avenue midway up the hill and pulled up in front of a tidy white-frame house with a veranda wrapped around it. Snow was piled on the front lawn, but I envisioned well-tended flowerbeds in the summer.

A woman with frosted blond hair opened the door as I walked up the front steps. Veronica Collins looked like the late Princess Diana grown into middle age, but she wasn't smiling.

I held out a hand. "I'm Pat Tierney, Tracy's mom."

"Do you know where my daughter is?"

I shook my head. "Tracy hasn't heard from Jamie since Thursday morning."

She moved back so I could enter the house. "I call her Jenny," she said. "Short for Jennifer."

I felt tension emanate from her as she watched me take off my parka. She put it on a bench by the door, and I followed her through the house.

It was bigger than it looked from the outside. An addition had been built onto the back, and the entire place was decorated in shades of white. Even the rugs were white, I noted as I followed Veronica into the gleaming white kitchen.

"Tea?" she asked.

"Thanks." I took a chair at the table. She set down two white cups and saucers, and smiled for the first time. "I haven't met Tracy," she said, "but she sounds like a nice girl on the phone."

I must have looked surprised, but she just shrugged. "I see you're not comfortable with it yet. Jenny told me twelve years ago so I've had plenty of time to adjust. Jen's thirty-two now, old enough to live her own life."

"Tracy only told me a few weeks ago."

She gave me a wry smile. "You'll get used to living with it."

I noticed then that she was perfectly put together, from her pale pink twin sweater-set down to the pearl polish on her fingernails. Perfectly put together, just like her home.

She joined me at the table with a teapot and poured the tea. "The police came by last night. They found your daughter's car in the public lot, and they said a woman with red hair was seen at Lyle's place on Thursday afternoon. Several hours before the fire."

"Where is the house?"

"About three miles east of town on Highway 123." She stared at her pearl fingernails. "It doesn't look good for Jenny. Lyle..."

"Tracy told me."

"Yes." She paused for a few moments. "It was ten years ago last summer, Carly had just turned seventeen. She was driving home from her weekend job at the garden center. She was making the turn onto 123 when Lyle hit her. The police said she died instantly." Her voice broke.

I gave her several moments to compose herself. "You just had the two girls?" I asked.

"Just the two of them." She tried to smile. "You see why I don't care about Jenny's lifestyle. What's important is that I still have her."

"Yes."

"We lived out at the lake in those days. I sold the place five years ago after Herb died." She looked around her. "Decided to make a fresh start here."

I sipped more tea and waited for her to continue.

"Lyle had been drinking that night, but he was never charged."

"Never charged? But—"

She took a deep breath. "He was hurt in the crash. Some cracked ribs and a concussion, and he was taken to hospital. In his condition, he couldn't take a Breathalyzer, and they never gave him a blood test. The upshot was they couldn't prove his blood alcohol content was above .08%." Her face crumpled.

"Good God!"

She nodded. "Only a fraction of impaired drivers who kill or injure people are ever charged, never mind convicted."

"Why didn't they do a blood test?"

She held out her hands, palms up. "Forgot? Didn't get around to it in time? Or maybe because he was a prominent business owner in the area."

"There was no closure for you."

She toyed with her spoon. "For months, I just went through the motions. I made meals, I did laundry. I thought of Carly getting into her car, driving to the intersection…"

After a few moments, she continued. "My Herb was one of those men who say little but feel things real deep. When Carly died, he held it all inside."

"And Jamie?"

"She was always feisty. She fought back, tried to get Lyle charged. But, as I said, there was no legal evidence against him."

She gave me a weak smile. "When she got nowhere with that, she lashed out—not that I approve of what she did. She strung up signs with the word *Killer* painted in red on Lyle's front gate. She's got plenty of spirit, my Jenny."

Two years earlier, a Jennifer Collins had led the legal team that secured a landmark judgment on behalf of an elderly widow. The court ordered a financial advisor at a prominent Bay Street securities firm to pay the woman more than a million dollars for shrinking her assets by putting them into high-risk investments.

"Your daughter was the young lawyer who got money back for Betsy Cornell, wasn't she?" I'd been impressed. The thirty-five-day trial in Toronto Superior Court brought the issue of investment fraud, especially fraud against small and elderly investors, to widespread public attention. Unless their investment firms carry expensive liability insurance, fraud victims usually suffer in silence or settle out of court for pennies on the dollar, with the deals sealed by nondisclosure clauses. Cases of bargaining rather than justice.

Veronica's face lit up with a smile. "That was my Jenny. She's got a passion for justice."

The more I learned about Jamie, the more I liked her.

"What happened with the signs she hung on Lyle's gate?" I asked.

"He threatened to sue her for libel, and the police spoke to her. But nothing came of it. You see, everyone around here, including the police officers, knew Carly. She was a sweetheart. And the way she died…well, it could've just as easily happened to their daughter or sister."

But the police probably had a record of what Jamie did, even though they didn't charge her.

Veronica was thinking the same thing. "So when Lyle is killed, who's the first person the cops look at?"

"Jamie was here in Braeloch on Thursday," I said.

"You know that for a fact?"

"She borrowed Tracy's car."

Her shoulders slumped. "She didn't drop by here."

"Do you have any idea where she could be? With a friend?"

She shook her head. "She stopped seeing her friends here when she went off to university."

"She got a letter from Lyle on Tuesday. He asked her for help."

Veronica looked surprised. "Lyle sent Jenny a letter? The police didn't tell me that."

"Tracy doesn't know what kind of help Lyle wanted, only that the letter upset Jamie. She'd destroyed it by the time Tracy got home. But she may have had a change of heart. She called Tracy at work the next day and asked to borrow the car."

"Did she say she was coming up here?"

"Not to Tracy. But as the police told you, her car was found here in town. And a red-haired woman was seen at Lyle's that afternoon."

Veronica gave a small sigh. "She's been coloring her hair that shade for years, ever since she started calling herself Jamie."

I remembered something Tracy had said. "She doesn't like to wear hats," I said. "Her red hair would have been a beacon against the snow."

"So she was at Lyle's that afternoon. So what? The fire broke out hours later."

But she looked defeated, and my heart went out to her. She'd lost one daughter in a terrible accident. And now her other girl was in serious trouble.

"Would anyone else have a grudge against Lyle?" I asked.

"I don't know about a grudge, but he rubbed a lot of people the wrong way. He was like that."

"He was a heavy drinker?"

"He was known to be, but they say he never touched a drop after…" She gave a bitter laugh. "A lot of good that did my Carly."

CHAPTER THREE

When I left Veronica's house, I drove over to the municipal parking lot and got out of the car. This was where Jamie had left Tracy's Honda. She could have rented a car or someone may have given her a lift.

I took a walkway between two buildings and came out on Main Street. The blinds were drawn on the windows of the Norris Cassidy branch across the street and I saw a *Closed* sign on the front door. The branch was closed for the weekend.

From what I'd seen on my drive through Braeloch, there were a few possibilities for lunch. Two doors from me, the Tiger Lily Café offered Chinese-Canadian cuisine. Joe's Diner and Takeout was another block down and, across the street, the Dominion Hotel advertised its dining room. I headed for Joe's.

"Pat! Pat Tierney!" a woman called as I was about to open the diner's door.

I turned, surprised to hear my name in a town where I was a complete stranger. I did a double take when I saw my friend Sister Celia de Franco hurrying down the sidewalk toward me.

The petite brunette's dark eyes sparkled with merriment. "You walked by when I was in Stedman's," she said. "I thought,'That can't be Pat.' But it is!"

I gave her a hug. "Have you had lunch? I'm about to try this place."

"Good pick. Joe makes an awesome burger."

Inside, Barry Manilow whispered from the overhead speakers. Sister Celia waved at a stout waitress and led the way to a red leatherette booth. "My spot," she said. "I'm here every day."

The waitress came over to us. "You brung a friend today, Sister."

"This is the best place for lunch in Braeloch, Sue."

Joe's was a clone of the diner my friends and I had hung out in in my final year of high school. I ordered my old favorite—a burger, fries and a chocolate milkshake.

"Make that two," Celia told Sue.

When Sue had gone to fill our orders, I gave Celia's arm a squeeze. "Good to see you." I hadn't heard from her since she left Safe Harbor, the home for refugees she ran in Toronto, two months before. I had no idea where she'd gone. "You're living here?"

"For the next little while, I'll be at the Catholic parish in town while the pastor recovers from heart surgery."

She grinned and ran a hand through her head of dark curls. "Would you believe the parish is called Jesus of the Highlands?"

I burst into laughter. The name made me think of a plaster statue of Jesus dressed in a kilt and sporran. "What kind of name is that for a parish?"

"Yeah, too cute for words. It was Holy Rosary until the diocese changed the name five years ago. Figured it would appeal to the cottagers, I guess."

"What do you do at the parish?"

"I run it," she said with a smile. "You look surprised. Of course, I can't celebrate Mass, but I hold a prayer service on Sundays—hymns, readings from Scripture and a short homily. I'm spiritual advisor to the parish groups. I go out on sick calls. And I run the office. Keeps me busy."

"I bet. Where are you staying?"

"Father Brisebois, the pastor, didn't want me to stay in the rectory. Considers it a male bastion. So I'm boarding with an elderly woman in town." She shrugged. "It's okay. I don't want to put her to too much trouble, so I eat most of my meals here."

Our food arrived, and we focused on our plates for a few minutes. It wasn't the healthiest lunch I've had, but it was darn good.

Celia signaled Sue to bring us coffee. "I've been dealing with the police for the past two days. Listen to this, Pat. Our seventy-four-year-old parish sacristan was murdered. Out here in the middle of nowhere. Can you believe it?"

"Lyle Critchley was your sacristan?" I wasn't sure what a sacristan was.

"You know? Of course, it's been on the news."

"Sorry to have to ask, but what's a sacristan? A caretaker?"

"It's the person charged with care of the sacristy, the room in a church where the priest's vestments and the sacred vessels are kept. But Lyle ran the entire church. Made sure the floors were washed, the walks shoveled, the lawns mowed. Served morning Mass for Father Brisebois every day. I take it he's been lonely since his wife died."

I gave her a tight smile. "Lyle Critchley is the reason I'm in Braeloch today."

I told her about Tracy and Jamie. She placed a hand on top of mine while I tried to explain how surprised and confused I'd been. And how I'd let Tracy down.

"Don't let anything come between you and your girls," she said.

Then I told her about the letter Lyle had sent Jamie and that the police were looking for her. I told her about my visit to Veronica that morning.

"I don't know what else I can do to find Jamie," I said. "There doesn't seem to be anyone I can talk to."

The coffee arrived, and Celia stirred cream into her mug. "Can't Veronica point you to some of Jamie's friends?"

"She says she's lost contact with people around here."

She shook her head, setting her dark curls dancing. "I find that difficult to believe. She must see people she knows when she visits her mother."

Celia was right. There had to be people Jamie could have turned to. I should have pushed Veronica more on that point.

"I wonder why she abandoned the car," Celia mused.

"Maybe Jamie—" I sat up straight and coffee sloshed over my sweater. My mind raced as I dabbed at it. "Jamie went to see Lyle in the afternoon but he wasn't there. She didn't see Veronica because she didn't want to tell her about Lyle and his letter. Maybe she went back to his house that evening and saw the fire. Maybe she was the one who called it in. She may have left Tracy's car in the municipal lot and spent the night at that hotel across the street, the Dominion. When she went to get the car in the morning, she found the police looking at it. Whoever saw her at the Critchley place also saw the car she was driving."

Celia raised an eyebrow. "What was in Lyle's letter?"

"Tracy doesn't know. Only that he asked Jamie for help."

"Legal help?"

"I don't think so," I said. "There must be lawyers around here he could have gone to."

"She didn't rush up there to kill him for hitting her sister," Celia said. "She would have done that years ago if that was her inclination."

"She wanted to talk to him, not kill him." As soon as the words were out, I knew in my heart that Jamie hadn't killed Lyle.

"Unless he was blackmailing her."

I didn't buy that. "For what?"

"Maybe she did something—something that affected his business."

"His business?"

"He ran Critchley's Heating and Cooling. Sold it a few years ago when his wife took sick." She stared at me, her mouth partly open. "A heating business would be open to all kinds of complaints."

"You bet. Liability claims, too. If a fire broke out because of a faulty furnace…"

"A fire."

"Maybe someone decided to fight fire with fire," I said.

I set my mug on the table. "The way to clear Jamie is to help the police find Lyle's killer. And that's what I'm going to do."

Tracy was at the front door when I let myself in late that afternoon. "Did you find her?" she asked.

"No." My heart twisted when the smile left her face. "Sorry, honey. And I didn't learn very much either."

Tommy came into the hall with Maxie. "Can we have pizza tonight?" he asked.

I hadn't given any thought to dinner. "That's a good idea, Tommy," I said. "We'll wait till Laura comes home, then I'll order it."

"Double cheese," he said, and returned to the television at the back of the house.

Tracy and I sat on the front sofa, and I told her about my visit with Veronica. "Apparently, Jamie doesn't keep in touch with her old friends up there," I said.

"That's not true. She got a birthday card from her friend, Al, last month. Al as in Alexandra."

"What's Al's last name?"

"Jamie may have mentioned it but I don't remember."

I told her that I'd met Sister Celia in Braeloch and that Lyle had been the sacristan at the parish she was running.

"I take it he stopped drinking," she said.

"Veronica said he went cold turkey after the accident that killed her daughter."

Laura came in and I ordered two large pizzas. After we'd eaten, Tracy returned to the condo and Laura went off to a party. I put on a video for Tommy, and booted up the computer in my study.

I did a search for Lyle Critchley. *The Highlands Times*, the weekly newspaper that calls itself "the eyes and ears of the Glencoe Highlands," had a small article about a fire that broke out on Thursday night in a garage. "An unidentified man died in the blaze," the article said. I assumed the newspaper had gone to press before Lyle's remains were identified.

But the Toronto daily newspapers were on top of the story. "Glencoe Highlands resident killed in garage fire," read the headline in Saturday's *Toronto World*. "Murder investigation under way," the deck under it added. A photo of an elderly white-haired man, his lower jaw jutting out like the prow of a ship, accompanied the article. The cutline under the photo identified him as Lyle Critchley.

The only thing I didn't already know was in the final paragraph.

"Police are now looking for Jennifer Collins as a person of interest. Ms. Collins grew up in Glencoe Highlands Township and graduated from Highlands Secondary School. She is now a lawyer at Optimum Capital Corp. in Toronto."

So Jamie had left the law firm where she and Tracy had met and moved to Optimum, a large investment firm, even larger than Norris Cassidy. I wondered why she'd joined Optimum when she'd made a name for herself in claims against investment houses and their financial advisors. And why hadn't Tracy told me?

I logged into Norris Cassidy's intranet and did a search for the Braeloch branch. It hadn't opened yet. Its launch was scheduled for the coming Wednesday.

In the kitchen, I poured a glass of chardonnay and a tumbler of apple juice, and joined Tommy in the sunroom where *Toy Story* was on the wide-screen TV. I sipped the wine and thought of how despondent Tracy had looked that evening. For her sake, I wanted to find Jamie and clear her name. But to do that, I needed to spend more time in Braeloch.

I closed my eyes and the image of Norris Cassidy's Braeloch branch popped into my mind. That branch was my ticket to finding Jamie.

CHAPTER FOUR

Early the next morning, I took my coffee into my study. Bach's "Violin Concerto in D Minor" washed over me as I turned on the computer and Googled "Norris Cassidy, Braeloch." A page of articles from *The Highlands Times* popped up on the screen. The newspaper seemed to have carried an article about the branch in almost every issue for the past few months. Local news, they say, sells local newspapers.

There were articles about Nuala Larkin, the woman who had been hired to run the branch, and Paul Campbell, the young financial advisor who would work under her. There were articles about renovations to the building. Two years back, the newspaper ran an interview with Dave Dwyer, Norris Cassidy's vice-president of corporate development, who said the Braeloch branch was the first of many the company planned to open outside large urban centers.

I turned off the computer. The Braeloch branch was a major step for Norris Cassidy. A lot of money had gone into that grand old house on Main Street. The firm wanted to tap the wealthy cottagers with vacation homes in the area.

It was just past eight. I toasted a bagel, poured another cup of coffee and sat down at the kitchen table to map out my strategy.

"See ya, Mrs. T," Tommy said as he left the house at nine-thirty.

I'd asked Tommy to call me Pat. I didn't expect him to call me Mom because his mother had died only three months before. But now that he was part of our family, Mrs. T was too formal.

I watched through the front window as he crossed the street to spend the morning with his new friend, Jake Mackenzie. When the door to the Mackenzie home closed behind him, I dialed the home number of Keith Kulas, our CEO. I hesitated to make that call, but I couldn't wait to reach him at his office on Monday.

A woman with a foreign accent picked up after the second ring. "The Kulas residence," she said.

I gave her my name and asked if I could speak to Keith. Moments later, he came on the line.

"Pat," he said. "How are you?"

I told him I needed to talk to him.

"Right now?"

"I'm sorry, Keith, but if you have time…"

"Can you come right now? Evelyn and I are driving to Oakville in an hour to visit our daughter." He gave me an address.

I went upstairs and told Laura I'd be gone for a few hours. Then I called Peggy Mackenzie and asked if Tommy could stay with Jake until I returned.

"No problem," she said. "I hoped he'd stay for lunch."

I changed into a pair of black dress pants and a black sweater, and left the house.

Ten minutes later, I was in the heart of Rosedale, the enclave for Toronto's wealthy residents just north of the downtown core. In front of me was a stately stone home from a bygone era. I rapped the brass knocker and a Filipino woman in a maid's uniform answered. She led me to a room at the back of the house, where Keith, a distinguished-looking man with a head of silver hair, was seated on a sofa. He was dressed in his version of weekend casual, a cream-colored cashmere cardigan and pressed gray pants.

The maid set a tray with two mugs of coffee and a plate of miniature blueberry muffins on the low table in front of him.

"This must be something very pressing if it can't wait until tomorrow," he said when the woman had left the room.

Keith has a type A personality. A as in anal. I'd get nowhere by playing on his sympathy. I had to show him how I could help Norris Cassidy.

I gave him my best smile. "I was in Braeloch yesterday and I saw the new Norris Cassidy branch. Very impressive."

A frown crossed his face as he picked up a mug. "That building has taken a ton of money to renovate."

"You'll go up for the opening?"

"Can't. Shareholders' meeting on Wednesday."

"None of the other directors will be there?"

He shook his head. "Bad timing. Shareholders' meeting and a branch opening the same day? Shouldn't have happened." He sighed. "Too late to go back to our day planners."

"I could go for you. I can cut the ribbon, serve the cake or whatever's planned."

Keith is shrewd. "There's something else, Pat. What is it?"

I hesitated. "It's…family business." *I have to find my daughter's lover.* "It's…complicated." *Because she works for our chief rival.* "I'd rather not say anything more."

He leaned back in his chair and his pale blue eyes studied me. "What's in it for Norris Cassidy?"

"The people you've hired at the branch are new to the company. We need to show the locals that Norris Cassidy is interested in them and their community, not just their money."

"Hmm." He sipped his coffee before turning his attention back to me. "It's not a bad idea, Pat. Go up to Braeloch and fly the company's colors on Wednesday. Then stay on. Vet all client accounts. Make sure everything runs according to our standards. Get out in the community and find businesses that need our services."

He wants me to stay on after the opening. "For how long?"

"Three weeks maybe. You can stay at Norris Cassidy's executive vacation home. Great place out on Black Bear Lake."

This was the opportunity I'd wanted, but three weeks of it? I had Laura and Tommy to think of. But my mind started to scramble for ways to make it happen.

"We've put a lot of money into this venture, Pat. You get it off to a good start."

There was something about the way he looked at me that gave me pause. "Any reason why it wouldn't?" I asked.

"I don't have to tell you that the Glencoe Highlands is not Toronto. A much smaller population base. And there's been talk of a recession looming. We have to think long-term, but we can't let costs outweigh revenue. The Braeloch branch needs clients. Affluent clients. If we can't find them…"

He cleared his throat. "Last week, we received an anonymous letter. It said a thief is working at the Braeloch branch." His mouth turned down in an expression of displeasure. "Clearly nonsense, but it shows that not everyone is happy about Norris Cassidy's arrival in the area. There are two banks in town, and we're competition for them."

"Nuala Larkin is the branch manager. What's her background?"

His face brightened. "The woman's a born leader. Hell of an addition to our team. She was at Optimum in Lindsay for a few years and approached us when she heard we were opening in Braeloch."

Optimum Capital was the company that Jamie had moved to.

"She'll have to build her business up from scratch," I said. Like Norris Cassidy, Optimum has a policy that a financial advisor's clients belong to the firm.

He smiled. "Next year, some of Nuala's Optimum clients may follow her to Norris Cassidy. Optimum's policy only applies to the first year."

The same as ours. But I didn't ask how he'd react if one of his advisors made a similar move.

"How many other advisors at the branch?" I asked.

"Just Paul Campbell, the junior. A go-getter, that young man. You wait and see. He'll have my job one day."

"Experience?"

"Worked at a Bank of Toronto branch here in the city for a few years. Grew up in the Glencoe Highlands. His family's all still there. A local boy will bring in local business."

Keith pulled a small notepad from his shirt pocket. "It's settled, then. Monty Buchanan can fill in for you. He's been at loose ends since he sold his business last summer. Drive up to Braeloch tomorrow. I'll call Shirley Corcoran, our caretaker, and tell her you'll stay at the house. And I'll let Nuala know that you'll be at the branch on Tuesday."

He scribbled down directions and a telephone number, and handed me the piece of paper. "Shirley's phone number."

My head spinning, I took it.

He stood up and held out his hand. "Get us off to a good start, Pat."

I'd been dismissed.

In the car, I phoned Shirley, who told me that the house at Black Bear Lake had four bedrooms and a pullout sofa in the basement. I said I'd arrive early that evening. I had my opportunity to look for Jamie and I was determined to make the most of it.

Then I called Stéphane Pratt, my business partner. I gave him some background on Tracy and Jamie, and I told him about Lyle's murder. Then I dropped the bombshell that I'd be at the Braeloch branch for the next few weeks.

"Monty Buchanan?" Stéphane said when I told him who would replace me. "Don't be up there too long, Pat. There's a limit to how long I can put up with old Monty."

"I'm sorry."

"We'll be fine, *ma chère*. You get the Braeloch branch off to a great start. So, have you come to terms with Tracy being gay?"

I hesitated. "I accept—at least I believe I've come to accept—Tracy's lifestyle. I'm her mother and I'll always be there for her." I paused. "How did your family take it?"

"My parents were shocked, of course. They're French-Canadian Catholics in a small city in Northern Ontario. How can they have a gay son? Where did they go wrong? There were some rough patches, but they eventually came to accept it.

"This is a period of adjustment for you," he added, "but it will turn out fine. *Bonne chance* in Braeloch, Pat."

Tracy was back at the house when I returned. She greeted me at the door, and we joined Laura in the kitchen where she was eating a late breakfast. I told them my plans.

"No! I'm not spending my winter break babysitting in the back woods!" Laura shook her head, her long blond hair swinging from side to side. "No way!"

I strove for patience. "Laura, I just explained—"

"Why can't Farah stay with Tommy up there?"

I reminded Laura that Farah Alwan, our housekeeper, had asked for the following week off. "Tracy can drive Farah up next weekend and take you back to Toronto. You'll be here when school opens."

"And I'll miss winter break!" she wailed. "Parties, ski trips if the snow's good. This is my last year of high school. I won't see some of the guys after this year."

I remembered that when I was eighteen my whole world revolved around my school friends, but I pushed that thought aside. "You've got almost four months till the school year ends," I said. "Plenty of time to say your goodbyes."

"And Kyle…"

I'd been worried about what Laura and her boyfriend Kyle Shingler would be up to when school was out the following week and I was at work. But over the years I'd learned to pick my battles.

"We wanted Tommy to live with us," Tracy told her. "We promised Mom we'd pitch in. Now's your chance."

"Tommy can stay with his grandmother," Laura said.

"Tommy's grandmother is an old woman with a heart condition." Tracy's voice was stern.

I pointed to the stairs. "Pack your bags, Laura. I'll get Tommy's stuff together. We'll leave in an hour. We have to stop for groceries on the way."

Laura glared at me defiantly, then dragged herself to the staircase.

"You and Tommy can—" I called out.

Her bedroom door slammed shut.

I took my cell out of my handbag. Celia picked up at the rectory.

"I'd love to!" she said, when I invited her to join us at Black Bear Lake. "Pack your outdoor clothes and your winter boots. Bring books. You may not be able to use your laptop or your cell phone at the lake. Rock cuts on the highways block the signal in many parts of the township."

That news was a downer. I like to be connected at all times. There'd be computers at the branch, but what would I do in the evenings?

"I'm going with you, Mom," Tracy said when I got off the phone.

I took her by the shoulders and looked into her eyes. "You have to finish your articling year. You've come this far."

I thought of something else. "And you need to keep your distance from the investigation. The police are looking for Jamie, and you're an officer of the court. You have a duty to tell them if you hear from her."

Tears filled her eyes. "I haven't heard from her for days."

"She hasn't contacted you because she doesn't want you involved. But I'll be up there. I'll do my best to find her."

"You'll be busy at the branch."

"Not that busy. There are two advisors and I'm sure they have everything under control. I'll just be the token rep from headquarters."

My mind flashed back to the article in *The Toronto World*. "I read an article yesterday that said that Jamie works at Optimum. I thought she was at your law firm."

"She joined Optimum three weeks ago as its client ombudsman."

"But she's specialized in claims against investment firms."

"She thinks it's her chance to bring about change within a company. Optimum wants to beef up its compliance department to ensure that trades are properly vetted."

She paused. "And she said we shouldn't work at the same firm. Optimum had been wooing her for months so she…"

"Crossed over."

"Yes."

"Jamie did that for you," I said. "She wouldn't want you to jeopardize your articling year."

Darkness had fallen when we turned into the long driveway that led to Norris Cassidy's vacation home, but lights on both sides illuminated our way. We pulled up in front of a two-story log structure. A rusty Toyota pickup was parked at the front door. Behind it was Sister Celia's blue Hyundai and a humongous black snowmobile on a trailer. I knew zilch about snowmobiles, but this one looked like the king of its species.

"Hey, guys!" Celia stood at the open front door beside a gray-haired woman dressed in a plaid shirt and blue jeans. "Welcome to the Glencoe Highlands. Meet Shirley Corcoran."

I waved at them and helped Tommy out of the back seat. Laura heaved a sigh and opened the passenger door.

At the door, Shirley handed me two sets of keys. A smile wreathed her weathered face. "Welcome to the Highlands, Mrs. Tierney. My Hank will keep the driveway plowed. If ya need anything else, just holler."

Celia took Maxie's leash from Tommy.

"Who does this snowmobile belong to?" I asked.

"Me!" Celia's face wore a delighted grin. "At least it's mine for the next few weeks. I've rented it till the end of March."

"Can I ride on it tomorrow?" Tommy asked as we went into the house.

"Sister Celia will be at work tomorrow, Tommy," I said.

"Monday's my day off," she said. "Are you at the branch tomorrow, Pat?"

I looked at my bedraggled family. Laura sat slumped on the bottom step of the staircase, holding her head in her hands. Tommy was about to fall asleep on his feet. And I didn't feel too perky myself. Maxie was the only one of our party with any energy. She raced around the ground floor of the house, barking at the top of her lungs.

I'd uprooted the kids and dragged them up there. We needed time to acclimatize.

"No," I said. "They expect me in on Tuesday."

The house was a luxury country home with pine woodwork, cathedral ceilings, skylights, a granite kitchen and a massive stone fireplace flanked by comfy leather sofas and armchairs. But it had no Internet or cell phone access. "How can I work on my history paper?" Laura asked when she came down from the bedroom she'd claimed.

I was disappointed, too. I'd brought my laptop with me, assuming that Norris Cassidy's executives would want to remain connected, even on their vacations. My cell, as well, because I never drive without it. "I'm sorry, honey. You'll have to go to the library in town. Or come into the branch."

We sat down to a dinner of cold cuts, salad and bread. After we'd eaten, Laura and Tommy turned in for the night. While Celia stacked the dishwasher, I saw them up to their rooms and got Tommy into bed. Then I left a message at Keith's office that I'd arrived at Black Bear Lake and I'd be at the branch on Tuesday.

Celia lit a fire in the fireplace and poured two glasses of cognac. I sat down beside her and she clicked on the television remote.

A fanfare of music announced the local TV station's evening newscast. The camera zoomed in on the face of an attractive young woman with shoulder-length dark hair. "I'm Mara Nowak, your host on *The Highlands Tonight*," she said. "Police are continuing their investigation into the murder of Lyle Critchley, the Glencoe Highlands resident who died in a fire in his garage on Thursday evening."

A picture of Lyle filled the screen.

"Police are still looking for Jennifer Collins as a person of interest," Mara said and moved on to another topic.

Celia turned down the sound. I got up and brought the telephone book back to the sofa. "The people who bought Lyle's business would know if he had any unhappy customers."

"I don't know who bought it," she said.

"They may have kept the company name." I flipped through the pages of business listings. "Doesn't look like it. Nothing listed as Critchley Heating and Cooling Systems."

"I'll ask around. Everyone knows everyone else around here."

"What was Lyle like?"

She sighed and took a sip of cognac. "He was a difficult man. Or maybe just set in his ways."

She paused for a moment or two. "He resented my presence. Complained last week when I put a vase of flowers on the altar.'Father Brisebois don't like flowers,' he said. "I told him that Father Brisebois wasn't there now.'I can see that,' he said.'Father would never let you wear blue jeans in here.'"

"I suppose he wanted women to wear dresses to church," I said. "Hats, too."

She smiled. "Women's fashion has always been a topic of great interest to Catholic clergy."

"Lyle shouldn't have criticized you."

She ran a hand over her eyes. "Here I'm going on about his shortcomings and the poor man is dead."

After Celia went up to bed, I called Devon Shaughnessy, the current man in my life. He runs a software business in Connecticut and I reached him at his home in Stamford.

"Too bad you're not near Kincaid. You could have stayed at my place," he said when I told him where I'd be for the next few weeks. Devon has a great home in another part of Ontario cottage country. That's where I met him. I rented the place next to it the previous summer.

"Why don't you come up here for a weekend?" Then I remembered Celia. A Catholic nun might not want my lover spending a weekend at the house. "Or I could drive over to your place for a few days."

Devon said he'd be busy with work for the next several weeks and didn't think he could get away. But he told me he'd make up for lost time when we got together.

"Promises, promises," I said. "Will you be up for—"

"No worries there. I'll even bring my Barry White CD."

"Barry who?"

"R and B singer, big in the '70s. 'Can't Get Enough of Your Love, Babe' was his No. 1."

I smiled. Devon can be a bit of a cornball, but he's a sweet guy.

"I'm picturing you right now, babe, in that black negligée." His voice was husky over the phone line. "You're incredibly hot in that gown."

I closed my eyes. "Tell me what you'd do if you were here."

His voice dropped lower as he did what I asked.

I added a few moves of my own.

We both sighed, then said our goodnights.

I was smiling from ear to ear when I hung up.

I splashed more cognac into my glass, and my thoughts returned to Lyle. He was a cantankerous old guy who seemed to have a knack for getting on people's nerves, maybe even on their bad sides. A lot of people may have wanted to get rid of him. I needed to check out his former clients and see if anyone with that particular leaning stuck out.

CHAPTER FIVE

The phone rang as I relaxed with a coffee after breakfast the next morning.

"A client has been murdered," Keith said. "We can't have this, Pat."

I'd expected him to object that I'd taken Monday off, but he was holding me accountable for murder.

"Good morning to you, too, Keith," I said. "If someone's been murdered, that's police business, not ours." I paused. "Who was this client?"

"Guy named Lyle Critchley. His garage burst into flames when he drove into it last week."

So Lyle had been checking out Braeloch's newest business. "Was he signed up as a client?" I asked. "Or was he just a prospect?"

"I expect anyone who walks into one of our branches to leave as a client." He paused. "Critchley had an appointment to meet with Paul on Thursday."

I closed my eyes. Lyle was only a prospect. Maybe Paul, the Wonder Kid, would have signed him up. Or maybe not.

"Dammit, Pat, we can't have Norris Cassidy's name associated with people getting murdered."

I stifled a sigh. "But it *isn't* linked to Lyle's murder. Paul, Nuala, you and now myself are the only ones who know that he was considering having us manage his money. He wasn't a client yet."

"Investment management is a sensitive business," he barked. "Our good name is everything."

"Norris Cassidy has an excellent track record. And I'm sure most people realize the Bernie Madoffs are just a few bad apples in the barrel."

"Would-be Madoffs can be anywhere. Even in a small center, as Optimum discovered."

The hairs on the back of my neck stood up. "What do you mean?"

"That letter I told you about gnawed on my mind all day. When we got back from Oakville, I went on the Internet and there they were."

"There what were?"

"News reports about the fraud at Optimum's Lindsay branch last year. One of their people dipped into the accounts of twenty retirees, took $50,000 out of each and moved the $1 million to an account in the Cayman Islands. But they caught the guy."

"And you think the wrong person was arrested?"

"Oh, no. They had the guy dead to rights. All the transactions were done from his computer. Police checked the other advisors' accounts and computers, and they came up clean. This guy—Ken Burrows—was arrested. He insisted he knew nothing about the theft or about the Cayman account. Hah! He's in jail now."

"The money was recovered?"

"No. The Cayman account was closed, and the money was moved who knows where. Burrows still insists he doesn't know where it is."

"Optimum reimbursed its clients?" I asked.

"It dragged its feet for a few months hoping that Burrows would confess and say where the money was. But, yes, Optimum paid those investors, although one of them died while she waited for her money."

Keith paused. "Optimum got a hefty fine from the regulators for failing to supervise Burrows appropriately. So it hired someone from outside to be a client ombudsman. Jennifer Collins, the lawyer in the Betsy Cornell case. And now the police are looking for *her* in connection with Lyle Critchley."

"It's a small world." As soon as the words were out of my mouth, I realized how true they were.

"Too small for my liking, which is why I want you to steer Norris Cassidy away from this mess as soon as possible."

"We're not in any mess. Lyle wasn't a client."

"Pat, get the branch off to a good start. If we don't have a solid base soon…" He paused. "You know our quotas for assets under management. If we don't see a substantial revenue base by the end of the year, we may have to pull the plug on Braeloch. Get in there tomorrow morning and kick ass. We're counting on you."

He hung up before I could ask whether Norris Cassidy had plans to get Internet service at Black Bear Lake. And courtesies like saying goodbye weren't among Keith's priorities that morning.

CHAPTER SIX

Just before noon, Laura burst into the house, followed by Celia.

"You've got to try it, Mom!" Laura peeled off her jacket. "It's awesome out there."

Celia had spent the past three hours taking Tommy and Laura out on the snowmobile. The sparkle in Laura's eyes told me the morning had been a success.

"I wanna go out again!" Tommy cried, coming into the kitchen.

"Pat's turn after lunch," Celia said.

"Aww," Tommy lamented. "I never get to have *any* fun."

"We'll go out again, kiddo, just not today," Celia said.

"Promise?" he asked.

"Cross my heart. Now go wash your hands." She shooed him off to the washroom.

Laura took plates from the cupboard. "Take a trip after lunch, Mom. I'll watch a movie with Tommy."

I stared at her, wondering for a moment or two whether I'd heard correctly.

"Aren't you up for a spin, Pat?" Celia asked.

I arranged slices of cold roast beef on a platter. "When I saw you head across the lake, I wondered whether the ice would hold." I didn't mention the fear that had sliced through me.

Celia helped herself to a piece of meat. "That ice is solid, even with the thaw last week. The winter's been pretty cold. Spring breakup is weeks away."

"Go on, Mom," Laura said.

Celia slid a laminated map across the counter. "This creek links Black Bear Lake to the next lake in the chain." She ran a finger over the plastic. "There are five lakes. The fifth is Serenity Lake. When we get to it, we'll be in Braeloch."

"How long would that take?" And how long, I wondered, would Laura's patience with Tommy hold out?

"Probably less time than a drive to Braeloch on the highway." She held up the map. "We'd have to drive down Highway 36, then east on 187. But the lakes cut through the area on the diagonal."

"Okay." I turned to my daughter. "Laura, you can give me a hand here after lunch."

She waved a hand grandly. "I'll wash up."

"We'll be gone for a few hours," I warned.

"No problem."

I decided to make the most of her expansive mood.

Down by the lake, I found Celia astride the snowmobile. She waved me over.

I approached cautiously. I half expected the beast to spring on me.

She patted the machine that was purring under her. "A beauty, isn't she? Pat, say hello to Molly."

"Hi, Moll." I gave it a little wave, feeling silly. "You grew up in the city, Celia. When did you learn to operate a snowmobile?"

Her dark eyes sparkled. "My mother came from Northern Ontario—a four-hour drive north of here—and we spent Christmas and winter break up there. My cousins all had snowmobiles. I thought it would be fun to get out into the great outdoors while we're here."

I looked at the tiny woman in the navy blue snowmobile suit astride the giant machine. "But this creature is so…big."

"It doesn't take muscle to operate a snowmobile."

She got off the machine and came around to where I stood. "She's powered by a four-cylinder, four-stroke—"

"Stop." I held up my gloved hands in mock surrender. "I'll never remember any of this."

She grinned. "That's okay. You don't have to know the specs to operate one of these machines. Although you'd impress the men around here if you could rhyme off a few." She paused. "You can drive a car, so you can drive Molly."

She pointed to the lever near the right handlebar. "This is her throttle. Use your right thumb on it to get her engine up to speed."

Then she showed me the brake lever and the handlebars. "Turn them the same way you would to steer a bike. See? Nothing to it."

She pressed the throttle and Molly sprang to attention. "Hop on!" she called out over the roar.

I glanced down at the ski jacket and jeans that I was wearing and wondered whether I was dressed for the occasion.

"You'll be fine," she shouted. "It's pretty mild today." She handed me a helmet with a face shield.

I fastened it on my head, then carefully seated myself behind her. Molly vibrated under me. Celia turned her head. "Hold on to the handgrips."

I grabbed the metal grips on either side of my seat and hoped for the best.

"Ready to roll?"

"Guess so," I yelled.

"Hold on tight."

Molly lurched forward, and we zoomed onto the lake. I tightened my hold on the grips, my heart in my mouth. I really was too old for this kind of adventure.

By the time we'd reached the other side of the lake, my fear had melted away. Laura was right, it *was* fun! Celia pointed the snowmobile down a wide trail through trees. A few yards down the trail, she pulled up beside a birch and cut the motor. She flipped up her face shield. "Okay?"

I nodded. "Do we have enough gas?"

"Enough to get us to Braeloch. We'll fill up there."

"Let's go for it." I pulled down my face shield.

"One more thing, Pat."

I flipped up the shield.

"When I raise an arm, it means we're about to make a sharp turn in that direction," she said. "Lean to the opposite side to keep the machine on both skis."

"Got it."

The trip down the frozen creek was like driving into a Christmas card. Snow-covered spruce and cedars hugged both shores. At one point, the trees gave way to a granite outcropping that rose high into the air.

We emerged from the creek onto an expanse of white that was crisscrossed by snowmobile tracks. A bay dotted with ice fishing huts was on our left. Ahead of us, two machines inched across the white canvas.

Celia raised her right arm. I leaned left and we flew across the ice. The sun beat down on us and the snow-covered lake sparkled. Exhilarated, I lifted my face to the sky. I pictured the scene at the beginning of *Easy Rider* when Peter Fonda and Dennis Hopper are on the road with Steppenwolf's "Born To Be Wild" on the soundtrack.

Rock 'n' roll gave way to classical, and "Ride of the Valkyries" ran through my head. Man, machine, speed, power. There was no more fitting accompaniment than Wagner's magnificent music.

The music faded and Jamie Collins' face flashed into my mind. *What had Lyle told her?* But I shelved that thought for later and focused on the moment. Moments like those out on the frozen lakes are too few and far between.

The lakes and the creeks that joined them flew by. We waved at the people on the snowmobiles we passed and they waved back at us.

On the fourth lake, a crowd had gathered on the far west side, and Celia pointed Molly in that direction. As we got closer, I saw that a strip of black water about six feet wide bridged the frozen bay we were on to the bay beyond it. Celia cut the engine. "It's a snowmobile skip over the narrows," she said. "Let's check it out."

We left Molly on the ice and walked over to the group of people on the beach. Their eyes were riveted on a black-and-yellow snowmobile that zoomed across the ice on the farther bay headed for the strip of open water.

I stared at it in horror. "The driver's going to drown!"

Celia put a hand on my arm. "Watch this."

The snowmobile hit the water at top speed and kept on going, spray flying out in all directions. "He's going across the top of the water just like a stone does when you skip it," Celia said.

A cheer went up from the crowd when the machine landed on the ice in our bay.

"Mark Nicholson," a man said over a loudspeaker. "His seventh run of the day at 26.04 seconds."

We watched two more snowmobiles skip over the water.

"The heavier the rider and the machine, the faster they need to go. And they can only go in a straight line, no turning," Celia said as we walked back to Molly. "If they don't make it across the water, they sink like stones. It takes only seconds for a snowmobile to drop to the bottom of the lake."

"And the drivers?"

"They're wearing wet suits. They'll come back for their machines in the spring."

"Why would anyone—?"

"Want to do it? Challenge. Personal best." She held up her hands. "Hey, I know. It's dangerous and it's unregulated. But some people are hooked on it."

I wondered what she would do if a stretch of water got in our way. One look at the grin on her face and I had my answer.

As we crossed the lake, I noticed that the needle on the gas gauge was near the empty mark. Fear flickered in my heart. If we ran out of gas it would be a long trek over the ice to Braeloch, then back to Molly. We'd be out on the lakes in the dark.

Celia gunned Molly down a small creek and the fifth lake opened before us. On its far shore, a village sat under a hill topped by two outcroppings.

"Braeloch!" Celia cried.

We filled Molly's gas tank at the municipal dock. We left her there and walked along the road that ran up to Main Street. At the town's west end, Main inclined upwards toward Jesus of the Highlands Church. Then it turned into Highway 123 that cut through the farm country east of town.

The church stood on a lower flank of the hill behind the town. A steep staircase led to the double front doors, and a network of ramps across the sloping lawn provided easier access to the entrance.

"Our stairway to heaven," Celia said as we stood at the foot of the staircase. "The church was built in 1910. People were either more mobile in those days or they didn't live as long. Now, at least half of our parishioners are over seventy and they use the ramps."

She studied the stairs with a frown on her face. "Bruce didn't put salt down today." She turned toward the bottom ramp, and I followed her up it.

She pointed to the two-story brick house beside the church. "My place of business."

"What's your title here?"

"The official moniker is pastoral coordinator. There's quite a few of us around these days, what with the shortage of Catholic priests and all."

She unlocked a side door to the church and led me into a small room behind the church proper. She flicked on a light switch. "The sacristy."

Pine cupboards and drawers had been built along one wall. A wooden clothes rack on the wall across from it held priest's vestments.

She flicked off the light and motioned me to follow her through the doorway.

The small church was unremarkable except for a round stained-glass window behind the altar. "A rose window," I whispered. In a few hours, the setting sun would illuminate the church with reds and blues and purples refracted from the window.

"Lovely, isn't it? A gift from the Greeley family, its plaque says. I haven't met any of them yet."

She entered a pew and knelt in prayer. I sat beside her.

A parish community, with its committees and clubs filled with wannabe leaders, could be a breeding ground for petty rivalries. Lyle had spent a lot of time in that church and its rectory. Had the crabby old man pushed someone past all endurance?

Celia turned to me. "On to the rectory."

"When is Lyle's funeral?" I asked as she locked the church door.

"Friday morning. They're sending a priest up from Lindsay."

"You said Lyle's wife had died. Did he have any other family?"

"He and Edna had no children," she said as we made our way along the path between the two buildings. "And there don't seem to be any relatives."

She unlocked the rectory door and pushed it open. "Welcome to the men's club."

The interior was gloomy. When she flicked on the hall lights, I saw that several doors opened off both sides of a long central hall.

"This could be a handsome building if some of these walls were taken down." She stopped in front of the first door on the left and pushed it open. "My office."

She reached inside to turn on the light. "Oh!" she cried.

I looked over her shoulder into the room. On a sofa against the far wall, a figure roused itself. A shaggy, salt-and-pepper head emerged from under a blanket.

"Bruce Stohl!" Celia said.

A rumpled man swung his feet to the floor. Tufts of hair stood up on his head.

Celia went over to him. "Fast asleep at two in the afternoon. That icy staircase out front is an accident waiting to happen."

The man staggered to his feet and blinked his red-rimmed eyes. "Sorry, Sister, I…I…"

"You reek of booze."

He hung his head.

"Bruce, where are you living?" she asked in a kinder tone.

"Got kicked out."

"Of where?"

"Mrs. Collins's basement. She kicked me out yesterday. Didn't want me smoking in the house."

"Here in town?"

He nodded. "Got no wheels, Sister. Can't get far around here without them."

"Veronica Collins?" I asked.

He turned to look at me. "Yeah, that's her."

"This is Pat Tierney, Bruce. Pat, Bruce Stohl is our maintenance man."

"Veronica is Jamie's mother," I said to Celia.

"Did Mrs. Collins give you notice?" she asked Bruce.

He hung his head. "She warned me about smoking a couple of times."

Celia let out a big gust of breath. "You can stay on the sofa here tonight. Just for tonight."

His eyes brightened.

"But no smoking. I don't want the rectory going up in flames." She glared at him. "You have cigarettes on you?"

He reached into his quilted vest and pulled out a pack.

She took it from him and stashed it in her pocket.

He winced as though he'd been hit.

"And no booze." She unzipped the nylon pouch that was fastened around her waist and handed him a $10 bill. "For supper at Joe's Diner. Joe's, Bruce. Not the Dominion Hotel bar."

He gave her a sad-dog smile.

"I mean it, Bruce. No smoking and no drinking in here. Don't let me down."

"I won't, Sister."

She moved toward the door, then stopped and looked back at him. "Did the police speak to you yesterday?"

Bruce nodded. "Guy with a gray moustache came back to the church after you left."

"Inspector Foster."

He nodded again. "He wanted to know where I was Thursday evening. Told him I was at home and he could check with Mrs. Collins. That's the night she smelled my cigarette smoke through the heating vents."

"Did he speak to anyone else at the church?"

"No one else was around then. I'd just finished mopping the floor."

"I'll see you in the morning, Bruce," Celia said. "Throw some salt on those stairs right now. And if it snows overnight, you'll need to shovel first thing."

A police cruiser pulled up in front of the church as we walked down the ramp. Foster and a uniformed officer got out.

"The guy in plainclothes is the big gun from Orillia," Celia said in a low voice. "He's here to investigate Lyle's murder. The one in uniform is Roger Bouchard who runs the local cop shop."

"What brings you to Braeloch, Ms. Tierney?" Foster asked.

Celia looked surprised.

"Inspector Foster and I have met," I said to her.

"Quite the coincidence to find you here. But I don't believe in coincidences." He gestured to the younger man beside him. "This is Sergeant Bouchard. He's in charge of the Braeloch detachment. Pat Tierney."

"I'm here for the startup of Norris Cassidy's new branch," I said. "I arrived yesterday."

"I see." But Foster looked as though he didn't. "Where is your daughter's friend?"

"Nobody knows. Tracy hasn't heard from her."

"You'll be in Braeloch a while?" Bouchard asked.

"A few weeks."

"Then perhaps—"

"Sergeant Bouchard," Foster said. "I remind you that I'm in charge of this investigation."

"But—" Bouchard began

Foster fixed his gray eyes on me. "We need to speak to Ms. Collins. There were bad feelings between her and Lyle Critchley."

"That was years ago."

"And then she turns up here on the day he's killed. As I said, I don't believe in coincidences. We need to speak to her." He handed me his card. "Soon."

"The letter Lyle sent her…"

"The mystery letter your daughter said she knows nothing about."

"Yes, Lyle told her something in that letter. And whoever killed him might want Jennifer Collins out of the way, too."

A frown creased his face. "If he—or she—knew that Critchley told her something in a letter."

I nodded. "That may be why she's lying low."

"Have her give us a call."

Then he bowed in a courtly fashion. "And have yourselves a good day."

Celia and I watched as they got into the cruiser. "Do you need to visit your branch?" she asked when the vehicle pulled onto the road.

"I'll be there in the morning. But I'd like to check out the Dominion Hotel and the car rental place. Do we have time?"

She glanced at her watch. "You go to the hotel and I'll try the rental shop. Then we should head back. We don't want to be on the lakes in the dark."

The Dominion Hotel's lobby was deserted except for a stuffed moose head on the wall behind the reception desk. Christmas ornaments dangled from the antlers. A noisy bar beside the lobby seemed to be where the hotel made the lion's share of its money.

I rang the bell on the desk. A good minute later, a teenage boy, his face pitted and scarred with acne, ambled out of the bar carrying a tray of empties. There was no point in asking if he knew Jamie. He would have been a toddler when she lived in the area.

But his face brightened when I asked if Jennifer Collins stayed at the hotel the previous Thursday night. He put the tray down on the reception desk. "The police asked us that. They think she had something to do with Lyle Critchley's murder. That's what Mara Nowak said on TV. Are you a private investigator?"

"Just a friend."

"She's not here now. She checked out on Friday morning."

"She say where she was going?"

"I wasn't here when she left. I work after school and on weekends. And during winter break." He opened a door behind the desk. "Dad, someone's asking about the Collins woman again."

A man with a thatch of iron-gray hair came to the doorway and took off his glasses. "We don't give out information about our guests."

"Jamie—Jennifer—Collins is a friend. I need to find her."

"Sorry." He peered at me. "I can't even tell you whether she stayed here."

I smiled at his son who had picked up his tray. "I understand."

At the door, two men in leather jackets pushed past me on their way to the lounge. I wondered what their hurry was. It didn't sound like strip karaoke was in session.

Outside, Celia hurried down the sidewalk toward me. "Jamie stayed at the Dominion on Thursday night," I said when she caught up with me.

"Well, she didn't rent a car when she checked out. Sign on the door says the place is closed until Victoria Day weekend."

"Damn! I wanted to rent a car for Laura this week. Is there another rental place around here?"

"Haven't seen one."

I decided I'd worry about Laura's transportation later. "Then somebody gave Jamie a lift."

Celia nodded. "As Bruce said, she'd need wheels to get anywhere around here. Unless she's still in town. C'mon, we've got to get back to Molly."

I followed her across Main Street, my mind in overdrive. Jamie must have known about the fire at Lyle's place. It may not have made the ten o'clock news that night, but someone could have told her about it. She decided to drop out of sight and asked a friend to pick her up on Friday morning.

"This way." Celia didn't break her stride as she turned into a walkway between two shops. Behind the buildings, a flight of stairs led to the waterfront. I followed her down them.

"What's Bruce's story?" I asked.

"A lost soul, although a very bright one. He has a doctorate in philosophy."

Surprised by what I'd heard, I nearly missed the last step. "What happened?"

"Taught at a university out in Alberta for a few years, then he had a breakdown. Drifted for a while, then turned up here last year. Father Brisebois took him on at the church."

"How old is he?"

"My age. Forty-two."

He looked a good decade older than her. Too much rough living, I guessed.

"Bruce is a classic example of the huge economic disparity in these parts," she said.

She patted Molly's hood and I waited for her to go on.

"The mega-cottages on the lakes sell for $1 million-plus. But there are people around here who are unemployed or earn the minimum wage. Like Bruce, they can't afford a vehicle to get to jobs around the township."

She kicked a snowbank beside the dock. "I'll put Bruce up in the rectory until Father Brisebois returns. On what we pay him, he can't afford much around here, and we have a heated building standing empty."

"You're not afraid he'll pass out with a cigarette?"

"I'll think of some way to keep him in line," she said with a chuckle. "Lyle would have a fit."

"He didn't like Bruce?"

"Bruce has been known to be...somewhat irregular in his duties. Lyle never had a good word to say about him."

Somebody else Lyle didn't get along with.

CHAPTER SEVEN

I walked into the Braeloch branch at the stroke of nine the next morning. At the front desk, a plump young woman with short fuchsia hair smiled at me. Ivy Barker, Administrative Assistant, her nameplate read.

"The branch officially opens tomorrow," she said, "but one of our advisors would be happy to—"

"I'm Pat Tierney from Toronto." I handed her my business card.

Ivy glanced at the card. "Ah, the lady from headquarters."

I nodded and looked around. The old house had been completely renovated. Norris Cassidy really *had* put a lot of money into it. But if the business didn't fly, the firm should be able to recoup its investment as long as real estate prices held strong.

The large waiting area to my left held several brown leather armchairs, coffee tables with magazines and a stately gas fireplace. Three offices were on my right. The door to the front office was open, displaying dark wainscoting, a bay window that looked out onto Main Street and a ginger blonde behind an oversized mahogany desk. A brass plaque on the wall identified the occupant as Nuala Larkin, Branch Manager.

I stepped into the office. "Hello, Nuala. I'm Pat Tierney."

She got out of her chair, drew herself up to her full five-foot height and extended her hand. "Welcome to Braeloch, Pat."

I took in her artfully tousled hair, charcoal tailored suit and spike heels. She was in her mid-thirties, a power dresser, and by all outward appearances, a woman who was going places.

Her turquoise eyes smiled at me.

I took her hand. *Smart cookie. You don't want me here but you're not about to show it.*

"And here's Soupy," she said.

I turned to see a tall, dark-haired young man at Nuala's door. The smile on his handsome face displayed nice white teeth. "Paul Campbell's the name." He held out his hand.

"Pat Tierney. Good to meet you." I winced as his big paw crushed my hand.

"Everyone around here calls me Soupy."

I flexed my hand to see if any bones were broken. "I get it. As in Campbell's Soup."

He actually looked impressed. "It's Paul Campbell on anything official," he went on, "but I've been Soupy since back in high school when our band got started."

"Band?"

He smiled. "The High Lonesome Wailers. Country, rock and reggae. From Johnny Cash to Creedence Clearwater to Bob Marley. I'm lead guitar."

"An interesting mix," I said.

"Soupy," Nuala chided. "Pat isn't here to discuss your music career."

"The Glencoe Highlands is a hotbed of music," he said.

I held up a hand. "I'm sure it is. But right now, I'll take a look at your client files. I understand you've got quite a few already."

"The Wailers are playing a fundraiser on Saturday night. I can put tickets aside for you."

I flashed him a smile. "I'll see if I can make it."

I spent the morning in the spare office looking over client accounts. Nuala and Soupy had already drummed up seventeen clients. One of them was Veronica Collins, who had a little more than $200,000 for the branch to invest. Not a bad beginning, although not the numbers that Keith wanted.

At quarter to twelve, Soupy poked his head around the doorframe. "Have time for some lunch?"

"I'm taking the four of us out for lunch," I said. "By the way, I see Veronica Collins is your client."

"You know Veronica?"

"We've met. So what's the best place in town for lunch?"

He laughed. "If you like burgers, that would be Joe's."

Ivy appeared beside him. "The really good places to eat are at the resorts. The Winagami is the closest. It's a twenty-minute drive."

"Let's go there," I said. "We don't officially open for business till tomorrow."

Ivy looked at her watch. "Nuala's gone to see a client, but she said she'd be back by noon. I'll make a reservation for twelve-thirty."

Fifteen minutes later, I joined Soupy and Ivy in the reception area. Nuala still hadn't returned.

"We were talking about Lyle Critchley, the guy who was murdered out at his place last week," Soupy said. "He came in here the day he died."

"I hear you nearly had him signed up as a client," I said.

He nodded solemnly. "Almost."

"Mr. Critchley was at the door when Soupy and I got back from lunch," Ivy said. "We saw him peering through the front window. Said he wanted a look at the place. So we opened up and asked him in. He checked the place out like he was thinking of buying it."

"'Swanky place like this, you folks must charge a pretty penny to handle people's money.'" Soupy mimicked an old man's voice. "'Fancy fireplace. Leather couches, too.'"

Ivy tried to hide her laughter. I laughed too, then felt badly because the man was dead. But he did sound like an aggravating old coot.

"But I knew Lyle would be a good catch," Soupy said. "Ran that heating company for years, probably had pots of money. I gave him one of our brochures. We made an appointment for this Thursday."

He sighed. "You win some, you lose some."

Ivy's mouth puckered. "I know I shouldn't say this, but he seriously creeped me out. You know what he said before he left?'I'll be back.'"

"Sounded more like a threat than a promise," Soupy said.

Nuala arrived just then, and we headed out to the small parking lot behind the building where I'd left my Volvo beside a cherry-red Lexus.

"Nice car, Nuala," Ivy said, looking at the Lexus.

Keith must have given her a whopping signing bonus.

"I could walk to work," Nuala said, "but I never know when I may have to visit a client."

I clicked open the Volvo's doors and got in behind the steering wheel. Soupy took the seat beside me, and Nuala and Ivy sat in the back. I drove through Braeloch and onto the highway.

"Watch out for cars coming up," Soupy said as we rounded a curve.

I gritted my teeth. Backseat drivers are a pain in the butt, and Soupy wasn't even in the backseat.

"Pat's driven a car before," Nuala put in behind me.

"Not up here," Soupy said cheerfully. "You take your life in your hands on the roads around here. More people get killed on the stretch between Braeloch and Donarvon than on any other road in Ontario."

I resisted telling him I'd driven through the Canadian Rockies and all the way down the west coast of the United States to the Baja Peninsula.

"Some say it's these rock cuts," he continued as we drove between two towering walls of rock. "This is the Precambrian Shield. Rocks millions, maybe billions, of years old. That spooks some people."

In the rear-view mirror, I saw Nuala roll her eyes.

"But what bugs me about these rock cuts is they screw up cell phone reception," he said. "That's been the hardest thing about coming back here."

"Oh, you big city boy," Ivy scoffed. "Life is so hard out here in the bush."

The Winagami's dining room was almost full. Many of the diners were families on winter break vacations. The waitress seated us in front of windows that looked out on a snow-covered lake. Half a dozen snowmobiles zoomed across it.

"Aren't you and Mara having your wedding reception here?" Ivy asked Soupy when the waitress had taken our orders.

He nodded. "July 21. Mara's folks booked it last year."

"Congratulations," I said. "Would that be the Mara Nowak on *The Highlands Tonight*?"

"You bet!" His face beamed. "That's my girl."

Across the table, Nuala smiled. "No winter wedding? Some say winter is the best time of year in these parts. No bugs, no bears."

"But tons of snow," I said. "The place where I'm staying has a long driveway. If anything prevents the Corcorans down the road from plowing, I'll be housebound."

"A lot of businesses rely on good snow conditions for snowmobiles and cross-country skiing," Ivy said as she looked around the room. "Especially during Christmas and winter break."

Our drinks arrived. White wine for Nuala and myself, beer for Soupy and Ivy. I raised my glass. "To the Braeloch branch," I said. "May it prosper and grow."

The others raised their glasses.

"I'm really impressed," I told them. "Seventeen client accounts and the branch hasn't even opened."

"Quite a few are Soupy's friends and relatives," Nuala said.

He gave a sheepish grin. "Figured I should call in some favors to get off to a good start."

He took a folded newspaper from inside his jacket and opened it. "Here's our ad." He passed the paper to me.

A full-page advertisement in *The Highlands Times* announced the opening of the Braeloch branch the following day. A series of financial planning seminars scheduled for the coming weeks caught my interest.

"These seminars are a great idea," I said.

"Nuala's idea," Soupy said. "First one's on Thursday night."

"We hope it will bring in some clients," Nuala said. "The topic is retirement planning. Next month, we'll do ways to reduce debt."

Soupy drew his chair closer to the table. "In May, when the cottagers return, we'll hold a Saturday session on cottage succession planning." His dark eyes shone. "We need to target the cottagers. They're putting in master-chef kitchens and Jacuzzis."

"There's a lot of wealth in this area," Nuala added.

"Wealthy cottagers have driven up lakefront real estate prices," Soupy said. "We have a place on Three Hills Lake that's been in our family for three generations. We'd never be able to afford it today."

"Don't overlook the local people," I put in. "Many cottagers have financial advisors in the city."

Nuala nodded.

"It's young people you should go after," Ivy said. "People my age are moving here for jobs in construction and the trades."

I smiled at her. "Young families may not have a lot of savings, but they'll grow. And they probably aren't working with a financial advisor yet."

The waitress arrived with our starters.

"This afternoon, I'd like to go over the seminars you've planned," I said as the woman placed a bowl of tomato bisque in front of me.

Soupy glanced at Nuala, then speared a shrimp from his plate. Nuala looked at me too brightly.

Tread carefully, I told myself. "Maybe I can pass along a tip or two. And I'm sure that you have ideas I can take back to Toronto."

Nuala lowered her eyes and dipped her spoon into her bisque.

I decided that they didn't need to hear Keith's caution that the branch had to deliver—and quickly. "You're doing all the right things," I said. "It takes time to build a business."

"My kids are with me this week," I said on the drive back to Braeloch. "My daughter was talking about cross-country skiing this morning but my…little boy hasn't done much of it. I don't think he can keep up with her."

I wondered if I'd ever get used to calling Tommy my son.

"Snow's still good," Soupy said. "Have them try Highlands Park out by the reservoir. Trails don't ice up like other places."

"Braeloch College has an art program on this week," Ivy said as I pulled into the parking lot behind the branch. "Drawing, painting, pottery, you name it. Your kids might like it. The college is across the lake from here."

"I'll check that out." Laura could hit the ski trails while Tommy was in the art program. But first I had to find them some form of transportation.

The four of us went over the agenda for the launch the next day, and gave it a few tweaks. Then Nuala and Soupy showed me their plans for the seminar series. I made a few suggestions, but I mainly showed a lot of enthusiasm.

When we'd adjourned, I followed Soupy into his office. It wasn't as large as Nuala's and it didn't have a bay window, but it had a fireplace with a beautiful carved wooden mantle.

"Does the fireplace work?" I asked.

"Yeah, it does. It's wood-burning, not like the gas one out front. I'll have to get some firewood."

I sat myself in the chair across from his desk. "Soupy, what investment firm was Lyle with?"

"I don't know."

"You don't know?"

He lowered his eyes. "I offered my services and he said he'd be back this Thursday. I told him to bring his last quarterly statement if he had one."

I sighed. "Soupy, the first thing you ask a prospective client is whether he's already working with a financial advisor. The client can take his business wherever he chooses, but we don't want to look like we're poaching another firm's clients."

"I figured he was on his own," he said. "Old-timer like him probably had his money stashed away in a bank."

"But you didn't know."

"Well, I would've known this Thursday if he brought in a statement of his holdings at another firm." His face brightened. "Police should've have found it among his papers. If there was anything to be found."

"Was Lyle's company doing well before he sold it?"

He smiled. "It was a terrific business. Mara's dad bought it. Couldn't believe his luck."

"What's Mr. Nowak's business called?"

"Nowak Heating. It's north of here on Highway 36 just past Donarvon."

Back in my office, I looked up Nowak Heating on the Internet. Its website listed Greg Nowak as the owner, and it included a map that showed where its office was located. I printed it out, then started compiling a list of companies in the area from the local Yellow Pages.

Shortly after four, voices in the reception area caught my ear. I rolled my head to stretch the kinks out of my neck and got up from my desk. It was time for a break.

I found Nuala talking to a couple in front of Ivy's reception desk. She raised a hand to me in greeting. "Pat, this is our new client, Bea Greeley."

I recognized the name Greeley—the family who installed the rose window in the church.

The white-haired woman smiled at me. She had a round, freckled face like a raisin bun.

"And Ted Stohl, who runs *The Highlands Times*," Nuala added. "He's writing another article on the branch."

Ted had the same surname as Bruce, Celia's new boarder at the rectory.

Nuala turned to Ted. "Pat Tierney is here from Toronto for our opening. You should talk to her."

Ted took my hand in a firm grip. He was some years younger than Bea, and wore his silver hair brushed back from his face and tucked behind his ears.

"Nuala's given me a rundown of your services," he said. "We'll use a shot of the building's exterior."

"Nuala's the person to talk to here," I said. "She's the branch manager."

He handed me his business card. "*The Times* comes out once a week. The article will be in Saturday's paper."

"I'll have your portfolio ready in a few days," Nuala said to Bea. "Come in on Monday and I'll go over it with you."

Ted smiled. "We'll both come in. Around two okay?"

"Fine," Nuala said and moved toward the door.

I looked at Ted. "Mr. Stohl—"

"Please. It's Ted."

"Ted, I met another Stohl yesterday. Bruce. Any relation?"

His face shut down and he didn't answer.

"I'm sorry. I didn't mean to pry," I said.

"My son," he said curtly. He held the door open for Bea and helped her down the stairs. He didn't look back.

"It's a small world up here," Nuala said when the door had closed behind them. "Not only does everyone know everyone else, but they all seemed to be related. If you wanted to prove the idea of six degrees of separation, look no further than the Glencoe Highlands."

I'd seen the movie by that name. The theory was that everyone is on average about six steps away, by way of introduction, from any other person on Earth.

"That wasn't what I'd call a display of fatherly affection," I said as I followed her into her office. "What's the beef between Ted and his son?"

"I haven't been here long enough to know." She perched on the window seat in the bay window.

I slipped into the chair in front of her desk. "Are there other family ties I should be aware of?"

"Well, Bea's related to Soupy. Second or third cousin. Soupy passed her on to me."

"As he should have," I said. "An advisor should never work with family members."

She smiled. "He thinks she's a dotty old bird. I have no problem with her, but her boyfriend..." She rolled her eyes. "Bea is an affluent, seventy-nine-year-old widow. Ted mentioned that he's sixty-eight. What does that tell you?"

"That she's eleven years older than him."

"And he's too old to be a boy toy. If he was a woman, he'd be called a gold digger."

"They're a couple?"

She examined her fingernails, which were painted the same shade of coral as her lipstick. "I assume so. He wants to know everything I'm doing with her money."

"Relax. You're managing it. He hasn't talked her into letting him invest it for her."

"That will come." She ran her tongue over her coral lips. "He'll question every move I make. Then I'll get a call from Bea saying she wants to close her account."

"Does she seem mentally competent?"

"She's one of those clingy women. Looks to Ted as an authority on everything. Otherwise seems sound of mind."

"Children?"

"A married daughter in Toronto."

"Does the daughter have power of attorney?"

Nuala nodded. "For now."

"Encourage Bea to bring her into the loop. Ask to meet her when she visits Bea."

"Ted would go for that? I don't think so."

"Bring it up on Monday."

Nuala locked eyes with me. "Maybe I'm making a mountain out of a molehill here, but I don't like to see vulnerable people like Bea get hurt."

My heart warmed to her. The woman had talent, energy and, best of all, integrity. Keith was right. She was a terrific addition to the firm.

"Does that come from your time with Optimum in Lindsay?"

Nuala bowed her head slightly, then nodded. "You know about that?"

"Yes." I paused. "Do you want to talk about it?

She seemed to hesitate. "Sure, but what more I could tell you..."

"I just want to see if there's a lesson to be learned from that sad business, something we might watch out for here." I paused. "Tell me about Ken Burrows."

"Soupy reminds me of Ken," Nuala said. "Young, confident, a go-getter, brought in a lot of clients. Charmed the retirees he ended up stealing from."

"Anything in his behavior that suggested he would—"

"No. Everyone at the branch was stunned."

"Any large purchases before this happened? Expensive tastes?"

She shook her head. "He liked to dress well and wore expensive suits." She motioned to her own outfit. "But so do I."

"What's your take on the investigation? Thorough enough?"

"Oh yes. The forensic accountants, the police—they were there for months. They went over all our accounts, checked hard drives on all the computers at the office and even our home computers. In the end, they found Ken's client accounts were the only ones with money missing. And that his computer was the only one that had been used to make offshore deposits."

"How did he expect to get away with it?" I wondered aloud. "I've heard of cases where crooked advisors have taken small amounts over long periods of time to try to conceal their thefts but this seems so...so..."

"Blatant?" Nuala said. "The police say Ken planned to take the money and run. Well, he took the money but he never got the chance to run. He was arrested at his home."

She paused to examine her nails again. "What really upsets me is that Ken stole hard-earned money from retirees. Those people depended on that money. Why he won't own up to what he did, I don't understand."

"How did Optimum or the police get wind of the fraud?"

"I don't know. A client complaint, probably."

I thought of the letter Keith had received. "What do you think of the way Optimum handled it?"

"Everything was aboveboard and by the book, from what I could tell. And they did make restitution."

"Why did you leave?"

"I saw an opportunity for advancement with Norris Cassidy, pure and simple. It's a solid company and I'm now a branch manager. Who knows, maybe I'll have a shot at an executive suite one day."

I smiled. "Maybe."

I rose to leave. "Have you settled into your new home?"

Her face lit up. "I have. I bought a little bungalow here in town. I can walk to work if I have to. This summer I'll get myself a kayak. Explore the chain of lakes."

"Are you on your own?" She didn't wear a wedding band but that didn't mean anything.

"Oh, yes."

She wouldn't have made friends in the area yet. "Come over for dinner this weekend," I told her.

When I left the branch later that afternoon, I drove up Highway 36, past Black Bear Lake, to the village of Donarvon. Nowak Heating was a few miles north of the village. With its yard full of fuel tanks and trucks, my first reaction was that it was a blight on the forest landscape. Then I realized that the business employed several people, which allowed them to live in a part of the world they liked. I waited for a fuel truck to pull into the yard, then I swung into the parking lot.

Inside the building, I found a toothy redhead zipping up her parka. "Is Greg Nowak in?" I asked.

She smiled and stepped into an office behind the reception desk. "Lady here to see you, Mr. Nowak," I heard her say.

A man with a dark moustache emerged from an office behind the reception counter. Mara seemed to have inherited her good looks from him.

"I'm Pat Tierney. I—"

"The investment woman from Toronto. Soupy's told me about you. The missus and me will be at your seminar tomorrow night."

I smiled, unsure how to begin. "Soupy hoped to take on Lyle Critchley as a client."

"He told me that. Missed out on a good one."

"I understand you bought Lyle's business a few years ago."

"Lyle decided to sell when Edna took sick. Made good sense to roll it into Nowak Heating."

"There wasn't anything about…how Lyle did business that—"

He rested his elbows on the reception counter. "Made a former customer set fire to his garage? That's what the police asked me."

"Well?"

"We don't solve our differences that way'round these parts."

"Somebody did."

He paused for a moment. "Lyle was a cranky old bugger, but I got to say he knew the business inside-out. He was up to scratch on all the latest industry regulations, and the sheet metal shop he had over on Highway 187 was as clean as a cat's whiskers. The furnaces and cooling systems he installed were first-rate."

"So—?"

"Ma'am, I haven't heard one peep of complaint from Lyle's customers."

CHAPTER EIGHT

Snow began to fall on the drive back to Black Bear Lake. By the time I'd pulled into the driveway, I had my windshield wipers going full blast in order to see what was ahead of me.

"Welcome home!" Celia called out when I opened the front door.

Laura lay sprawled on a couch, flipping through a magazine. Tommy and Maxie were on the rug in front of the hearth. Celia was curled up in an armchair.

I sat down at the end of the couch that Laura had taken over and shook her foot. "You haven't started dinner yet, honey? I called an hour ago."

Celia held up her hands. "Dinner is coming to us tonight."

"There's pizza delivery out here?"

She grinned. "Who needs pizza? The chef at the Winagami has cooked dinner for us."

"Chef at the Winagami?"

"Devon's arranged to have dinner delivered from the hotel." She glanced at her watch. "Should be here in about ten minutes."

I was upstairs changing into jeans and a flannel shirt when the telephone rang. "It's Tracy, Mom," Laura called. "She wants to speak to you."

"I can pick up my car in Orillia tomorrow," Tracy said when I got on the bedroom extension. "My boss says I can leave work early and my friend Hannah will drive me."

Orillia, where the Ontario Provincial Police has its headquarters, is a 90-minute drive north of Toronto. "The police told you not to leave the city," I said.

"They must be okay with it because a police officer called this morning and told me to come for my car. Have you found anything about Jamie?"

"I've been focusing on Lyle," I said. "We need to find out as much as we can about him to know why he sent Jamie that letter. The letter's key to everything."

I told her about my visit to Nowak Heating, and that I'd ruled out unhappy customers. I felt pretty pleased with myself, but it wasn't good enough for Tracy.

"Mom, focus on Jamie," she snapped. "We still don't know what's happened to her."

"I've been here all of two days," I shot back. "What do you expect? I'm an outsider here. If Jamie doesn't want to be found, anyone who knows where she is won't tell me."

"I'm sorry, Mom, it's just that...I'm worried."

"Honey, Jamie has her reasons for keeping out of sight. She'll turn up." I told her about Lyle's visit to the branch the week before.

"He sounds like an old curmudgeon," she said.

"My sentiments exactly. But that's probably not why he was killed."

My second Winagami meal of the day started with a sublime cream of mushroom soup with duck stock, followed by spinach-and-goat-cheese salad. The main course was succulent pork tenderloin with green beans and slivered almonds, and roasted potatoes. Dessert was chocolate mousse. There was a container of macaroni and cheese for Tommy. And a bottle of French Merlot and a bottle of New Zealand sauvignon blanc. We tucked into the meal as if we hadn't seen food for days.

Celia wiped her mouth with a napkin. "Devon's some guy."

"You should marry him, Mom," Laura muttered as she scraped the last of the mousse from her plate.

Celia raised an eyebrow at me.

I gave a dismissive wave of my hand.

"You're gonna marry Devon, Mrs. T?" Tommy asked with his mouth full. "I never been to a wedding."

"There's not going to be a wedding, Tommy." Devon was a great Mr. Right Now but I wasn't looking for Mr. Right.

"So, Sister Celia," Laura said, "what's celibacy like?"

I scowled at my daughter. She thought she was making a statement of some sort, but she was just being rude.

"It means I don't have to worry about a date for Saturday night," Celia said.

I couldn't help but laugh.

"What's celi...celi...?" Tommy wanted to know.

"Something grownups do—or don't do," I said.

"Like drinking wine?" he asked.

"Something like that."

"Can't say it's for me," Laura said. "No thanks."

Partly to change the subject, I brought up the art program at Braeloch College. Ivy had found a flier for it at the public library that afternoon. I took the flier out of my handbag and handed it to Laura. "Why don't I drive you and Tommy over to the college in the morning, and you can check it out? The launch party at the branch is at ten, but I can drop you off and come back for you around noon."

Laura looked at the flier, then flung it down on the table.

"Like art at school?" Tommy asked.

"Sounds like it. The flier mentions puppets and jewelry, too."

Laura slouched down in her chair. "I'm not interested."

"Tommy might be." I said. "You could work on your paper while he's in class."

She rolled her eyes. I braced myself for an outburst, and I wasn't disappointed.

"I gave up my winter break to come up here," she said. "I'm living like a celibate with Kyle back in the city. A hermit, too. There's no Internet access in this house, and I have no transportation to get to the library. How can I work on my paper?"

"Tommy, would you and Maxie like to watch a video?" I asked.

He wiggled off his chair. Celia took him to the entertainment unit in the living room. Maxie followed them.

"Our launch is tomorrow," I said. "But I'll make sure you get into town on Thursday. I'll come up with something for Tommy to do while you're at the library."

She fixed her eyes on me. "I thought I should let you know."

"Know what?" I held her gaze but my heart was sinking.

"About next year."

"Yes?"

"Kyle and me, we want to go to the University of Guelph. We'll get an apartment. Together."

The wineglass in my hand crashed to the table. Red wine stained the green-checked cloth. Guelph is a two-hour drive from Toronto, and Laura had promised to do her undergraduate degree in the city if we adopted Tommy. But I didn't want to discuss that within earshot of the boy. And this business of living with Kyle would have to wait as well.

"We'll talk about this later." I blotted the stain with paper napkins. "Help me clear the table."

When Tommy was in bed and Laura had retreated to her room with her iPod, Celia poured two snifters of cognac.

I took one of them. "How much did you hear of Laura's outburst?"

"Not much. Tommy and I were looking through the DVDs you brought." She threw another log on the fire and squatted down in front of it.

"Laura just announced that she's going to the University of Guelph next year—even though she promised to stay in Toronto to help with Tommy."

Celia turned to face me.

"She and her boyfriend want to get an apartment there. They're eighteen years old! It's not the fact that they're having sex that bothers me—sorry, Celia."

I sometimes forgot that Celia was a Catholic nun, and lived according to a code of poverty, chastity and obedience to her religious order. I was brought up a Catholic myself but I hadn't been what you'd call "practicing" for years.

She smiled. "I wasn't born a nun. I'm well aware that sex is a powerful urge for young people. And not only young people."

"I don't want Laura cocooning at eighteen. She should be out meeting people, doing things."

"Joining the green movement. Protesting tuition fee hikes. "

"Sure."

"Pat, September is months away. Plenty of things can happen between now and then."

"And I don't want to think about any of them," I said with a sigh.

I must have dozed off because what seemed like minutes later the local television station launched its evening news broadcast with the now-familiar musical fanfare. My watch told me it was ten o'clock.

I sat up on the sofa and rubbed my eyes. Mara Nowak was on the screen. "A snow front has moved into the Glencoe Highlands, Haversham, Barrie and Muskoka. Plows will be on the main highways in the township throughout the night, and snow should have stopped falling by morning."

Coverage of Lyle's murder was limited to a shot of his driveway gate over which scene-of-the-crime tape had been draped. "That's the gate Jamie hung her signs on 10 years ago," I said.

I wondered for maybe the hundredth time whether Lyle had wanted investment advice when he stopped by the branch or if he was just curious about the town's new business. He had no children to leave his money to, but maybe he wanted to set up a charitable trust or a foundation.

"Police are still looking for Jennifer Collins," Mara said on the television set. "Anyone who knows her whereabouts should call..."

I turned down the sound and told Celia about my visit to Nowak Heating. "Seems like we can eliminate unhappy clients from the suspect pool."

She smiled in agreement.

"And I met Bruce's father today. He runs *The Highlands Times*."

"I heard that Bruce and his dad had a falling out." She paused for a few moments, looking thoughtful. "Some people can't make allowances for what they see as others' failings. Even in their own children."

Like I did with Tracy. I felt a stab of guilt and I strengthened my resolve to clear Jamie's name.

Celia stretched in her seat. "I need more background on Lyle for the eulogy I'm writing. I have almost nothing to go on. The man lived here in the township for most of his life but nobody seems to have known him."

"Lyle wasn't from here?"

"He grew up in Lindsay. Came here as a young man to work for the heating company, and several years later he bought it."

"Soupy may be able to help you find people who knew Lyle. He seems to know everyone around here."

Her face brightened. "I'll drop in on your launch party tomorrow."

"Will you go back to Toronto when Father Brisebois returns?" I hoped she wouldn't be transferred across the country.

"I don't think so," she said. "The Toronto archdiocese didn't take kindly to the shenanigans at Safe Harbor."

"That was so unfair," I said.

"Someone had to take the fall, and I'm content to move on. Sister Roslyn has my old job so Safe Harbor is in capable hands. But the powers that be in Toronto aren't happy with me, and my superior thinks I'll do more good outside the archdiocese. The boys at the top will have it in for me for some time to come."

She reached over and patted my arm. "We're here now. Let's make the most of it."

She turned off the television. "And find Jamie."

CHAPTER NINE

I was in bed when the telephone rang at seven the next morning.

"Shirley Corcoran here," a woman said. "Hank's battery's dead and our son's on his way over to give him a boost. Hank'll be with you as soon as he can."

I looked out my bedroom window. The world was a winter wonderland with fresh snow everywhere.

Downstairs, I found Celia pouring orange juice. "No sign of spring today," she said.

I told her the driveway wouldn't be plowed until Hank got a boost from his son, and I had no idea how long that would take.

"I've got to be at the rectory by nine." She handed me a glass of juice. "You'd think the locals would know how to keep their batteries from freezing."

"I've got to be in Braeloch, too," I said. "Our launch starts at ten."

I went to the window at the front of the house and looked out at the driveway. Acres of snow separated us from the highway.

"I'll be outside," Celia said at the front door.

I sighed. "We could be here for hours."

I looked in on Tommy and Laura upstairs. They were both asleep.

I shook Laura's shoulder and told her we wouldn't be plowed out for some time. "Sister Celia and I are going out to shovel snow," I said. "Get Tommy up and give him some breakfast. Then come out and help us."

She pulled the duvet over her head.

Outside, Celia had cleared the front steps. Her Hyundai was still capped with snow, but its engine was purring.

I inserted the key into the ignition of my Volvo and the motor turned over. "At least we don't have to worry about our cars."

"The temperature didn't drop last night," Celia said, "so I didn't think we'd have a problem."

"Seems strange that Hank needs a boost. His battery can't have frozen."

Celia looked at her watch. "It's a quarter to eight. If Hank isn't here by eight-thirty, I'm taking Molly across the lakes into town. Coming with me?"

I looked at all the snow between us and the highway. "I guess I am. I can't miss the launch."

Then my eyes picked out movement at the end of the driveway. A dark insect seemed to be munching its way toward us through the white stuff. "Look!"

Celia clapped her hands above her head. "Hank's here. Thank you, God!"

"What gives?" Laura bounded out of the house in her parka and jeans. "Hey, you're leaning on your shovels. We have snow to clear."

"What's Tommy up to?" I asked her.

"Eating cereal." She looked down the driveway. "Hey, the plow is here!"

It inched toward us, veering off to the side of the driveway every so often to drop a load of snow. We cleared snow from around the cars, and when the plow drew near, its driver waved at us. When he'd cleared the driveway up to the cars, he cut the engine.

I walked over to him. "You must be Mr. Corcoran." I figured he was too young to be Shirley's husband, but he was probably the son she'd mentioned.

"Nope," he replied cheerfully. "I'm Kerry Gallant, your next-door neighbor. When Shirley phoned to say that Hank would be late this morning, I decided to try out the plow we bought last week. Shirley said you people leave for work early."

"You are an angel from heaven," Celia said coming up behind me.

The man laughed. "Not me." He took off his tuque and displayed a head of wavy brown hair. He was in his mid-thirties and very easy on the eyes. He put the hand that held the tuque on his chest and gave us a bow. "I'm just a kid playin' with a new toy."

He put the tuque back on, flashed a grin and headed back to the highway.

"He's a hottie," Laura said as she followed Celia and me into the house.

At the branch, I found Soupy on a ladder in the reception area. He was stringing green and white streamers across the ceiling. Nuala was helping the caterers set up coffee urns on a long table.

"You made it in," Soupy said to me.

I looked up at him. "Yes."

"We had a whack of snow last night."

Ivy followed me into my office. "Phone call, Pat. Mr. Kulas at Toronto headquarters."

I closed my office door wondering what Keith wanted now. "Good morning, Keith," I said into the receiver.

"I understand there'll be media coverage."

"I'll handle it."

"And remember what I said about meeting quotas for assets under management."

"We're pulling out all the stops, Keith."

"You'll have things to do, then," he said and hung up.

I slammed down the receiver and scrunched up a piece of paper. "Up your assets, Keith!" I lobbed the paper ball at the wastepaper basket across the room.

Just then the door opened and Soupy stepped into the office. He yelped as the ball hit him in the groin. "I shouldn't have barged in," he said. "But Mike from the catering company asked if we'll need more soft drinks."

"Ask Nuala." I shrugged off my coat. "She placed the order."

"I'm sorry—"

"Forget it. We've got less than an hour to get everything ship-shape."

Soupy wasn't a bad kid, I thought as I followed him out of my office. Just young and gauche.

He and Nuala and Ivy deserved a chance to further their careers at the Braeloch branch. I vowed to do my best to make the venture fly.

At ten-thirty, I introduced the Braeloch team to clients and prospects in front of Mara Nowak and her camera crew. Then the party moved into full swing.

The snowstorm hadn't hurt us. There must have been fifty people in the reception area and halls. There were plenty of sandwiches, pastries and drinks.

I turned to see Soupy behind me with his arm around Mara, a goofy grin on his face. "My fiancée, Mara Nowak. Mara, this is Pat Tierney from Toronto."

I took her hand. "I watch your television show. There's lots of news to report in this area." The local media must have been having a feeding frenzy. Lyle's murder was probably the biggest news to hit the area in a long time. That and the Norris Cassidy branch.

"We've got our very own murder investigation," Soupy said. "Mara wants to talk to Jen Collins. Or at least find out where she is."

Mara smiled at him, then turned to me. "Jen's mother won't talk to us."

I wondered if Mara and her team could flush out Jamie. "Why don't you try some of her friends? People she went to school with."

Mara's caramel-colored eyes looked thoughtful. "I went over to the high school and got a copy of the yearbook from the year she graduated. Familiar names but not many familiar faces. A lot of them moved away, like Jen did. It's going to take legwork to find those who still live around here."

A light went on in my head. *Jamie's yearbook. Her own copy.*

"Good luck with that," I said. "If you'll excuse me…"

I made my way through the crowd. On the other side of the room, I found Ted Stohl leaning against the wall.

"Here for the newspaper?" I asked.

He held up a notebook. "Thought I'd add a few more lines to my story."

It occurred to me that he probably knew Lyle and that he might remember Jamie. "Lyle Critchley's murder must have been a shock to people around here," I said.

He was silent for a moment, probably sizing me up. Both of us knew this wasn't small talk. "That's putting it mildly." He ran a hand over his chin. "It's kept us on our toes at *The Times*. We go to press at noon on Friday, so we only have a small item in this week's paper. But we're working on full coverage for the next issue."

"Do you remember Jen Collins? She grew up here."

He shook his head. "I was in Toronto for a long time. Came back two years ago when I bought the paper. "

He looked at me with new interest. "She a friend of yours?"

I'd decided to be open about Tracy and Jamie's relationship. As they were. "She's my daughter's partner."

He didn't blink an eye. "Emotions can get the better of anyone."

If Jamie wanted to kill Lyle to avenge her sister's death, she'd have done it years ago. But I let his comment pass. "My daughter hasn't heard from her for days. She's worried. Veronica's worried."

A handsome, gray-haired woman came up to us. She smiled at Ted, then turned to me. "I'm Lainey Campbell, Paul's mother. Ted's given my cousin, Bea Greeley, a helping hand since her husband died last year. It was his idea that your company manage her money."

"I'm grateful," I said. "Ted and I were just talking about the fire last week."

The smile left her face. "Edna, Lyle's wife, and I were pals when we were young, but they kept to themselves in recent years. Edna died last year." Her face clouded. "And now Lyle. That kind of thing don't happen around here. Sure, there's accidents on the highways and on the lakes. Shooting accidents in the woods. But a murder…" She shuddered.

Ted turned to me. "Lyle bought property at the lake where Lainey spends the summers."

Lainey sighed. "He did indeed. Bought four lots the year before last. Never built a cottage, but he bucked our plan to put up a satellite tower for high-speed Internet service. Thought the tower would lower property values."

She looked thoughtful. "What will happen to his lots now?"

"That will be up to his heirs, whoever they are." Ted paused. "I hear the police want to speak to Jen Collins."

"Poor Jen," Lainey said. "They haven't forgotten her run-in with Lyle years ago."

"Do you know who her friends were when she lived here?" I asked.

Lainey smiled. "Al Barker. They walked around town holding hands. Set a lot of tongues wagging."

Now I had a surname for Al, the friend Tracy had mentioned. "Does Al still live around here?" I asked.

"Sure does." She inclined her head toward the reception desk. "Older sister of your Ivy."

Another family connection. I headed over to the coffee station and poured myself a coffee. When I turned back to the party, I found Inspector Foster beside me.

"Heard from Ms. Collins yet?" he asked. His gray eyes bored into mine.

"No, but I've found out something you should know."

He raised his eyebrows in a silent question.

"Lyle Critchley dropped by here last Thursday."

"Thursday?"

"The day he died."

"He came for investment advice?"

"I don't know. He may just have been curious about the renovations. As you can see, this building's been turned inside out."

Foster waited for me to continue.

"He was probably here less than five minutes. Paul Campbell gave him one of our brochures and made an appointment with him for this week."

"Did he say where he was going when he left?"

Lyle said something before he left. What did Ivy say it was?

"You'd better speak to Paul." I pointed out Soupy across the room and Foster headed over to him.

I made a beeline for Ivy at the reception desk. She was chatting with two young women about her age, but they backed away as I approached. I pulled up a chair beside her.

"Ivy, where can I find your sister, Al?"

She stared at me for a moment. Then she lowered her eyes and toyed with a pen on her desk. "Do you—?"

"I'm looking for my daughter's friend. Jennifer Collins. Al might know where she is."

She looked up at me. "The woman the police want."

"They want to talk to her, yes. Did you know her when she lived around here?"

"I was just a kid, but I remember Jen coming to the house with Al. A few years later, Lyle Critchley killed her sister in a car accident, and Jen hung those signs on his gate."

"No one's heard from her in days. Her mother's worried."

"The police think she killed Lyle?"

"They want to talk to her."

"Do you think she killed him?"

I sidestepped her question. "Your sister may have some idea of where I could find her."

She took a steno pad out of a desk drawer, and wrote down directions.

"Drive out there." She tore the page from the pad and handed it to me. "Al and Ruby screen their calls. If they don't recognize the name on call display, they won't answer the phone."

Only a few guests remained when Sister Celia blew into the branch. She looked like a teenager in her purple parka and red boots.

"Pretty cool place," she said.

"I've met someone who should able to tell you more about Lyle." I took her over to Lainey, who was putting on her coat in the reception area.

"This is Sister Celia de Franco," I said. "She's running the Catholic parish here while the pastor is on sick leave. She'd like some background on Lyle for her eulogy."

I turned to Celia. "Lainey Campbell was a friend of Lyle's wife."

"I can't seem to get a handle on Lyle," Celia said.

Lainey shrugged off her coat and seated herself on a sofa. "Lyle wasn't what you'd call a people person."

Celia sat beside her. I took the leather chair across from them.

"He wasn't always like that, though," Lainey said. "When Burt and I first started stepping out, and that's going back a good many years, Lyle and Edna had just got married. The four of us sometimes went dancing. Lyle was older than the three of us, but he was always the life of the party. A big fan of Elvis Presley back then."

"Lyle?" Celia looked astonished.

"Lyle," Lainey confirmed. "He became a different man after—"

"The accident that killed Carly Collins," I said.

Lainey winced. "That was a terrible thing. But, no, long before that. After he and Edna lost their baby boy."

"Their baby died?" I asked.

"He was kidnapped."

"Kidnapped?" Celia said. "They were asked to pay a ransom?"

"No ransom. Lyle and Edna lived in town then, and some of us moms used to meet for afternoon coffee at Kresge's lunch counter. On nice days, we'd leave our babies sleeping in their carriages in front of the store. One day Edna went back outside and found her carriage empty. Little Lyle was gone."

I couldn't imagine leaving an infant unattended in public.

"No one would do that today," Lainey said, as if she'd read my mind. "But those were different times. Everyone knew everyone'round here. Burt and I never locked up at night."

"The child was never found?" I asked.

"Not a trace. The police kept the case open for years."

"That's terrible," I said.

"No wonder Lyle was so bitter," Celia added.

"It changed Lyle and Edna," Lainey said. "It took them years to have little Lyle, and they had no other children after they lost him. They pulled away from their friends. I saw Edna from time to time, but Lyle started drinking and he was an ugly drunk. He sobered up after the accident that killed Carly Collins, but he kept his distance. Probably knew he wouldn't be welcome in most circles."

"Did he have brothers or sisters?" Celia asked.

"One sister, Pearl. A year or two older than him. She lived in Lindsay, but I heard that she died last summer."

Lyle had recently lost both his wife and his sister. I couldn't help but feel sorry for this man who'd lost all that had remained of his family.

Celia looked hopeful. "Did Pearl have children?"

"No, Pearl never married. She was a high school teacher and she must have retired a good ten years ago."

She told us a few anecdotes about Lyle in his younger days. Celia took a pen and notepad from her handbag and scribbled them down.

"You'll be at the funeral on Friday?" she asked Lainey.

"Of course."

"Would you give a reading from Scripture? I'll hand you a copy when you get to the church and tell you when to come up to the pulpit."

"Sister, I'm not a Catholic."

"Doesn't matter. You were a friend of Lyle and his wife."

When Lainey had left, Celia glanced at her watch. "I have to get back to the rectory. We're cleaning the parlor and the dining room for the reception after the funeral." She chuckled. "Father Brisebois never used those rooms."

Then she tapped a hand against her head. "Promised Bruce I'd drive him over to Veronica's place this afternoon to collect his stuff."

"I'll take him over."

"You're sure?"

I nodded. I wanted to talk to Veronica again.

CHAPTER TEN

As I drove through Braeloch with Bruce, I saw there was no longer a Kresge's store on Main Street. It occurred to me that I hadn't seen a Kresge's five-and-dime anywhere since I was a child.

Cars and trucks drove by us in the opposite lane. On the sidewalks, pedestrians headed for shops, Joe's Diner and the town's two banks.

The image of a half-dozen baby carriages lined up on the sidewalk flashed through my mind. How could someone take a baby out of a carriage on this street without being seen? At three o'clock on a Wednesday afternoon, Braeloch, while not exactly bustling, was far from empty.

Perhaps the town had been a much smaller place four decades earlier. But the buildings on Main Street dated back to the late nineteenth century. Braeloch had been an established community for more than a hundred years.

"Turn right at the next street," Bruce said.

I snapped out of my reverie. "How are you doing at the rectory?"

"Okay."

"I guess there's more work to do now with Lyle gone."

Bruce's mouth was set in a grimace. Celia had said Bruce and Lyle hadn't got along.

"I hear he was a difficult man to work with," I said.

Again, Bruce made no reply. He clearly didn't like Lyle, but did he dislike him enough to kill him? The fire had been deliberately set.

I pulled into the driveway behind Veronica's white Mazda. We made our way through several inches of slushy snow when we left the car.

Veronica opened the door as we climbed the front steps. Her face was gaunt and the circles under her eyes had deepened. She looked surprised to see me.

Bruce doffed his tuque. "Here to get my stuff," he mumbled and bent down to pull off his boots.

"Hello again," I said to Veronica. "I'm in town for a few weeks for the opening of the Norris Cassidy branch."

She led us into her kitchen. "Don't tell me Bruce is one of your clients."

He scowled at her before he disappeared down a flight of stairs.

"I'm Bruce's chauffeur," I said. "He's staying at the Catholic church rectory. My friend, Sister Celia de Franco, couldn't get away this afternoon so I volunteered to drive Bruce over here."

"Business must be slow at your investment place."

"The branch was jumping today. We had our official opening. Sorry you couldn't make it. I see you're one of our clients."

She pulled out a chair for me at the kitchen table. "Jenny told me I should get some investment advice. And when Lainey's son said he could help me, I thought, why not? But I won't let him have all my money till I'm sure he knows what he's doing."

"Of course. But I'm sure Soup—Paul—will do an excellent job for you."

I took the seat. "Have you heard from Jamie?"

She sat down across from me, her face a mask of worry. "Not a word. She didn't call on Sunday night like she always does, even when she's away on business. Lyle told her something, then he was killed. She knew too much."

I repeated what I'd told Tracy. "Everyone knew that Lyle and your daughter weren't on friendly terms. Who would think he'd confide in her? I'm pretty sure she's following up whatever he told her."

She searched my face. "You are?"

I gave her a smile. "Yes. I heard that Al Barker is her friend. Maybe…"

She looked at me sharply and frowned. "Jenny wouldn't go there. She's a lawyer, after all."

"What do you mean?" Veronica was the second person to react strangely when I mentioned Al.

"Out of the question." But she didn't elaborate.

"Who does Jamie see around here when she visits?"

"No one, really. Summers, she hikes. If the snow's good at Christmas, she'll go cross-country skiing. Jenny likes the outdoors."

She doesn't bring her friends around. She's afraid you'll be critical of them.

I didn't want that kind of relationship with my girls, and I strengthened my resolve to find Jamie. I decided I'd visit Al Barker the next day.

Something crashed in the basement and Veronica hurried over to the staircase. "What's going on down there, Bruce?"

"Dropped some books," he shouted back.

She sighed as she returned to the table. "I feel badly about Bruce."

I gave her what I hoped was a sympathetic smile. "I've met his father. He runs the newspaper."

"Ted bought *The Times* two years ago and moved back to Braeloch. He and his wife, Vi, are from around here, and he worked at *The Times* years ago when he was starting out. Then he got a job at one of the big Toronto papers, and they went down there. They were there for years. We were all surprised when he came back."

"And his wife?"

"Vi's in Highlands Ridge, the old folks' home here in town. Alzheimer's."

I made a mental note to tell Nuala that Ted's wife was alive.

"Sister Celia doesn't think Father Brisebois will let Bruce stay in the rectory when he returns," I said. "Would Ted have room for him?"

She frowned. "He and Bruce don't get along. Ted can't understand why Bruce won't pull himself together." She sighed. "I'm not much better, I suppose. But I told Bruce not to smoke in the house. He's got a fondness for the bottle, and I don't want my home going up in flames while he's passed out. When his cigarette smoke came up through the heat register last Thursday night, I decided enough was enough."

"What time was that?"

She looked surprised at my question and fingered her pearl necklace. "Ten-thirty. *The Highlands Tonight* had just ended."

That would have been enough time for Bruce to get out to Lyle's place and back—if he had a car. I looked around the spotless kitchen. Not a thing was out of place. Veronica's keys hung from a rack of pegs beside the kitchen door, arranged according to size. One of them was a car key.

Veronica saw me looking at the key rack. "I keep all my keys there. That way, I always know where they are."

She frowned and glanced at the stairs to the basement. "Now I'll have to find someone to shovel the snow and mow the lawn. I had to clear the stairs and the walkway myself today. Didn't get around to the driveway."

"Did Bruce run errands for you in your car?"

"No, I'd never let Bruce—"

"Let me what?" Bruce emerged from the basement stairwell with a bulging green garbage bag in one arm and a stack of books in the other.

"Nothing," Veronica said. "Got all your things?"

"Clothes are here. Okay if I leave some books down there for a while?"

She nodded. "Good luck to you, Bruce. Don't burn down that

rectory."

"Yeah, right," he muttered as he made his way out the door.

"The car's open. Be out in a sec," I called after him and turned back to Veronica.

"I was wondering, does Jamie—Jenny—keep her high school yearbook here?"

Veronica's eyes narrowed. "Why?"

"I might get an idea of who her friends were in high school. One of them might know where she is."

She shook her head. "The best and the brightest, like my Jenny, moved away. Nothing to keep them here." She sighed. "I don't know that Jenny would approve, but if it would help you find her…"

"I won't tell her, Mrs. Collins," I said.

"Will you tell the police—if you find her?"

I swallowed hard. "I'm not sure."

"I see."

To my surprise, she pulled a book out of the bookcase behind her and handed it to me. "I hope I'm doing the right thing."

Celia had a pot of meat sauce on the stove when I got in. I was startled to see Kerry Gallant at the table with Laura, glasses of wine in front of them.

"Kerry's here for dinner, Mom," Laura said.

"Your daughter came over and invited me." He gave me a look that telegraphed, *That okay with you?*

"You deserve dinner for plowing us out this morning, Kerry," I said. "Several dinners, in fact."

I went into the living room and bent over Tommy, who was watching a video. I gave him a hug.

He kept his eyes on the screen. "Hi, Mrs. T."

I went upstairs and telephoned Tracy. I told her that Al Barker still lived in the area.

"That's the friend who sent Jamie the birthday card," Tracy said.

I didn't tell her I had Jamie's yearbook. That was between Veronica and myself. "I'll see you on Saturday," I said. "Make sure Farah is still up for a visit to the country."

When I came downstairs, Celia was ladling sauce onto plates of spaghetti.

"Get over here, Tommy," I called.

I sat down beside Kerry and smiled as Tommy skidded up to the table.

"What do you do around here?" I asked Kerry.

He heaped salad onto a side plate, and passed the bowl to me. "As little as possible. I'm a kept man."

Celia stared at him, her ladle in midair. Laura flashed me a wicked grin.

"Kept by whom?" I asked.

"Wendy Wilcox." He smiled. "That's her place next door. She comes up on weekends."

"Wendy Wilcox, the Bank of Toronto's chief economist?"

"The same Wendy Wilcox."

So the Dragon Lady of Bay Street is a cougar!

"Kerry doesn't do as little as possible, Mom," Laura put in. "He's an artist. You should see his paintings."

She looked at Kerry. "Does Wendy, like, give you spending money?"

"Laura!" I said.

He smiled at her. "Some."

"Way to go!" she cried.

"Am I a kept kid?" Tommy asked, his face smeared with sauce.

Tommy was the beneficiary of a large trust fund that had been set up by his late mother's wealthy family. It would pay for his education and a lot more. But I didn't see any reason to discuss that. "You and Laura will both be kept until you finish school and find jobs. When you're older, you can help out with a summer job like Laura does."

"Good salad, Laura," Celia said.

"I keep thinking about that cat," Celia said when we were alone in front of the fire that night.

"Cat?"

"Lyle told me he had a cat."

"The police probably took it to an animal shelter," I said.

"I asked the lead detective, Foster, if it was being fed. He told me they hadn't seen a cat. But if it was out the night Lyle was killed, it might still be out there," she said. "It may be frightened of strangers."

I clinked my glass against hers. "You can't rescue everyone. You're doing a great job with the two-legged animals."

"Don't see why I can't try."

I smiled and told her about my visit to Veronica's home that day. "She said that Ted and Bruce don't get along. Ted can't understand why Bruce doesn't pull himself together."

A cloud passed over her face. "A lot of people don't understand mental illness. I haven't met Bruce's father, but he probably had high hopes for his son. Sent him to Central Canada College, the boy's boarding school north of Toronto. Then he was at the University of Toronto for several years. He was their only child."

"Bruce suffers from depression?" I asked.

"I'm no expert, but he may be bipolar. The right meds could mean a world of difference to him. I've tried to get him to see a psychiatrist in Lindsay but I haven't got very far."

We sipped our drinks in silence for a while. There was still a good half-hour to go until the evening news. "Kerry's a colorful character," Celia finally said.

I chuckled. "Wendy has to be a good fifteen years older than him."

"Must know how to keep her happy."

I stared at my friend, surprised to hear that from a nun. Then we both burst out laughing.

After Celia went up to bed, I flipped through Jamie's yearbook.

The blur of smiling, hopeful faces meant nothing to me. I didn't have time to track down alumni as Mara planned to do, so I decided to concentrate on the one person I knew was still in the area—Al Barker.

According to Lainey, Al and Jamie had walked around town holding hands. They were more than just friends back then, yet Veronica had dismissed the possibility of Jamie turning to Al as "out of the question." I wondered why.

I looked up Alexandra Barker. I found a photo of a girl with shoulder-length blond hair, a lovely face that reminded me of the actress Candice Bergen and a determined set to her mouth.

I turned to the back of the book where Jamie's classmates had penned their memories and their best wishes.

Best of luck to a cool kid…Wish you every happiness…

I scanned the signatures looking for Al's, and there it was.

Sweetheart, the world is yours for the taking! Love, Al.

I closed the yearbook, hoping that Al was the key to finding Jamie.

CHAPTER ELEVEN

The temperature plummeted overnight. In the morning, the front steps of the house were coated with ice and the driveway had turned into a skating rink.

I inched the Volvo along the driveway. Vehicles flew by on the highway, which told me that the road crews had put down salt and sand. Something I wished Hank had done on our driveway.

At the mouth of the driveway, I saw a black Mercedes coming toward me on the highway. I waited for it to pass, but it slowed down and pulled onto the shoulder of the road. Kerry got out.

I rolled down the window as he ran up to me. He leaned in, his face close enough that I could smell his morning scrambled eggs. "Come meet Wendy," he said.

I ground my teeth at the idea of courting the Dragon Lady. But I got out of the car and made my way through the snow. I was doing this for Kerry, I told myself.

He introduced me to an attractive woman with auburn hair. Wendy was on the far side of fifty but her face could have served as an advertisement for Dr. Stanfield's Toronto makeover clinic.

"Wendy got in while I was at your place last night," Kerry said.

She gave a throaty chuckle. "Made a surprise visit and found my boy gone."

She searched my face. "Have we met before?"

"The investment fund awards banquet last fall," I said.

"I remember. You run one of Norris Cassidy's branches." She glanced at her watch. "I'm taking Kerry into town to pick up his Jeep. Then I have to be in Toronto for an eleven-thirty meeting. Let's get together this weekend. Kerry will organize something."

"I'm headed for Braeloch," I said to Kerry. "I'll give you a lift."

"That's right," Wendy said. "Norris Cassidy opened a branch up here."

I glanced at my watch. "And I should be at it now."

I walked back to the Volvo while Kerry said his goodbyes to Wendy.

"A good night?" I asked when he jumped into the seat beside me.

His lips curved into a smile. "Nights are always good when Wendy's here."

I eased the car onto the highway. "How long have you two been together?"

"Three years. The bank bought one of my paintings for the lobby of its Bay Street tower. Wendy was on the selection committee. We, ah, got to know each other. She wants me to paint full-time."

Whatever works for them.

Midway through the morning, I called Laura and told her I'd come by the house around twelve-thirty. I planned to drop her at the library and spend the afternoon with Tommy.

"I have something to do this afternoon," she said.

I knew better than to ask what it was. I assumed she wanted to visit Kerry. That was the only place she could get to without transportation. "Take Tommy with you if you leave the house," I told her.

I'd just turned back to the computer when there was a knock on my door. I looked up and saw Kerry in the doorway, a Norris Cassidy pamphlet in his hands.

"They did an awesome job on this building." Then he pointed to the pamphlet. "You're holding a seminar tonight."

I wondered where this was going.

"Financial planning basics," he read. "I think I'll come. Wendy tells me to take more interest in my finances. Maybe I'll surprise her with a few investment ideas."

"I'm having an early dinner with the kids," I said. "Drop by the house at five for a bite to eat and we'll drive in together."

I didn't tell him he could expect a visit from Laura and Tommy that afternoon.

"I'd like to drive over to Lyle's place," Celia said when she phoned me just before noon. "Want to come?"

"You want to rescue that cat."

"It may be shivering at the door."

I was curious to see the Critchley place. And Keith had told me to get out and about in the community, although he probably didn't mean rescuing cats.

"All right," I said with feigned reluctance.

"I'll pick you up in an hour. We'll stop at Joe's for a bite."

"It should be somewhere around here." Celia slowed her Hyundai as we approached a stretch of houses along Highway 123. "Sherry Vargas at the church said it was just past the Art Hut."

"What's the roadside number?" I asked.

"1-9-0-5-6."

"There," I said when we'd rounded a bend. Crime-scene tape was stretched across the driveway ahead of us.

She pulled onto the shoulder of the road. A stone house was set back on the wide lot.

"We can't see if the cat's around from here." She pulled back onto the highway.

The driveway on the next property was plowed, but the walkway to the house hadn't been cleared of snow.

"Doesn't look like anyone's home," I said. "Let's park here."

She swung into the driveway.

I looked at the expanse of trees and snow that separated the property from the Critchley place. "We can't walk through the woods."

"We'd be up to our armpits," Celia agreed.

The temperature had risen since I'd set out that morning but I pulled on my tuque as we walked along the highway.

"Do you think this is illegal?" Celia asked, as we ducked under the crime-scene tape.

"Probably."

We grinned at each other.

The Critchley driveway hadn't been plowed. Celia led the way down it, walking whenever possible on the patches of gravel that had started to appear through the snow.

"I wonder if the police found tire tracks or footprints here after the fire," I said.

"It was cold that night," Celia said, "but there'd been a thaw at the beginning of the week. Rain, too. Might have cleared some of the snow from the driveway."

My eyes were riveted on the charred remains of the garage at the end of the driveway. We slowed our steps as we approached. Celia stood still for a few moments, her head bowed.

I shivered. A man had died a terrible death in that garage.

I turned and looked at the house. Its first story was constructed of gray stone. A second story with dormer windows was clad in white metal siding and capped with a sloping red metal roof. The house was attractive, cared for, maybe even loved.

"No sign of a cat around," I said.

"I'd like a look inside the house."

"Should we?" But I was curious, too. I wanted to know more about Lyle Critchley.

I'll be back. That's what he said when he left the branch. Lyle had an appointment with Soupy, but his words sounded like a threat.

"The police probably have the place locked up." Celia headed for a wooden porch that had been built onto the back of the house. "But let's try the back door."

"Not a good idea. There's an investigation going on." But I was right behind her. For all my sanctimonious talk, I was as ready to snoop as she was.

Inside the porch, shovels, hoes and rakes hung on the walls. A pair of work boots stood at the back door to the house.

An orange cat squeezed through a hole at the end of the porch, brushed our legs and let itself into the house through a flap in the wall.

"Lyle didn't have to put out the cat," Celia said. "It comes and goes as it pleases."

"There's probably a bowl on the floor inside. The police may have put food in it."

"I doubt it. And if it hasn't been fed, we can't let it starve." She put a gloved hand on the doorknob, then quickly withdrew it.

"They'll have dusted for prints by now," I said. "It's been a week since the fire."

She grabbed the knob, and it turned.

The house smelled stale and musty. *Dead air.* I shivered and not because the heat was turned down low.

Copper pots and pans hung from the kitchen ceiling. A shelf over the stove held a row of cookbooks. A rack of knives stood on the butcher-block countertop. Not even the film of white power that dusted all the surfaces could hide the fact that some serious cooking had once taken place in that kitchen.

The cat meowed and rubbed itself against my legs. There was no cat bowl on the floor. I opened cupboards with the tip of a leather-clad finger. No boxes of kibble. No tins of cat food.

"Here!" Celia fished something out of the dishwasher.

"Careful."

"Like you said, the police have finished in here." She held up a white plastic bowl with "Cleo" stamped on it in big red letters. "We have the bowl. Now where is the cat food?"

"Probably downstairs." I turned on a light at the top of a flight of stairs. "I buy big bags of chow for Maxie and keep them in a bin in the basement."

Bowl in hand, she headed down the stairs, the cat close behind her. I stepped through the kitchen doorway into a room where a maple dining set held pride of place. Beyond it was the living room. A flowered chintz sofa and matching armchairs were grouped in front of a brick fireplace. They were attractive, comfortable rooms, but nothing out of the ordinary.

Nothing that told me anything about Lyle Critchley.

Several framed photos on the mantle caught my eye. I crossed the room to look at them.

A large picture in a gilt frame displayed a couple in out-of-date wedding finery. A much younger Lyle than in the photo that *The Toronto World* and the TV station had run, and a woman I assumed was Edna. They looked happy and hopeful. Another photo showed them a few years later with a baby in Edna's arms.

Sadness washed over me. A few years after Tracy was born, I'd had a miscarriage that had left me inconsolable for months. But the sadness had gradually lifted and Laura had arrived. Lyle and Edna never learned what happened to their son. And they never had another child.

Lyle was a lonely man who had come to the branch looking for help or maybe just a diversion. For some inexplicable reason, I felt we'd let him down.

The mantle held several other photos. A much older Lyle with a woman of around the same age, probably his sister. Photos of places I didn't recognize. A picture at the far end of the mantle caught my eye. Three people, in their twenties or early thirties, smiled at the camera, their arms on one another's shoulders. Lainey Campbell was in the middle, Lyle and Ted on either side of her. The photo had probably been taken in Lyle's dancing days.

"Come take a look down here, Pat," Celia called from the basement.

At the bottom of the stairs, the basement divided into two rooms. The area to the right was an unfinished furnace and laundry room. A big bag of dry cat food sat on the washing machine.

"Look in there." Celia inclined her head to the room on the left side of the stairs.

The cat let out a rasping noise, something between a meow and a squawk.

"Okay, Cleo, I hear you." She dipped the bowl into the bag of chow and set it on the floor.

I went into the room she'd indicated. The ceiling track lighting had been turned on. Pine paneling covered the walls. A large wraparound desk stood in the center of the room. It held two printers and two fax machines. The desktop in front of the chair was empty. All surfaces were filmed with white powder. "Looks like the police took the computer," I said.

With a gloved finger, I opened the drawers of a large filing cabinet. They were empty. "They took the files, too."

Celia circled the desk. "What do you think the police found in Lyle's computer and files?" she asked.

A light clicked on in my head. "They may have found the letter he sent Jamie."

Celia bent over the desk between the two fax machines. "What's this?" She blew on the powder that covered an open newspaper. "*The Highlands Times*. Why didn't the police take this?"

"Don't touch it," I said. "Can you read the date and the pages it's open at?"

"March 2. Pages six and seven."

"Last week's issue. We'll look at a copy in the public library."

The cat followed us up the stairs.

"Should we take Cleo with us?" Celia asked at the top of the stairs. "We can't come over every day to feed her."

"We'll have to take her," I said. The last thing I needed was something else to look after.

"It may just be for a few days." She gave me a sidelong look. "Someone may want to adopt her."

Fat chance of that, I thought as I returned to the basement for the cat carrier I'd seen. While I was there, I grabbed the bag of chow.

"Adult female," Celia said when I returned from the basement. "About three years old."

I hoped Cleo would get along with Maxie, but I somehow doubted it.

I kept my eyes on the highway as we walked down the driveway. I hoped the police had urgent business in a distant part of the township.

"If the police come along," Celia said, "we can say we're on a rescue mission."

"I'd like to see the March 2 edition of *The Highlands Times*," I said to the forty-something brunette behind the checkout desk at the Braeloch Public Library.

"You'll find the two most recent issues in the reading room." She inclined her head toward an adjacent room.

An elderly man in an armchair raised his eyes from the newspaper he held and nodded at us. I took two newspapers from a rack and pulled up a chair at the long table in front of the window. Celia sat down beside me.

The entire page six of the March 2 issue was taken up by a photo spread of a craft and bake sale at Highlands Ridge, the old folks' home Veronica had mentioned. I wondered if Lyle had attended the sale. Vi, Ted's wife, lived at Highlands Ridge, and Lyle probably knew other residents there. The bottom half of page seven carried an ad for a local carpet and linoleum business. On top of it was a roundup of events scheduled around the township during winter break. On the far right side of the page, a single-column article reported on a township council meeting held earlier that week.

I scanned the article. "This is it.

"'One of the topics under discussion was a proposal to construct a satellite tower for high-speed Internet access on Three Hills Lake,'" I read in a low voice."'The tower would be lit at night to warn low-flying aircraft.'"

I turned to Celia. "We need one of those towers at Black Bear Lake."

I picked up where I'd left off."'The proposal was approved despite a letter from a property owner at the lake who claimed that the tower would lower real estate values.'"

"Lyle didn't live near a lake," Celia said.

"He owned four lots at Three Hills Lake. Lainey said he was against the tower."

I turned to the Letters to the Editor page. Three letters were on the page, one of them written by Lyle.

I continued reading."'The Glencoe Highlands is renowned for its natural beauty. Metal towers will ruin this wilderness paradise. The township needs to restrict these eyesores to towns and ban them in the countryside.'"

We looked at each other.

"The people who wanted a tower at Three Hills Lake wouldn't have liked Lyle," I said.

"But would they have wanted to kill him?"

"I doubt it. Most people want to be as connected as possible these days, and the township would try to ensure that they are. Lyle might have held things up a bit, but not much more than that. Three Hills Lake residents probably dismissed him as an old crank."

I picked up the current edition of *The Times*, the March 9 issue. On its front page, I saw the small item about the fire that I'd read online. I turned back to the article about the council meeting in the previous issue. "And the proposal to build the tower was approved the week *before* Lyle was killed."

"Then we can rule out a killer at Three Hills Lake." Celia got out of the chair. "We'd better see how Cleo's doing."

"Up for another visit?" I asked as we left the library. "It's time I met Al Barker."

CHAPTER TWELVE

On Main Street, I saw Laura and Tommy leave Joe's Diner with a young man with a long, dark ponytail. "Kyle!" I cried.

"What—?" Celia started to ask.

But I was sprinting down the street. "Laura!"

She saw me and said something to Kyle, who turned and waved.

"Hey, Mrs. T!" he said when I got closer.

Laura looked sheepish. "Kyle came by today."

"And we went to Joe's," Tommy said. "I had fries and a Coke."

"What brings you this far from home?" I asked Kyle.

"Haven't seen Laura for ages. So I took Mom's car and drove up here."

"Ages? We're talking, what, four days?" I said.

The diamond stud in Kyle's earlobe winked in the sunlight as he nodded. "Yeah, about four days."

"You'll need to head back within the hour," I told him. "I don't want you on the roads around here in the dark."

"Can Kyle stay with us for a few days, Mom?" Laura asked. "Tomorrow's Friday. The week's almost over."

"He needs to get the car back to his mother."

"No problem, Mrs. T," Kyle said. "It's Mom's old car. She just got a Ferrari."

"Kyle can take us out on the snowmobile," Tommy said.

Three pairs of eyes looked hopefully at me. Laura and Kyle had planned this all out.

Celia inched the Hyundai down a slippery lane that snaked through the forest. "We slide off this road, we're stranded," she said. "We don't know if anyone's home at the Barker place, and our cells may not pick up a signal out here."

I didn't like the lane either, but I needed to talk to Al.

After several more minutes of twists and turns, a weather-beaten red barn came into view. Behind it was a white house, badly in need of a fresh coat of paint. Snow-covered fields stretched out behind the house, and they gave way to dense forest beyond. A split-rail fence edged the front of the property, but the gate stood open. On one gatepost, a metal sign cautioned against trespassing. *Beware Of Dogs* warned a sign on the other post.

Celia ignored the signs and drove into the muddy yard where a wiry figure was replacing the windshield wipers on a blue Ford pickup. Celia pulled up beside the truck.

I rolled down my window. "Hi!" I said.

A barking German shepherd bounded from the house and headed straight for our car. A shrill whistle brought the dog to a stop.

"Fang, sit!"

The dog sat but kept his eyes on us.

"Can't you read them signs? Fang don't like strangers." The voice was husky but it belonged to a woman. She was dressed in cut-off jeans, work boots and a green-plaid jacket. A battered baseball cap covered her head. Her face was an older, weathered version of the face in the yearbook photo.

"You're Al Barker," I said.

"Might be."

Fang growled. Cleo squawked in her carrier cage on the backseat.

I didn't like the look of Fang, but I got out of the car. "My name is Pat Tierney. Can you tell me where I might find Jen Collins?"

Al's cobalt-blue eyes took in my navy wool coat and polished boots. "You'll find Jen down south. Toronto."

She saw me look at the barking dog, but she made no move to calm him.

"No one's heard from her for days," I said. "Her mother's worried."

"Jen's a big girl. Shouldn't have to report to her mom every day."

Fang bristled and showed his sharp teeth. I gulped.

"A lot of people are worried about her," I went on. "Including my daughter, Tracy. Can you tell us where she is?"

Al studied my face. Then she pulled off her cap and thick, fair hair tumbled onto her shoulders. She took a deep breath and was about to say something when a black van with ELK TV emblazoned on it in gold careened down the lane.

Fang started to bark fiercely.

"Sheee-it!" Al slammed the cap back on her head. "Last thing we need." She turned to the dog. "Fang, stay!"

The dog stood beside her and snarled at the van.

The passenger door opened, and Mara hopped out. "Al, is Jen

Collins here?"

"Get outta here!" Al roared. "This is private property."

Damn it, Mara! Al was about to tell me something.

Al glared at me. "Both of youse!"

With that, she stomped off to the house, the muscles in her bare calves pumping like pistons.

Fang barked at Mara and me, then trotted after Al.

Mara groaned. "I heard Al and Jen used to be an item. Before Jen went down to the city." She looked up at the house. "Do you think she's in there?"

I ignored her question. "What does Al do out here? Is this a working farm?"

"You don't know?"

I shook my head.

"Al and Ruby Taylor run a grow-op."

I looked at Mara in disbelief. "Out here?"

She nodded. "Everyone knows about it. So when a stranger asks questions…"

It explained the reactions I got whenever I mentioned Al.

"Al and Ruby are nervous," she said. "There's been talk of bikers trying to move in on them."

I groaned inwardly. If Jamie was staying with Al and Ruby, she was digging herself into an even deeper hole with the law. She was a "person of interest"—I translated that as "suspect"—in a murder investigation. And now it looked like she was mixed up in a drug operation that, if the talk about bikers was true, had the potential to turn violent very quickly.

"The police haven't clamped down on the grow-op?" I asked.

Mara's cell phone rang. She fished it out of her jacket pocket and checked a text message on the screen. "Sorry, gotta run." She sighed. "New sponsor's just let us know about a ribbon cutting. Station manager wants it on the news tonight."

I nodded and headed back to the car.

"Hey," Mara called as I opened the car door, "maybe we should team up. Share what we know about Jen."

I waved at her and got into the car.

Celia turned the key in the ignition. "You may not have noticed, but two women came out on the veranda while you were talking to Al, before ELK TV showed up. A tall, slim gal and a heavy woman. Didn't stay out long."

"What did the slim one look like?"

"Spiky black hair."

Tall, slim, only the hair color was wrong. "The heavy woman was probably Ruby who runs this place with Al. The slim one might be…"

We looked at each other.

"She changed her hair color," I said.

"Wants to lie low."

"I'll be back tomorrow," I said as we pulled out of the yard. "There's something else to worry about."

"The grow-op."

"You know about it?"

She nodded. "I hear things. I don't know why the police haven't shut it down."

"Have you heard anything about bikers?"

"Yup." She paused. "Those girls are in for big trouble."

At the house, we found Kyle and Tommy playing Concentration. Kyle had the telephone receiver to his ear.

Maxie took one look at Cleo's carrier cage and began barking.

I handed Cleo's cage to Celia, and grabbed Maxie's collar. Celia took the cat upstairs.

"Where's Laura?" I asked Tommy and Lyle.

"In her room," Tommy said.

Kyle held the telephone out to me. "My mom. She wants to talk to you."

Liz Shingler thanked me for inviting Kyle to spend the rest of the week with us. I didn't tell her the invitation hadn't come from me.

I went up to Laura's room where she was sprawled on the double bed and closed the door behind me. "This room is out of bounds to Kyle," I said. "He'll take Tommy's room, and Tommy will sleep in the twin bed next to mine."

"Devon sleeps with you when he visits."

"When you have your own home, Laura, you can do as you like. Right now, I'm the one who pays the bills, so you'll follow my rules. If you don't like it, Kyle can get in his mother's car and drive back to Toronto."

She stared at me, poker-faced.

I paused at the door. "I know you arranged this behind my back."

She turned her back on me and slammed a pillow over her head.

"Sister Celia said Kyle can use the snowmobile," I said. "He and Tommy can go out on it tomorrow. You drive into town and work on your paper at the library."

I heard a groan from under the pillow.

After dinner, Kerry and I raced back to Braeloch in his Jeep. Nuala gave her presentation to an audience of twenty-six in the branch's small basement auditorium. From my seat at the back, I spotted Greg Nowak and Lainey Campbell.

Nuala was an impressive speaker. She was clear and concise, and included plenty of examples and a few jokes. She answered all the questions that followed, then we chatted with our guests over refreshments.

"That went very well," I told her as people left the building.

"You think so?" she asked.

"Your talk was great."

She lowered her eyes, but she couldn't hide the pleasure that blossomed on her face.

"And we had a fabulous turnout for a winter evening," I added. "I'd have been thrilled with fifteen people. And they all seemed interested in what we can do for them."

"You bet," Soupy said. "I'd be surprised if Nuala's talk doesn't bring in a dozen new clients."

The front door opened and Greg Nowak hurried back in. "Forgot to give you these, son." He handed Soupy a parcel.

"Tickets to our gig at the Legion on Sunday night," Soupy said to Nuala and me. "You've got to come out and hear us."

"The missus and me enjoyed your talk," Greg said to Nuala. "Gave us plenty to think about."

"I can't take you on as my clients," Soupy said. "Conflict of interest. But Nuala would be happy to."

She smiled and handed Greg a card.

He saluted us, and Soupy walked him to the door.

"Let's call it a day," I said to Nuala. She was staring at Kerry who was seated in front of the fireplace.

"Kerry," I said, "come meet our team."

Nuala's eyebrows nearly hit her hairline. Soupy joined us as Kerry came over.

I saw Nuala take in Kerry's wavy brown hair, black leather sports jacket and designer jeans. She appraised me as I made the introductions.

I suppressed a chuckle. She thought he was my guy, and I didn't try to set her straight.

"Shall we be off?" I asked him.

He gave me a wink and took my arm.

I grinned at him. He knew exactly what Nuala and Soupy were thinking.

Kerry opened the front door with a grand sweep. I smiled at him, then turned around. "You'll be okay tomorrow, Nuala?" Soupy and I planned to attend Lyle's funeral in the morning.

She gave me thin smile. "I think I can manage on my own for a few hours."

"So?" Kerry said when we were in his Jeep.

"So what?"

He turned the key in the ignition. Then he sat back in his seat while the engine warmed. "Nuala was sizing us up."

"She assumes we're a couple," I said breezily. "And that surprises her because you're…younger."

"Hey, I like older women."

I laughed but I felt uneasy. "Nuala doesn't know you're spoken for."

"I don't ask Wendy what she's up to in the city all week." He slipped a CD into the player. "And she doesn't ask how I spend my time up here."

To change the subject, I blurted out the first thing that came into my mind. "Have you heard of any grow-ops around here?"

He frowned. "I'm not very well plugged into this community, but I can get you some weed if you want it."

"Oh, it's not for me. Somebody mentioned a grow-op the other day, and I wondered how they operate."

He grinned. "Thinking of getting into the business? Well, those plants need plenty of UV light and grow farms are usually traced by their high hydro bills. Smart operators use generators."

Al and Ruby's place was out in the middle of nowhere, with no neighbors to hear the generators. I remembered the forest behind the house and barn. The grow houses were probably in a clearing in those trees.

"You're sure I can't get you some weed?" Kerry asked as we pulled out of the parking lot.

"Thanks, but no." I slid down in the passenger seat and turned my attention to The Tragically Hip on the sound system.

I found Kyle stretched out on a sofa, headphones over his ears and Cleo curled up on his chest. Maxie was nowhere to be seen.

"Pat, come up here," Celia called from upstairs.

On the second floor, Laura's door was closed. Behind it, Maxie barked a greeting.

Celia sat at her desk, her laptop open in front of her. "I'm not sure about the music I've chosen for tomorrow. Lainey said Lyle was an Elvis fan back in his dancing days. But I don't think Monsignor Frank McCann would appreciate'Love Me Tender' or'Hound Dog' at a celebration of the Rite of Christian Burial."

I just looked at her. She was going way beyond the call of duty with the funeral arrangements.

"I have no idea what he liked in religious music," she said, "so I kept to the old standards."

"Best to err on the side of caution." I sat on the edge of the bed. "I take it Monsignor Frank will do the honors for Lyle."

"That's right." She sighed. "Lyle's send-off will be presided over by nothing less than a monsignor. He'd be tickled pink."

"How's the eulogy coming?" I asked.

"It'll be short." She chewed the end of her pen. "I've found someone to give another reading. Sister Doreen, one of our sisters, runs a group home in Lindsay. I called her, and it turns out that Lyle's sister, Pearl, was her high school English teacher. Pearl stayed in touch with many of her students. Doreen gave me the number of a Gavin Ridout, who'd been close to Pearl."

I held up a hand. "Don't tell me. Gavin will be at the funeral tomorrow."

She grinned. "He'll give the first reading."

CHAPTER THIRTEEN

Jesus of the Highlands Church was jam-packed, but there wasn't a handkerchief in sight. The people seated around me were bright-eyed and alert. They clearly anticipated that something out of the ordinary would happen at a murder victim's funeral.

The only flowers in the church were three white roses that Celia had placed in a vase on the altar. The absence of flowers spoke volumes about a man who had lived most of his life in that community.

Gavin and Lainey gave the two Bible readings. A man in his early forties with cropped red hair, Gavin was a powerful speaker, and his mellifluous voice captured the beauty of the Old Testament passage. Lainey wasn't the orator that Gavin was, but her reading from the Acts of the Apostles came straight from the heart. At one point, her voice broke and she paused for a few moments to compose herself. Finally, someone was mourning Lyle.

Monsignor Frank kept his homily short and focused on Lyle's work at the church. "After he lost Edna, Lyle found consolation in the work he did here. Now that he's in heaven, he wants you to continue it."

The woman in front of me turned to the man beside her. "That old fart? Cared more about keepin' the church clean than about the folks who come here to worship."

Celia's eulogy was a brief summary of Lyle's life, peppered with stories about his fondness for *Hockey Night in Canada* and his love of dancing. "Let's think of Lyle jiving up in heaven with St. Peter on drums," she concluded.

Monsignor Frank scowled at her as she returned to her pew.

After the final blessing, he sprinkled holy water on the casket, then he walked around it, swinging the incense censer. When the casket was perfumed to his satisfaction, he gestured to someone at the back of the church, and an accordion wailed the opening bars of "Amazing Grace."

The accordion player, in a red-plaid lumber jacket, walked down the center aisle, the music swelling in volume as he approached the altar. He stopped in front of the casket, and waited for Monsignor Frank and the altar servers to put on their coats and jackets over their robes. When they were assembled in front of the pallbearers, he led the procession up the aisle and out the front door of the church.

Snow had begun to fall. Mara Nowak and her crew filmed the procession as it proceeded down the ramps and around the church to the cemetery at the back of the property. I watched from the church steps for a few minutes, then made my way to the cemetery.

Blankets of plastic grass covered the ground around the grave that Lyle would share with Edna. Monsignor Frank recited a prayer, and the casket was lowered into the ground.

"May his soul, and the souls of all the faithful departed, through the mercy of God, rest in peace. Amen," the monsignor said and gave the casket a final splash of holy water.

Celia handed a small clod of earth to Gavin. He tossed it into the grave.

Bruce pushed his way through the crowd. I saw Ted, who stood with Bea at the edge of the group, start to go after him, but Bea placed a restraining hand on his arm.

Bruce strode up to the grave and pitched a rock the size of a baseball into it. It landed on the casket with a thud.

The crowd gasped. "Is this customary at Catholic funerals?" a woman behind me asked.

Celia appeared beside Bruce and whispered something to him.

She turned to the crowd. "You are all invited for sandwiches and coffee in the rectory." She beckoned to me.

I hurried over and took Bruce's arm.

"World's a better place since Lyle Critchley left it," he muttered.

I smelled whiskey on his breath.

Celia took his other arm. He tried to pull away but we held his arms. Suddenly he deflated, and we frog-marched him across the cemetery.

"I thought it would be nicer to get together in the rectory than in the church basement," Celia chattered as we steered Bruce through the cemetery gate. "Father Brisebois will have conniptions when he hears about it."

"I cleaned the chimney," Bruce said.

She patted his arm. "You did a fine job. Now we can light a fire in the fireplace."

Inside the rectory, the double doors on the right side of the hall stood open in welcome. Celia steered Bruce through the doorway and over to a table laden with sandwiches and two large metal urns.

"Sherry, here's your first customer," Celia said to the busty platinum blonde behind the table. "Bruce will have a mug of coffee. Black. And some sandwiches."

Sherry glared at Bruce. "You're supposed to help me." She poured coffee into a mug and slapped two egg-salad sandwiches on a paper plate.

Celia added a few more sandwiches to the plate and picked up the mug. "Bruce needs to rest for a bit."

I took the plate, and followed her and Bruce into the hall. We were at the foot of the stairs when the front door opened and Soupy and Lainey Campbell came in.

"That was a lovely reading you gave, Lainey," Celia said. "Thank you."

"This is Lainey's son, Paul Campbell," I said. "He's an advisor at our branch. Sister Celia de Franco."

"Most folks call me Soupy." He smiled at his mother. "Except Mom."

"Oh, call him Soupy if you like." Lainey shook her head. "Don't know why I bothered giving him a good saint's name."

She put an arm around Bruce. "You okay, dear?"

He ducked his head and mumbled something I couldn't make out.

"Bruce will rest upstairs for a while," Celia said.

"Why don't I take that mug, Sister? You get back to the reception." Lainey slipped off her coat and gave it to her son. She took the coffee mug from Celia.

"Give me the sandwiches," Lainey said to me. "Bruce don't need two of us to tuck him in."

"Stay in your room till the reception is over," Celia told Bruce. "Out of harm's way."

I handed the plate to Lainey, and she followed Bruce up the stairs.

"I hope he stays upstairs till he sobers up," Celia said. "I don't want him to play the fool again in front of Monsignor Frank."

She opened the door to her office. "Put your mother's coat in here, Soupy. And would you take coats from people as they come in? Pile them on the sofa and the chairs in here. On the desk if you need to."

Back in the reception room, Sherry poured me a coffee. "Heard Bruce threw a rock into Lyle's grave." Her blue eyes twinkled with amusement.

I smiled but kept my mouth shut.

"Can't say I blame him. Shouldn't speak ill of the dead, but Lyle was the devil to work with. Everything had to be done his way. And his attitude toward women…" She groaned. "I didn't know Edna well, but she struck me as the timid kind of woman you'd expect a man like Lyle would be married to."

Sherry's tight sweater and the mass of platinum hair piled on top of her head told me that Lyle wouldn't have suffered her presence in silence.

She looked at me with new interest. "You run that investment place in town."

"I'm just helping out till the branch gets up and running. Nuala Larkin is the manager."

"Nuala Larkin?"

"She just moved to Braeloch."

Celia joined us. "Sherry knows everyone around here."

Gavin came in and looked around the room. Celia and I went up to him. "You did a great job with that reading," she told him.

"This is Gavin Ridout from Lindsay," she said to me.

I smiled at him. "You're Pearl's friend."

His face lit up. "Did you know Pearl?"

"No, I'm new to the area."

"Pat runs the Norris Cassidy branch that just opened," Celia said.

"I'm just here for the start-up. Nuala Larkin is the manager."

"Nuala Larkin. She ever live in Lindsay?" Gavin asked.

"She was an investment advisor at Optimum there."

"I've heard of her. Lindsay's a small place, although not as small as Braeloch." He paused for a moment or two. "Pearl was my high school English teacher. She helped me through a rough patch when I was teenager. Encouraged me to stay in school and now I'm a high-school teacher myself."

"Gavin told me that Lyle was devoted to Pearl," Celia said. "He was her mainstay when she took sick."

The smile left his face. "We lost her last summer."

Ted came in and whispered something to Celia.

"Upstairs," she said. "He's resting."

"I'll get him some sandwiches." Ted headed for Sherry's table, and Celia followed him.

Bea came over to us. "Where's Ted going?"

"To check on his son," I said.

A frown crossed her face. "Ah, Bruce."

I'd just introduced Bea to Gavin when Lainey entered the room. Her face was pale, and she looked troubled. She saw us and came over.

"What's wrong?" I asked.

She shook her head. "It can't be."

"Hello, Lainey," Gavin said.

Lainey's face broke into a smile. "Gavin's my summer neighbor at Three Hills Lake," she said. "Pearl was often at his cottage."

"I saw a fair bit of the Critchleys in the summer when Pearl visited Lyle and Edna," Gavin said. "I talked Lyle into buying those lots at the lake. But he never built a cottage."

"Why was he trying to stop our Internet tower?" Lainey asked.

"He thought it would spoil the rural charm," Gavin said.

Lainey snorted.

Bea looked up at Gavin. "Did you see the window behind the altar?" she asked him.

He stared at her, clearly puzzled by her question.

"Stained glass," she said. "I donated it in memory of my Floyd. He was the sacristan before Lyle."

She looked as if she was about to cry. "Lyle didn't want the window put in," she said. "He wanted the church kept simple."

Lainey put an arm around Bea. "It's a lovely window, dear."

Bea smiled at her gratefully. "There you are, Ted," she said as Ted joined us. "I need to sit down."

He helped her to an armchair by the window. Lainey and Gavin went over to the refreshment table.

I saw Celia greet Monsignor Frank as he entered the room. She took him over to Sherry, who handed him a plate of sandwiches. I joined them and helped myself to a sandwich.

"This is Pat Tierney," Celia said to the monsignor. "Monsignor Frank McCann."

He acknowledged me with a nod of his head. "Quite a spread you've put on," he said to Celia. It sounded like an accusation.

"Lyle was our sacristan. He gave a lot of time to this parish."

Monsignor Frank picked up a tuna sandwich and looked at it thoughtfully. "I visited Father Brisebois yesterday. He wonders how you're getting on."

Celia lifted her chin and looked him in the eye. "Very well."

He pursed his lips. "That incident at the cemetery. What was that about?"

"Bruce Stohl is a troubled man with a drinking problem."

The monsignor was shaking his head when Soupy came over. "Where's Bruce?" he asked Celia.

"Resting upstairs."

"Okay if I look in on him?"

She nodded and Soupy moved off.

Monsignor McCann cleared his throat. "Father Brisebois wants me to ask Fred Hall to take over the sacristan's duties."

Celia folded her arms across her chest. "Sherry Vargas asked if she could have the job, and I told her she could. She lives down the road, so it will be easy for her to get here every morning to set up for Mass."

He pursed his lips again. "Sherry...?"

"Sherry Vargas. She just handed you those sandwiches. Which she made, by the way."

He looked over at Sherry and frowned. "She's a woman."

Celia locked eyes with him. "Yes?"

Inspector Foster appeared at the doorway and crossed the room in a few strides. "Where is Bruce Stohl?"

"I'll get him," Celia said. "Pat, take Inspector Foster to the kitchen. He can talk to Bruce in there." She hurried out of the room.

Foster followed me to the kitchen where he stood in the middle of the room and looked around. I asked if he wanted a coffee. He nodded, but before I could head for Sherry's coffee urn, he held up a hand. "A question, Ms. Tierney."

I smiled politely.

"I spoke to Paul Campbell yesterday. He told me he doesn't know where Critchley invested his money before he came to your branch."

"That's right. Lyle made an appointment with Paul for Thursday, when they would have gone over his holdings. But then..." I held out my hands.

"So you don't know?"

"No, I don't. You didn't find a statement of his investments at his home?"

"Just his bank accounts."

"Then he probably didn't have an investment advisor."

"And that letter you told us about," he said. "It's not on Critchley's computer."

"Maybe he wrote it by hand."

"Or maybe it never existed."

Sherry was pouring Foster a cup of coffee when Celia came up to me. "Bruce isn't in his room," she said. "I can't find him anywhere."

CHAPTER FOURTEEN

Nuala chuckled. "That is too funny. I know it was a funeral but…"

"It wasn't your usual send-off," I said from my chair on the other side of Nuala's large desk. I wanted to tell her that putting a huge barrier between herself and her clients wasn't the way to build business relationships. But she'd take it as criticism.

"So who's Bruce Stohl?" she asked.

"The maintenance man at the church."

"The church where Lyle Critchley worked?"

"Yes. Bruce and Lyle weren't the best of buddies."

"I guess not." She raised an eyebrow. "Could Bruce have disliked Lyle enough to…well, kill him?"

"From what I've seen of him, Bruce is his own worst enemy. I doubt that he'd hurt anyone."

"He threw a rock into Lyle's grave."

"He couldn't hurt a dead man, could he? And if he killed Lyle, why would he draw attention to himself?"

She picked up a pen and began to doodle on a pad on her desk. "He'd been drinking, you said, so he wasn't thinking clearly. Maybe the drink loosened his inhibitions last week, as well. His feelings for Lyle surfaced and..."

"Lyle's murder was planned," I said. "Someone deliberately set that fire. The killer was waiting for Lyle to drive into his garage."

"Mom."

I turned to see Laura in the doorway.

"I just spent a few hours at the library," she said. "Thought I'd check out your new digs. Pretty swanky."

I introduced Laura to Nuala, who told her to pull up a chair.

"Cool neckpiece you're wearing." Laura was looking at the yellow chunks of stone strung together with silver that Nuala had teamed with a black angora sweater. "Amber, right?"

Nuala smiled and nodded. "Your mom's just told me about Lyle Critchley's funeral."

Laura turned to me. "How'd it go?"

I described what happened in the cemetery. Laura stared at me, speechless.

"Bruce and Lyle didn't get along," I said.

"No kidding!" she said. "Is Bruce a suspect? It looks like—"

"Bruce is a troubled man, but I don't think he's a killer."

"The cops need to look at him," Laura said. "They seem to want to pin the murder on Jamie."

"Jamie?" Nuala said. "Aren't the police looking for someone called Jennifer?"

"Yeah," Laura said. "Jennifer Collins. That's Jamie."

"You sound like you know her."

"I…I…" Laura stammered.

"Jamie's my older daughter's partner," I said.

Nuala raised an eyebrow. "They said on the news that she works at Optimum in Toronto. Why are the police looking for her here?"

"Jamie got this letter from Lyle last week and she drove here last Thursday," Laura said. "Nobody's seen her since."

"I have work to do," I said and got out of my chair.

Laura got up too, and gave me a peck on the cheek. "Good to meet you, Nuala." She gave her a little wave. "Gotta get back to the boys."

Nuala and I watched as Laura loped out of the office.

Nuala smiled at me. "Nice girl." She paused. "By the way, what did Lyle do at the church?"

"He set up the altar for Mass. Saw that work got done around the building."

"So he was Bruce's boss. He may have been impossible to please."

"Probably was. I gather he could be difficult."

She flashed me a 100-watt smile. "There you have it! Lyle was on Bruce's case because he didn't do things to his standards. Bruce couldn't take it anymore and set fire to Lyle's garage. But even after that, he still loathed the man. He had a few drinks today and gave Lyle the send-off he thought he deserved."

I was amused—and slightly annoyed—by her take on Lyle's murder. "We'll see if the police come to the same conclusion."

At the office door, I turned to face her again. "Come to the house for an early dinner on Sunday."

She beamed. "Anything I can bring?"

"Just yourself."

"What time?"

"Around five," I said, and gave her directions to Black Bear Lake.

The door chimes sounded, and a man's voice greeted Ivy. Moments later, the phone on my desk rang.

"Gentleman here to see you, Pat," Ivy said. "Name is Kerry Gallant."

I groaned. "Send him in."

A few moments later, Kerry stood in my doorway, a big smile on his face. "Having a good day?"

"I was at a funeral this morning."

He looked slightly taken aback. "Hey, it was that the guy who died in the fire last week, wasn't it? I heard on the radio his funeral was today."

"It was."

"They're calling it a murder. Do the police know who did it?"

"Why ask me? I've been around here less than a week."

I was about to ask the reason for his visit when he got around to it himself. "How about dinner at the Winagami tonight? I've eaten at your place twice now. It's about time I reciprocated."

I smiled at him. "There's no need for that. It's no trouble for us to set an extra place."

"I'd like to have dinner with you."

"Thank you, Kerry, but I have to keep an eye on the kids. I don't want to give Laura and Kyle any more time alone than I have to."

"They're cool kids."

"They may be cool, but they're eighteen years old and can't keep their hands off each other. Sister Celia has a meeting tonight, so I'm the chaperone."

He winked. "It's going to happen sometime."

It was none of his business. I should have shut him down there and then, but I went on. "Well, I'd rather it didn't happen under the same roof as my seven-year-old son."

"Monday, then? Wendy's driving up tomorrow."

"I don't know what Celia's plans for Monday are."

"I'll call—"

It was time to nip this in the bud. "Kerry," I said in my best no-nonsense voice, "I'm going to a fundraiser at the Legion tomorrow night. A young advisor at this branch is playing in the band. Why don't you and Wendy join me? Both of you."

"But—"

"Tomorrow night, Kerry. I'll call you with details. Now go paint some pictures."

At three, I'd finished all my work and wondered how I could justify my presence at the branch for much longer. Nuala and Soupy had everything under control. All they needed was more clients, but people couldn't be rushed into decisions that involved their life savings. Keith ought to know that.

I was in the parking lot behind the building when Soupy pulled into his parking space in a bottle-green Porsche. I knew what we were paying him, and I wondered how big a loan he'd taken to buy that car.

"Nice car," I said when he opened his window. "It looks new."

He flashed a grin. "Celebratin' my new job. Hey, your tickets will be at the door tomorrow night. How many?"

"Four. My daughter will be with me. And two neighbors want to come along, too." I opened my handbag. "How much do I owe you?"

"My treat."

"You're sure? Well...I'll see you tomorrow night."

"I'll be at Veronica Collins' place in the morning. Gotta do the know-your-client thing with her."

The know-your-client questionnaire is the cornerstone of the financial planning process. Soupy needed to go through the questions with Veronica before he put her into any investments. "Mind if I tag along?" I asked.

The smile left his face. He thought I was keeping tabs on him, but I didn't care. I wanted to see Veronica again.

"I'll meet you here," I said. "What time?"

"Said I'd be there at ten."

"I'll see you here at quarter to ten."

I pulled out of the lot and onto Main Street. I slowed down to wave at Lainey on the sidewalk across the street. She gave me a jaunty salute.

A vehicle barreled past me in the opposite lane, traveling faster than traffic usually moves in Braeloch. A white Mazda with Bruce behind the wheel.

So Bruce *did* drive Veronica's car.

Fifteen minutes later, I turned into the lane that led to Al and Ruby's place. I drove slowly. The ice had started to melt, exposing deep potholes.

There were no vehicles in the yard, and the window shades and curtains in the house were drawn. I pulled up in front of the barn and stepped out of the car into the muddy yard. Fang was nowhere in sight.

I picked my way along the path up the hill. Patches of grass were exposed where the snow had melted. In the snow near the house, I saw three different boot prints. That might have meant that three people were living in the house. Or one set of prints could have been made by a customer.

I banged on the front door. When no one answered, I followed the veranda around to a side door that I assumed opened into the kitchen. Again, no response.

Then I heard barking somewhere outside. *Fang!*

I drew a deep breath and ran to the front of the house. *Maybe he hasn't seen me.*

I heard the dog's paws scrabbling along the back porch as he searched for my scent. I dashed for my car. I looked over my shoulder to see the German shepherd race around the corner of the house.

Then my feet slid out from under me. I landed on my back on a patch of ice. Hard.

I scrambled up as Fang charged toward me. Heart thumping, I reached the car and fought to open the door. The dog leaped on me, his claws sliding down the front of my coat. The weight of him pushed me flat on my back again. I grabbed the scruff of his neck and held his snapping jaws away from my face. I knew I couldn't keep him at bay for long.

Just when I thought I was a goner, a vehicle pulled up beside me.

Fang froze at the sound of a shrill whistle.

"Fang, get off!" a woman ordered.

The dog backed off me.

"Back!"

He retreated a few more steps. He kept his eyes on me and growled.

Shaking, I struggled to my feet.

A heavy woman, her short, dark hair threaded with gray, stood beside the blue pickup I'd seen the day before.

"Fang, go!" She pointed to the house.

The dog growled at me again, then ran off to the house. I exhaled in relief.

"Can't you read?" The woman pointed to the *Beware Of Dogs* sign at the gate. "Yer lucky I got here when I did. Seen you here yesterday. Didn't Al tell you Fang and Killer don't like strangers?"

"Killer?"

"Our Doberman. Killer has barn duty. Fang's on yard patrol." She paused. "On yer way now."

"You must be Ruby."

She squared her shoulders. "Yeah?"

"I'm Tracy's mother. I'm looking for Jen."

"Al said you'd find her in Toronto."

"Tracy's worried sick about her. Ask her to leave a message at this number." I handed her a slip of paper with the rectory's phone number on it.

Inside the car, I sank back in the driver's seat and fingered the rips in my coat. I looked up at the house where Ruby had opened the kitchen door. A curtain twitched on the big window at the front of the house.

Relief washed over me. Ruby had taken the phone number. Jamie would soon be in touch.

Rosemary McCracken

Celia led me down the hall to the rectory kitchen. "A sandwich?" she asked. "Something to drink?"

"No thanks. I've got to get back to the kids."

"Well, I need to fuel up for the Catholic Women's League meeting tonight." She took four sandwich quarters and a bottle of Evian from the fridge, and sat down at the chipped metal table.

I sat across from her and told her about my latest visit to Al and Ruby's place. She gasped when I told her about my encounter with Fang. "Some pets those girls have," she said.

I replayed my brief conversation with Ruby. "You may get a message from Jamie," I said. "I'm not sure if the police have tapped phone lines, but I don't think they'll bother with the rectory's line."

"You really think she's out there?"

"If not, Al and Ruby know where she is. Ruby took the phone number from me."

I was about to tell her about seeing Bruce in Veronica's Mazda, when the kitchen door opened and Bruce stepped inside.

Celia pulled her chair back from the table. "Where did you disappear to earlier?"

He shrugged and opened the refrigerator door.

"Help yourself to the sandwiches in the plastic containers," she said. "Like some tea?"

"Yeah, thanks." He sat down at the table with a blue plastic box.

She brought a teapot in a red cozy and two mugs to the table. "Inspector Foster came by looking for you."

He shoved an egg-salad sandwich into his mouth. I averted my eyes from the sight of him chewing white bread and chopped egg with an open mouth.

She poured tea into the mugs. "You may want to think about what you'll say when he returns. He'll ask why you threw that rock into Lyle's grave. And where you went afterwards."

Bruce took another sandwich from the box and turned it over in his hand.

"I saw you driving a white Mazda an hour ago," I said.

He looked up quickly. "I borrowed it."

The sound of the front door knocker echoed through the house. Celia sprang to her feet and hurried down the hall.

"You borrowed Veronica Collins's car?" I asked Bruce.

He gave the sandwich his full attention.

Celia appeared in the kitchen doorway. "Inspector Foster's here to see you, Bruce. You'll have to talk to him at some point. Might as well be now."

He glanced at the back door.

"Stay right where you are." She hurried back down the hall.

A minute later, Foster pulled up a chair beside Bruce and gave me a curt nod. "Still no word from Ms. Collins?"

"No one's heard from her," I said. "Her mother and my daughter are worried."

He turned to face Bruce. "Where were you a week ago Thursday night, Mr. Stohl?"

"Already told you. At home. At Mrs. Collins's place."

"Veronica Collins says she smelled your cigarette smoke around ten-thirty. What were you doing earlier that night?"

"I was in all evening."

"Watching television?"

"No, I don't have a TV. I was reading."

Foster appraised him for a few seconds. "What was that scene you pulled in the graveyard all about?"

Bruce ducked his head. "I..."

"Bruce had been drinking," Celia said.

Foster held up a hand.

"And he lost it," she said.

"Let him answer for himself," Foster thundered.

He turned back to Bruce. "You threw a rock into Critchley's grave. You didn't like him, did you?"

Bruce ducked his head again. "Not much." Then he looked up at Foster. "Doesn't mean I killed him."

"Where did you go when you left the cemetery?" Foster asked.

Bruce studied the ceiling. "Came back here for a bit. Then I walked around town."

I pictured him behind the wheel of Veronica's car, but I kept that to myself.

"You wanted to avoid explaining why you threw that rock into the grave."

Bruce took another sandwich out of the box and stuffed it into his mouth.

Foster shut his notebook. "Don't leave town without letting us know, Mr. Stohl."

That reminded me of something. "My daughter, Tracy, is driving up here tomorrow for my birthday," I said to Foster. "We'd forgotten you said not to leave Toronto without letting you know."

"She'll see Ms. Collins while she's here?"

"I just told you we don't know where she is. Tracy wants to see me on my birthday."

"By all means have her come. She may lead us to her friend."

Celia took Foster to the front door, and I turned to Ross. "Why were you driving Veronica's car this afternoon?"

"Running an errand." He grabbed four sandwiches and left the kitchen.

CHAPTER FIFTEEN

"When does your first session start?" I asked Laura the next morning. She was seated at the kitchen table in her pajamas.

She rolled her eyes. "Nine, Mom. Life drawing for Kyle and me until noon."

"Crafts for me," Tommy chimed in.

"Nothing on at the college on Saturday afternoon, but we'll be busy little bees all morning," Laura said. "Happy, Mom?"

"You'd better call Kyle if you want to get to your class on time."

I checked my watch, thinking that Tracy and Farah would be on the road by now. The plan was for Farah, our housekeeper, to stay at Black Bear Lake to look after Tommy when Laura and Kyle returned to the city.

Laura flung one of her long legs onto the chair next to her that held a fabric bag. "Hey, what's this?" she asked, peering into it.

"That's mine," Celia said as she came into the kitchen

"Condoms," Laura said. "A big box of condoms!"

We both stared at Celia.

"I'm taking them to the church—"

Laura snorted with laughter.

"—to the teen group that meets on Saturday afternoons."

"Won't you get into trouble with the brass?" I asked.

"I don't care. The Catholic Church needs to rethink its position on contraception. Some of those kids are sexually active and they're in no position to raise children."

"Or get STDs," Laura put in.

Celia nodded. "I'll put out the condoms and let the kids help themselves. No questions asked."

"Good for you," Laura said.

I looked at them with admiration. That was one story I wanted to hear the end of.

"My first client in the Highlands deserves a house call," Soupy said as he led the way to the parking lot behind the branch.

It was a beautiful early spring day and I was up for a brisk walk. "Veronica lives a few blocks away. Why don't we walk over?"

"Too much slush on the streets."

My boots were waterproof, but I didn't bother telling him that. He wanted to show off his new car.

"Like it?" he asked when we were inside the Porsche.

I inhaled the new car smell. "Mmm."

He patted the dashboard. "When I saw this baby, I just had to have her."

"Must have cost a bundle."

"Yeah, it did. The loan, you wouldn't believe..."

I nodded, but I questioned his financial judgment. If you don't have the money, why spend a small fortune on a luxury toy?

He grinned. "Any chance of a raise?"

I laughed. "All in good time."

He gunned the car down Main Street a fair bit over the speed limit.

I gripped the arm of the passenger door.

He grinned. "Not scared, are you?"

I bared my teeth in a smile and hoped the police would show up before he wrapped us around a telephone pole.

We found Veronica sweeping her front porch. "Don't know why I'm doing this," she said as we came up the walk. "We're good for a few more blizzards yet."

She seemed more cheerful than she'd been on my other visits. The circles under her eyes had vanished. I had a strong hunch that she'd heard from Jamie.

She sat us at the dining room table and brought out a tray with a pot of tea and three cups and saucers from the kitchen. When the tea was poured, Soupy opened his briefcase and took out Norris Cassidy's know-your-client form. I watched closely as he went over the questions on it with Veronica. He clearly enjoyed working with people.

"That wasn't difficult," she said when they'd finished. "Now you can put me into some good investments. Mind you, nothing risky. I'm not one of your highfliers."

Soupy smiled at her. "That's why I had you answer these questions. Now I know your risk tolerance, and I can choose your investments according to it."

She gave a small sigh. "My risk tolerance is zero." But she didn't seem worried about letting him manage her money—or about anything else. The tension she'd shown before was gone. I was sure Jamie had contacted her.

"I'll get you into some blue chips and quality bonds," he said. "Maybe some conservative mutual funds. I'll get to work on it first thing Monday morning, and we can meet later in the week to go over your portfolio."

He glanced at me. His look telegraphed *How did I do?*

I gave him a thumbs-up.

"You have a lovely home," I said to Veronica as we got up from the table. Too much white on white for me, but the place was well put together.

She looked pleased.

"Veronica and Herb had a great place out on Black Bear Lake near you," Soupy said as we walked into the living room.

I wondered how he knew where I was staying, but news seemed to spread quickly in the Glencoe Highlands.

"A woman from Toronto bought our place," Veronica said. "She was in your line of work. Wendy...I've forgotten her last name."

"Wendy Wilcox?" I asked.

"That's it."

"Her place is next to ours."

She smiled. "Summers were lovely, but I didn't like being out there in the winter after Herb died."

I pictured the acres of snow between the house we were staying in and the highway. "Those long driveways can be hell after a snowfall."

"I've never regretted moving into town," she said. "Monday and Thursday afternoons, I volunteer at the public school library, and my bridge group meets every Friday afternoon. And I can walk everywhere in town. I don't like driving in the winter."

So she was playing bridge the day before when Bruce was out in her car.

"I can see that you're happy here." I paused. "And that you've heard from your daughter."

She looked startled. "No, I haven't."

She wasn't a good liar.

My birthday falls a few days before St. Patrick's Day, which was why I was named Patricia. When I hit forty, I tried to put a stop to celebrations of my birthday, but Michael wouldn't hear of it. Now the girls kept up the tradition. As I drove back to Black Bear Lake that day, I found myself looking forward to the lunch the girls had planned.

Tracy's Honda Civic was in the driveway. Inside the house, Tracy and Farah were putting the final touches on a lunch of my favorite cold foods—smoked salmon, pasta-and-artichoke salad, pita, hummus and ripe black olives.

"Where's Sister Celia?" Tracy asked.

"Handing out condoms at the church," I said. Seeing Tracy's look of surprise, I added, "It's a long story. The short version is she won't be here for lunch."

Laura, Kyle and Tommy came in, and we sat down to eat. For dessert, Farah brought a birthday cake with two candles to the table. One candle was in the shape of a four, the other an eight.

Laura, Tracy and Tommy sang "Happy Birthday."

Tommy clapped his hands. "Blow out your candles and make a wish, Mrs. T."

I made a silent wish for Jamie's safe return, and blew out the two candles.

"Your gifts now, Mom," Laura said.

I opened the gift-wrapped parcels the girls had placed on the table in front of me—a pretty scarf from Farah and a lightweight jacket from the girls. "For hiking around here when the snow's gone," Laura said. "The way it's melting, that should be in a few days."

"This is from Devon." Tracy set a vase that held a dozen apricot roses on the table. "He called the house last night and the flowers arrived at seven this morning. He didn't know if there was a florist around here."

After I was toasted with sparkling wine, Laura and Kyle announced that they were heading back to the city. With Farah there to look after Tommy, they wanted to be on their way.

"There's a party at Jessie's tonight," Laura said. "Everyone'll be there."

I was about to say that I didn't want an empty house at their disposal, but why put ideas into their heads? And I didn't want Tracy to drive back to the city that afternoon. She'd be exhausted. Besides, she wanted to find out everything she could about Jamie while she was in the area.

Laura and Kyle waited for my reaction. As Kerry had said, it was going to happen sooner or later. Probably already had. "Drive carefully," I told them.

When Laura and Kyle had said their goodbyes, Farah cleared the table and Tracy sat me down in front of the fireplace. "What about Jamie?" she asked.

"You haven't heard from her?"

"No."

I told her about my visits to Al and Ruby's place, and the change I'd seen in Veronica that morning. "I'm pretty sure she's heard from Jamie, but probably not by phone."

Tracy took one of my hands. "Take me to Al's place."

"I don't think—"

"I've got to see Jamie. She's been gone for ten days."

I knew she wouldn't take no for an answer, so we bundled up and headed outside.

"We'll take my car." She rummaged in her handbag for her keys. "When Jamie sees it, she'll know it's me."

Thirty minutes later, we pulled up front of the women's barn. Tracy parked the Honda Civic beside the blue pickup. "Stay in the car," she said.

"I'll go with you."

She placed a hand on my arm. "Stay here, Mom. I'll be okay. They'll feel threatened by two of us."

She was halfway to the house, when the front door opened. Al, with a barking Fang at her side, came out on the veranda with a rifle in her hands. She yelled something, but Tracy didn't halt her stride.

I jumped out of the car. "Tracy, get back here!"

Al aimed the gun at her.

I heard Tracy say something. "Jamie" was all I could make of it.

Al fired into a spruce tree beside the house.

"Tracy!" I called. "Come back here."

"I want to see Jamie!" she shouted.

The gun went off again. "Get outta here!" Al yelled.

I charged up the path. A bullet whizzed over my head.

"Both of youse! Do I have to blow yer fuckin' heads off?"

Tracy turned back down the path, her shoulders slumped in defeat. When she got closer, I saw that her face was covered in tears. I put an arm around her.

In the car, she leaned her head on the steering wheel. "I know she's in there."

"Honey, they don't want people coming around here. They're running an illegal business."

She blinked back her tears and stared at me. "What?"

"A grow-op. Seems everyone around here knows about it."

She shook her head. "I can't believe it. Jamie never told me her friends ran a grow-op."

"Strangers aren't welcome. Not even you."

A part of the puzzle fell into place. "Especially not you. Jamie's trying to protect you by keeping you away from here."

A police cruiser with Sergeant Bouchard at the wheel was about to turn into the lane when we reached the highway. He lifted a hand in greeting as I pulled onto the road.

Tracy turned around in her seat. "Cops are paying a visit." She turned back to me. "He's looking for Jamie."

"Al and Ruby are quite capable of taking care of her."

Everyone in the township seemed to know about Al and Ruby's business. The police weren't fools and they would have gotten wind of it.

It would have been a no-brainer to shut it down. Unless they were on the take.

"I think Sergeant Bouchard is making a social call," I said. "He probably expects a payoff."

CHAPTER SIXTEEN

The Royal Canadian Legion's Branch 696 Braeloch was hopping that night. Bob Marley's "One Love" blasted out the open back door as Tracy and I got out of the Volvo. What The High Lonesome Wailers lacked in musicality, they made up for in energy and volume.

Kerry's Jeep pulled into the parking lot. Wendy jumped out, dressed in a fringed leather jacket and hand-tooled western boots. The only thing missing was a Stetson. She let out a whoop, lifted her arms above her head and swayed to the reggae beat. "Time to party!"

I introduced them to Tracy, and we headed for the front door with Wendy leading the way. Kerry winked at me and hurried after her.

Tracy shook her head. "So that's the Bank of Toronto's chief economist."

"She's letting her hair down tonight."

Tracy rolled her eyes.

Soupy had saved seats for us at his parents' table. Nuala was already seated beside Lainey. Tracy and I draped our jackets over the backs of the chairs across from them.

A stocky, bald man extended his hand across the table. "The big financial players have arrived. I'm Burt Campbell." Soupy had told me his dad and his older brother ran Highlands Electric. Burt was also the township's reeve, its highest elected position.

When the introductions were over, Burt stood and picked up the empty plastic beer jug. "I'll get us a round. Beer for everyone?"

We all nodded. The Legion isn't exactly known for its chardonnay.

As Burt sauntered over to the bar, the band struck up Buddy Holly's "Peggy Sue." Wendy turned to Kerry. "Shall we?" She hauled him onto the dance floor before he could answer.

They elbowed their way to the middle of the floor. Then Kerry grabbed her hand, twirled her around and pushed her away. She sashayed out, then moved backwards to him, turned and took his hand. They touched hips, and he twirled her around again. The other dancers drew back to watch. They clapped and hooted when the number was over.

Kerry and Wendy returned to the table, flushed and grinning broadly. "That was awesome!" she cried, fanning herself with her hands as she took her seat.

The band launched into another Buddy Holly tune, "That'll Be the Day," and I studied the foursome on the stage. They were all in their late twenties, and I remembered Soupy had told me the band had started up when he was in high school. Our junior advisor was his usual exuberant self on lead guitar, his goofy grin a permanent prop. A fellow with cropped blond hair played bass guitar. A man with a shaven head and rings in his ears was on drums, and he shared the spotlight as lead singer with Mara Nowak.

The band slowed the tempo for Patsy Cline's "Crazy," and several older couples drifted onto the floor. Mara's husky voice floated through the room. She was pretty good.

"Dance?" Kerry shouted into my ear.

I glanced at Wendy's seat. It was empty.

"Washroom," he said.

I looked at Tracy. She was closer to his age; why hadn't he asked her to dance? She waved toward the dance floor. "Go on, Mom."

Reluctantly, I got up. Kerry took my hand and led me onto the floor.

He held me closer than I liked and breathed into my ear. I felt like a teenager at a high school social.

When the music stopped, he nibbled my earlobe. "Dinner this week?"

I smiled and shook my head.

Wendy gave me an appraising look when we returned to the table, then lifted a shoulder and turned back to her conversation with Nuala and Lainey.

Tracy wasn't in her seat, and her jacket was gone. Thinking she might have stepped outside for some fresh air, I checked the front door. People were huddled together outside smoking. But no Tracy. Same thing at the back door.

I headed to the washroom where several women were lined up for the three cubicles. "Tracy!" I called. No answer.

I remembered that she had a key to my Volvo. Had she gone back to Al and Ruby's place? I ran down the back stairs to the parking lot, my stomach churning. But the car was right where I'd left it.

Back at the table, I asked the others if Tracy had said where she was going.

"She said nothing. Just came out of the washroom with Ruby Taylor and grabbed her jacket," Lainey said. "Must've gone for a smoke."

But Tracy didn't smoke.

Burt gave me a wink. He probably thought she'd gone to score some weed.

Was Ruby taking Tracy to Jamie? I had no choice but to wait until Tracy returned to find out. And I've never liked waiting.

When the band took a break, Soupy and Mara came over. We told them how great they sounded. Mara took Tracy's empty chair beside me, and Soupy went to join Greg Nowak and his wife at the table behind ours.

"No *Highlands Tonight* on Saturdays?" Wendy asked Mara.

"Show's on every night of the year except Christmas, but I get every second weekend off. The station manager fills in for me. We'll have something on this fundraiser tonight. Our camera crew was here earlier."

Wendy and Nuala returned to their conversation, and a couple came over to chat with Lainey and Burt. I kept my eyes on the door.

"Heard anything more about Jen Collins?" Mara asked me.

"Not a thing."

"I think she's out there with Al and Ruby. I hear she still sees those two."

"They don't like visitors, do they?" I said.

"They try to keep a low profile. You're a stranger to them and I'm media." Then the smile fell off her face. "They've been having trouble lately."

"What kind of trouble?"

She shrugged and stood up.

I thought of Roger Bouchard turning into Al and Ruby's lane that afternoon. Was he giving them protection at a price?

And Lyle must have known about the grow-op. Had he threatened the women?

As I scanned the room for Tracy again, I spotted Foster. He came over and slid into the seat Mara had just vacated. I glanced at the door. Still no Tracy.

"Heard from Ms. Collins?" Foster asked as he took off his parka.

I shook my head.

"She must have friends around here."

So Foster didn't know about Al and Ruby. Bouchard probably wanted to steer him clear of them.

Foster surveyed the dance floor and turned back to me. "Might as well stay here a while. You never know, Ms. Collins might drop in."

The band launched into a boisterous version of "Proud Mary." Foster grimaced. "Wish they'd turn down the sound."

Kerry and Wendy got up to dance. A burly man in a black leather vest, tattoos on his bare arms, came over to our table. I remembered seeing him at the Dominion Hotel a few days before. He said something to Nuala, and she followed him onto the dance floor.

Foster kept his eyes on the dance floor until Nuala returned to the table.

"Someone you know?" I asked her.

She laughed. "Neanderthal's not my type. One twirl around the floor was enough."

We turned our attention to the stage as Soupy introduced the band. "And now for the door prize. Thanks to all of you, the Legion will be able to make a donation to the cenotaph restoration fund. Get your tickets out, folks, and our lovely Mara will do the honors."

Robbie rolled the drums while Mara reached into a basket and pulled out a ticket. I looked around the room. *Where is Tracy?*

The drums rolled again. "The winner," Mara announced, "is ticket number three-five-zero!"

Nuala yelped. "That's me!"

The band struck up "For She's a Jolly Good Fellow" as Nuala went up to the stage. Mara handed her an envelope, and everyone stood and cheered.

"Hope she likes fishin'," Lainey shouted across the table. "It's a gift certificate for Glencoe Rod and Tackle."

Leather Vest came up to Nuala when she returned to the table. She smiled at him and shook her head.

"Ruby Taylor still around?" he asked the rest of us. "Saw her here earlier."

We shrugged or shook our heads. *Where have Ruby and Tracy gone?*

"That guy's trouble'," Burt said and got out of his chair.

The bikers, I thought, as I watched him follow Leather Vest to the front door. Leather Vest had asked about Ruby and now the township's reeve was turning him out. Not only did everyone in the community know about the grow-op, but they were all connected to it in some way.

I stared at the door, digesting this, when it opened and Bruce came in. He saw me and wove his way across the room.

"Sister Celia here?" he yelled over the music when he got closer.

"She stayed home tonight."

"There…there was a message. From Jennifer Collins. On the rectory voicemail last night."

Foster pulled over a chair for him from the Nowaks' table. "Tell us about it."

"Bruce," I said, "why don't I drive you—"

"Let him finish." Then Foster continued in a softer tone. "This message?"

Bruce wedged himself in between Foster and me. "Forgot to tell Sister about it this morning. Jen said to let somebody called…Tracy Tierney know she's okay."

Foster leaned closer to him. "Did she say where she is?"

"No, that was it." He eyed the beer in Tracy's glass.

"The message was from Jennifer Collins?" Foster persisted.

"I'm not sure." Bruce sat up straighter in the chair. "It was a woman's voice. She said,'This is a message from Jennifer Collins for Tracy Tierney. Jen is fine, don't worry about her."

So Jamie was with Al and Ruby. If not at their place, at some safe place they'd found for her.

"Did you delete it?" Foster asked.

"Yup. Nearly forgot all about it, too."

I should have told Foster where Jamie might be. But I knew she was checking out something, something to do with what Lyle had told her in his letter. I had to let her go on looking. She wouldn't find anything if she was in jail.

Bruce looked at me. "Tierney. That's your name. Tracy's your...?"

"Daughter," I said. "Bruce, what were you doing in Veronica's car on Friday?"

He glanced at Foster, who was saying something to Lainey. "Errand."

But not for Veronica. She won't let you drive her car.

The band was blasting out Marley's "I Shot the Sheriff" when Tracy returned to the table. Relief washed over me. And I saw that she looked a lot happier. She even had a sparkle in her eyes.

Foster's jaw dropped when he saw her.

"I told you Tracy was driving up today," I yelled in his ear. "It's my birthday."

Across the table, Lainey pointed at the empty chair beside her. "Sit over here, dear. Burt's outside for a smoke."

"Up here to see your friend?" Foster shouted across the table.

"I'm here for my mother's birthday."

He got up from his chair. "I'd like to talk to you, young woman. Outside."

She got up and followed him to the door.

Lainey was staring at me, so I felt I should explain why Foster wanted to talk to my daughter. "Tracy's a friend of Jennifer Collins. Inspector Foster wants to know if she's heard from her."

She nodded. "Jen's probably with Al and Ruby."

Does everyone around here know that?

Tracy returned a few minutes later and came over to my chair. "We'd better get back, Mom. I've got to hit the road first thing in the morning."

Wendy elbowed Kerry, and they stood up.

"C'mon, Bruce," I said. "I'll drive you to the rectory."

We said our goodbyes to Nuala and Lainey. Bruce chugged down the beer in Tracy's glass and wiped his mouth on his jacket sleeve.

The High Lonesome Wailers were rocking to "I Heard It Through the Grapevine" as we crossed the parking lot. Wendy leaned into Kerry. "That was fun, sugar." She smiled at me. "How about a nightcap at our place?"

"Thanks," I said, "but Tracy has an early start tomorrow. We should get home."

Wendy opened the Jeep's passenger door. "Another time, then." She waved as the vehicle pulled out of the parking lot.

I turned to Tracy. "So what happened with Ruby?"

Tracy put a finger on her lips and inclined her head toward Bruce.

CHAPTER SEVENTEEN

Kerry's Jeep had disappeared into the night when I pulled onto Highway 123. I drove into Braeloch where I dropped Bruce off at the rectory. Then I turned the Volvo around and drove back to the highway.

"So?" I asked when we picked up speed outside of town.

"You can trust me," I said when Tracy didn't answer. I made a zipping motion across my mouth. "My lips are sealed."

"I know, Mom, but…" She leaned back and fell silent.

The sky was studded with stars, and I hoped that meant we wouldn't have to wait for Hank and his plow the next morning. I smiled to myself, thinking that I'd become a real country woman, attuned to all signs of weather. In the city, the weather doesn't affect us nearly as much.

Tracy slipped a CD from her handbag into the player, and the voice of k.d. lang crooning "Constant Craving" flooded the car. I turned the volume down.

"Mom!"

"What did Ruby have to say?"

She sighed. "All right. I promised, but I suppose I can tell you." She paused. "Ruby said Jamie's okay, that we should let her lie low for a while."

"What else? You were gone a long time. You didn't happen to see Jamie herself when you went outside?"

"No, I didn't."

I wasn't sure whether I believed her, but I decided not to argue the point. "Did Ruby say why she's lying low?"

Tracy said nothing for a few moments.

"Come on."

"Jamie's working on something."

"She's working on whatever Lyle told her in his letter. What was it?"

"Ruby wouldn't say."

Again, I wasn't sure that she was telling me the truth. "And Foster? What did he want?"

"The usual. Where is she? Why hasn't she contacted him?"

"Why did Ruby come to see you tonight? Jamie left you a message."

Glancing at her, I saw I had her full attention.

"What message?"

We passed the Legion. Judging from all the vehicles in the parking lot, the party appeared to be still in full swing. I told Tracy what Bruce had said.

"Hmm. I guess she doesn't want us to go back to her friends' house."

"That's where she's staying?"

"I think so, although Ruby didn't come out and say it."

I pointed out the Critchley place as we drove by it. The driveway gate was closed and crime scene tape was still strung over it.

"Jamie came here the day Lyle was killed?" Tracy asked.

"Someone with Jamie's hair color was seen on the property. Someone who was driving a Honda Civic."

The next stretch of highway passes the entrance to Glencairn Conservation Park, fifty acres of hiking trails through forest and around wetlands. We were driving through the park when I saw a set of headlights in my rear-view mirror. The vehicle—with its brights on, I couldn't tell if it was a car, a SUV or a pickup—must have pulled out of the park's driveway. It picked up speed and, in seconds, was bearing down on us.

"Jesus! Mom, what's that guy doing?" Tracy cried.

"I don't know, but I don't think Jesus has anything to do with it."

The vehicle bumped our rear fender. I pressed down on the gas pedal.

What seemed like seconds later, the Volvo was shimmying and sliding on the road. Black ice. I lifted my foot and tried to remember what I'd heard about driving on black ice. *Don't hit the brakes.* I gripped the steering wheel and hung on for dear life.

"Mom, he's trying to run us off the road!"

"He doesn't have to. Black ice is doing it for him."

I feathered the wheel, and tried to steer the Volvo toward the middle of the road. No sudden moves, I told myself. But the Volvo was drifting toward the snow-covered shoulder of the road. The drop down to the culvert was pretty steep along that stretch and there was no guard rail. If we went over, we'd probably survive the fall, but we'd never get the car back on the road without help. We hadn't taken our cell phones—if we could even get a signal—and it was a long walk back to town.

The Volvo started to spin just as the bright lights bore down on us again. *He wants me to panic. Wants me to pull to the right and slide into the culvert.*

"Mom, do something!"

Then the Volvo's tires gripped bare pavement and it steadied itself. Our pursuer pulled up on our left side. My instinct was to yank the wheel to the right, but I resisted the impulse.

Suddenly, the vehicle whizzed past us and zoomed down the road ahead, its tail lights disappearing in the darkness.

I steered the Volvo into the middle of the straight stretch of road where the tires got a good grip on the salted asphalt. I exhaled in relief, but my heart was still skittering around in my chest.

"Oh, my God!" Tracy moaned.

I looked at her quickly. "You okay, honey?"

She nodded.

"Notice the type of vehicle? Could you read the licence plate?"

"No, its lights were too bright. Couldn't make out anything. And it happened so fast."

I'd brought the Volvo up to sixty, when Tracy asked, "Mom, what was that all about?"

"Someone's trying to tell us something."

She groaned. "So what's wrong with picking up the phone?"

"Whoever it is doesn't want to talk. He just wants us out of here."

CHAPTER EIGHTEEN

At the house, we found Farah curled up at the end of a sofa, her dark eyes wide with fear. I placed a warning hand on Tracy's arm.

Celia got up from the chair beside the sofa. "Farah's had a scare."

Farah unfastened the metal clip that held her hair back from her face. She ran her hands through her long, dark hair.

Celia motioned for us to sit down. "Farah, tell Pat and Tracy what happened."

She gave a shudder. "Horrible. I hear banging noise out there." She glanced at the sliding glass doors that opened onto the three-tiered deck. "Then this face, it look at me through the glass."

I raised an eyebrow at Celia. I wanted her version of what had happened.

"It was about fifteen minutes ago," Celia said. "I was upstairs working in my room. Farah screamed and I ran down here. She was pointing at the doors, terrified. But by the time I got here, whoever was out there had gone."

"I saw him!" Farah cried. "Look at me like he want to—"

"Did he knock on the door?" I asked.

"No. He just look at me."

"A man?"

She nodded. "Ugly man. Fat, white face."

"Hair? Hat?"

"No hair," Farah said. "Just white face."

"He must have been dressed in black," Tracy said. "With a black tuque on his head."

We all looked at the deck doors. We'd always left the curtains open because the view of the lake—even frozen over and covered with snow—was spectacular. And, at night, the closest house in front of us was clear across the lake.

I pulled the heavy curtains across the doors. Farah sighed with relief. "Did he leave footprints?" Tracy asked.

"Somebody did," Celia said. "They lead around the house to the driveway where they meet tire marks that aren't ours. But I didn't hear a vehicle drive up."

Farah pulled the afghan tightly around her. "We are far from people here. I cannot stay alone with Tommy."

I pictured her packing her bag the next morning, but I shelved that thought for later. "We'd better call the police."

"Foster or Bouchard?" Celia asked.

"Both of them."

Roger Bouchard picked up on the first ring. I told him what had happened and he said he'd be right over. I left a message for Foster.

"Farah has a tendency to overdramatize," I said to Celia as we made hot chocolate in the kitchen. "But we'd better show the footprints and the tire marks to the police. It's clear outside right now, but they could be covered with snow in the morning."

I told her what had happened on the drive home. "I'd better let the police know about that, too. The vehicle appeared behind us around the same time that Farah saw our visitor."

"So they were two different people," she said.

"Who may have been working together."

But not Bruce. He was at the rectory.

Sergeant Bouchard arrived forty minutes later. He pulled the tuque off his curly gray hair and strode through the house.

"Doors haven't been tampered with, nothing's broken," he said looking at the sliding deck doors. His beak of a nose pointed at me. "Somebody dropped by to see if you were home."

I turned on the deck lights. "He could have knocked on the front door and asked for one of us."

"'Round here, everyone goes to the back door."

"You didn't just now."

"I knew who I was calling on. City folks don't use back doors."

I opened the sliding doors. From the doorway, he looked at the footprints on the deck. "Kodiaks," he said. "Size nine, I'd say."

I closed the door and led him to the dining table where the others were seated. He sat down and asked Farah a few questions about the face at the window.

Then he sat back and studied her. "How old are you?"

She looked startled. "I have twenty-three years."

"Where do you come from?"

Her dark eyes widened. She opened her mouth, but no words came out.

"Farah's from Iraq," I said. "She came to Canada three years ago. She and Tracy drove up from Toronto today."

"Would it be fair to say that you overreacted tonight?" he said to Farah. "You had a long day and you're in an unfamiliar place. So when this caller knocked on the door, you—"

"No!" she cried. "He not knock on door. He just stare at me."

"We have something else to tell you, officer," I said. Tracy and I took turns telling him about the vehicle that tried to run us off the highway.

He took a few notes. "Don't suppose you got the licence number?"

"No," Tracy said. "Those brights were blinding."

He closed his notebook. "Some moron was playing games with you. Real stupid. Someone could've gotten hurt." He stood and zipped up his parka.

"Aren't you going to look at the tire tracks in the driveway?" Tracy asked.

He sighed. "If it makes you happy."

We went out the front door and over to where the footprints from the deck met the tire marks. I stared at the tread marks in the snow and wondered if they would mean anything to the police. They probably had distinctive nicks and scrapes, and other signs of wear.

"Goodyear snow tires," Bouchard said. "Looks like it was a medium-sized van."

"Aren't you going send to someone over to take photos, and make casts of the footprints and these tracks?" I asked.

"Ms. Tierney, you had yourself a caller tonight. Nothing more."

I stared at him.

"Good night, ladies."

I was fuming when we returned to the house. Celia sat studying the dying embers in the fireplace. Farah had gone to bed.

Tracy put her arms around me."'Night, Mom. I'll probably be gone when you get up in the morning. I'll set my alarm for six."

"There's no rush to get back. Sunday's not a work day. Why don't you sleep in and leave after lunch?"

"I want to catch up on some work at the office."

I watched her go upstairs. Whatever Ruby had said had put her mind at ease about Jamie.

I sat down beside Celia. "Do you have a camera?" I asked.

She shook her head.

Then it dawned on me. "I can take photos with my cell."

I got my cell from my room only to find the battery had died. I hadn't used it in nearly a week, and I'd let it run down. I plugged it into its charger.

"As soon as it's charged," I told Celia, "I'll get pictures of the

CHAPTER NINETEEN

I woke up on the sofa when Tracy came downstairs the next morning. My watch told me it was five after six. *The footprints and the tire tracks!*

My cell was charged. I grabbed my parka from the chair where I'd left it and opened the curtains over the deck doors. The eastern sky was pink, a sign of a sunny day, but it had snowed during the night. Not enough snow to warrant plowing the driveway, but enough to cover the prints on the deck. *Damn!* Then I wondered if forensics could lift prints from under fresh snow.

Tracy was eating cereal at the table. I sat down across from her. "Anything more you'd like to tell me about what Ruby said last night?"

She put down her spoon. "I really didn't see Jamie. Ruby said she's working on something. But I don't know what it is. Really, I don't."

She sighed. "Ruby said we should leave her alone. Let her get on with it, she said."

I stared at her, exasperated. I'd hightailed it up north to find Jamie. Now that Tracy was no longer worried about her, the search was off as far as she was concerned.

But I was committed to stay in Braeloch for a few more weeks. And I was worried about Jamie. The police wanted to speak to her, and she was eluding them. And mixed up in a drug operation.

"We need to tell the police that Al and Ruby know where Jamie is," I said.

"I told Foster that I don't know where she is, and that's the truth. I don't know whether she's at their place or somewhere else. I'm going back to Toronto, and Jamie needs to get on with what she's doing."

She had that stubborn look on her face, and I knew I wouldn't get her to change her mind. "You'll stay at the house with Laura?" I asked.

"Yes."

"Keep an eye on her. And Kyle."

Tracy looked at me steadily as she finished drinking her orange juice but said nothing.

I watched her Honda Civic disappear down the driveway, then I went upstairs to shower and dress. I was back in the kitchen with a pot of coffee brewed when Foster called at seven-thirty. He said he'd turned his cell phone off when he returned to the hotel the night before and hadn't heard my message until now. He told me he'd be at Black Bear Lake within the hour.

Farah slipped into the kitchen and gave me a baleful look. "It is dangerous here for me and Tommy."

I handed her cutlery for four place settings and motioned her toward the table. "Sister Celia and I have to go to work tomorrow," I said. "But Kerry Gallant, the man who lives in the house on the next property, works at home. I'm sure he'll come over if there's a problem. Why don't I call him right now?"

Kerry answered on the second ring. I told him that Farah would be at the house with Tommy while I was at work, and asked if I could give her his number.

"Sure," he said. "I'll look in on them."

We were in the middle of breakfast when Foster arrived. I told the others to go on eating, and I took Foster out to the deck, then around to the driveway. There wasn't much to see.

"Sergeant Bouchard seemed to think whoever was out there was making a social call," I said when we returned to the house.

A frown creased Foster's face as he lowered himself into a chair in front of the fireplace.

"Visitors usually knock on doors, whether they're front doors or back doors," I went on. "They don't just peer in windows."

"Sounds like somebody tried to frighten you," he said. "Here at the house and out on the highway."

"They were two different people. Tracy and I were on the highway around the time Farah saw that man on the deck."

He raised an eyebrow.

"Maybe they were working together," I said.

"Bouchard didn't measure the prints or the tire tracks?"

"He didn't do anything."

Foster made me go over what had happened on the highway again. "When did you first notice the vehicle behind you?"

When I told him it might have come out of the driveway at Glencairn Conservation Park, he sighed. "I'll take a look, but any tire tracks out there will be covered with snow."

"Is there a way to get prints from under fresh snow?"

He looked thoughtful. "We can sometimes get photographs using oblique lighting. Provided the temperature doesn't rise above freezing."

He hoisted himself out of the low chair. "I'll get a forensics team over here." He inclined his head toward the glass doors. "They'll check for fingerprints on the glass. Don't use those doors today."

At nine-thirty, I headed out with Tommy and Farah. I dropped Farah off at Foodland to shop for groceries. I told her to get a coffee at Joe's when she finished and we'd meet her there. I parked the Volvo in the municipal lot, and Tommy and I walked over to the church.

Jesus of the Highlands Church was full again, but this time all eyes were on Sister Celia. A woman in the pulpit was big news in the Catholic Church I'd grown up in.

Celia wasn't in the pulpit, though. She had pinned a tiny microphone on the purple liturgical stole she wore, and she stood facing the congregation in the center aisle.

"Love God and our neighbor to the very best of our ability," she said. "That's the great commandment. It's what we were put on this Earth to do. But it's not always easy.

"I was a teacher for many years. First in elementary school and later in high school. When I taught Grade Five, one of my students brought a tree branch with a caterpillar cocoon attached to it to class. He asked if we could watch the butterfly emerge, and I agreed. We set up the cocoon inside a window in the classroom.

"A week later, the cocoon began to tear. A few days later, we could see the head of the butterfly with its tiny antennae. The next day, the tear in the cocoon was larger and we saw the butterfly's folded wings. At recess that day, one of the boys ripped open the cocoon and exposed a half-formed creature, part caterpillar, part butterfly.

"'Bobby!' I cried.

"'I was only trying to help it, Sister,' he said.

"Too late, I told him that the struggle to emerge from the cocoon is part of the process of becoming a butterfly. The exertion develops its muscles and its circulatory system. Deprived of that struggle, our little creature—our caterfly or butterpillar—died soon after that.

"A struggle is also integral to our own evolution, our journey to becoming the best people we can be. We come out of church on Sunday fired up with good intentions. Then someone cuts us off at an intersection. Grabs the last bag of milk right in front of us at the grocery store. Steals our handbag or wallet. And our good intentions fly right out the window. We crawl home and complain to our spouse or our friends. But the important thing is that, tomorrow we try again. The struggle builds our character.

"In the Apostles' Creed, we speak of the Communion of Saints. That's you, Tommy." Her eyes were on the boy seated beside me.

Tommy looked up at me, his eyes big brown circles in his face.

"And you, Sherry Vargas," she said to Sherry on the other side of the church.

"And you, Bruce Stohl." She smiled at Bruce, who was seated beside Sherry.

"And you in the blue jacket and you and you!" She pointed to people throughout the church.

Those she'd indicated smiled self-consciously. Some lowered their heads.

"All of us, we're all saints in the making. We all have the capacity to do wonderful, generous things for our fellow human beings and the planet on which we live. We can also do terrible evil. But the fact that we are here today means our intentions are in the right place."

She bowed her head and paused for a few moments. "The Lord be with you."

Then she raised a hand. An accordion wailed the opening bars of "When the Saints Come Marching In." A sax and two guitars joined in.

Celia began to clap in time to the music, and so did everyone else in the church as she and the two altar girls walked down the center aisle.

She'd done a good job beating the bushes for musicians, I thought as we filed out behind them. From what I'd heard of him, I didn't think Father Brisebois would approve of music in his church.

"Well done," I said to her at the church door where she stood greeting her flock.

"Am I really a saint?" Tommy asked.

She gave him a big smile. "You sure are, kiddo."

"Well," I said as I ruffled his hair, "maybe when you're asleep."

After lunch, Celia took Tommy out on the snowmobile. Farah loaded a tray with jars and bottles, and retreated to the upstairs bathroom for a beauty treatment. I slipped into my room and lay down on my bed with the novel I was reading.

I heard Farah come out of the bathroom and go downstairs. Not long after, rapping sounded on the front door. I got up and looked out the window. Kerry's black Jeep was in the driveway. After her fright the night before, I didn't think Farah would answer the door, but a few moments later I heard Kerry's voice in the hall. I sank back on my bed and chuckled.

When I went downstairs a half-hour later to put the roast in the oven, I found Farah and Kerry drinking tea in front of the fireplace. Kerry lifted a hand to me in greeting. "Needed to stretch my legs," he said.

The front door opened, and Celia and Tommy came in. "When can we go out on the snowmobile again?" Tommy asked her.

"Sister Celia has work to do this week," I told him.

"Tell you what, young man," Kerry said, "I'll take you for a spin tomorrow."

The boy's face broke into a delighted grin. "Right after breakfast?"

"You'll have to ask Sister Celia," I said.

"I've got my own machine," Kerry said.

Kerry said his goodbyes, and Celia fed Tommy crackers and cheese at the table. Farah followed me upstairs.

"Kerry, he make paintings," she said. "That is his work."

I smiled and thought of Wendy who paid the bills at the house next door.

"He is very nice man. He is rich?" Farah asked.

"I don't think so."

"He has big place over there. Maybe I see it tomorrow."

"Take Tommy with you if you go over. I don't want him here alone."

She stopped outside the room she'd taken over from Laura, and turned to face me. "Kerry, he is lonely there?"

"I don't think he is. But he enjoys company now and then."

Farah was entertaining romantic ideas about the man next door. She had been brought up in her homeland to marry and bring up children, but the war in Iraq had forced her family to flee to Canada. Farah still hoped to find a husband who could give her a nice house, fine clothes and a position in society, and Kerry seemed to fit the bill.

I smiled at her. I didn't have the heart to tell her about Wendy.

Not long after that, Tommy poked his head around my doorframe.

I smiled at him. "Hey, kiddo!"

"Hey, Mrs. T!" He jumped on my bed.

I gave him a hug. "Have fun out there on Molly?"

He grinned at me and nodded.

I hugged him, and inhaled the little-boy scent of shampoo and chocolate. His eyes closed, and I tightened my arms around him. I hadn't spent much time with him all week, and I felt badly about that. I kissed his head. He was part of my family now. I like having my family with me. *When Jamie...*

I smiled when I realized that Jamie had become a member of the family. From everything I'd heard about her, she was an exceptional woman. And Tracy loved her. That was good enough for me.

I lay on the bed with Tommy in my arms. I heard more rapping on the front door, but I let Celia deal with it. While Tommy slept, my mind drifted. Foster had said he'd turned off his cell phone when he got back to the hotel the previous evening. Was he at the Winagami? He might be at the Dominion Hotel where Jamie had stayed that first night. I wondered if he knew she'd been there.

I should have told him that Al and Ruby were helping Jamie. But I didn't think Jamie would want her friends—and their business—to come to his attention.

I groaned. *What a mess this has turned into.* Tommy squirmed in my arms. I pulled the duvet over him and eased myself off the bed.

Looking down at the sleeping boy, I knew he'd go stir-crazy cooped up in the house for another week. Farah would be hopeless at keeping him entertained. Kerry might take him out on his snowmobile once or twice but that wouldn't be enough to help the time pass.

I decided to book a day off work that week and take Tommy to the Glencoe Wolf Center. Maybe we'd go on a dogsled ride. Norris Cassidy had to give me time to look after my family.

Downstairs, I found Celia preparing vegetables for dinner. "The forensics people were here," she said.

"Could they lift the tire and boot prints?"

"Don't know. They knocked to tell us they'd arrived, but they just drove off when they were done. Made a mess of the deck doors."

I glanced at the doors, but she'd drawn the curtains over them.

"I hope Nuala eats meat," I said as I checked the roast in the oven. "Yes, she ordered chicken for lunch at the Winagami."

"Some people won't touch animals with four legs," Celia said.

I sighed. "That would be just my luck."

I heard a car pull up outside. I opened the front curtains as Nuala stepped out of her Lexus.

"Hmm," Celia said beside me. "Nice car. Fancy boots. Your company must pay well."

Nuala sniffed appreciatively when she walked into the house. "Smells wonderful. Should go well with this." She handed me a bottle of wine.

I looked at the bottle in my hand. Château des Grandes Maisons costs sixty-five dollars and change.

I watched Nuala take off her boots and slip on a pair of high-heeled sandals. They looked like René Caovilla footwear, which would have put her back six hundred bucks. I took in her black Prada pants and lime silk jacket, and thought of her Lexus and Soupy's Porsche. Our Braeloch advisors had a taste for the high life.

I introduced her to Celia, who was arranging a tray of snacks in front of the fireplace.

Nuala looked around the room. "Nice place."

"It's one of Norris Cassidy's executive vacation spots," I said. "I'd like to try out the Caribbean place someday."

I could almost hear the wheels in her head spinning as she tried to gauge my status at the company.

"You're certainly away from the crowds out here with that long driveway," she said.

"We are alone here," Farah said, coming downstairs with Tommy and Maxie. "My cell phone, it don't work at this place."

"Tommy Seaton and Farah Alwan," I said to Nuala. "Tommy and Farah, this is Nuala Larkin."

While Celia poured wine, Cleo wandered into the room. Maxie growled.

"Hold the dog, Farah," I said.

Farah grabbed Maxie's collar. "How long this cat is here?"

Cleo bolted upstairs. Maxie tried to run after her, but Farah held tight. It wasn't the time to tell her that Cleo seemed to be a permanent addition to the family. I went upstairs and put Cleo in my room.

"A good time at the Legion last night?" I asked Nuala when I returned.

"You bet," she said with a smile. "I stayed right till the end. But I never got a chance to talk to your daughter. Where did she go?"

"Off to meet a friend."

"Jennifer Collins?"

"No."

"Does Tracy know where Jennifer is?" she asked.

I shook my head.

"Pat," Celia called from the kitchen, "the roast is ready to carve."

Dinner turned out well. The meat was done to perfection, and Celia had whipped up a pan of Yorkshire pudding to go with it. Nuala's wine slipped down our throats as smoothly as honey.

"Cheers!" Tommy said throughout the meal, holding up his glass of grape juice.

Nuala told us about a trip she'd taken to a ski resort in British Columbia the previous winter. "I'd never skied before," she said. "I got myself up the mountain on the chairlift and I stood at the top wondering what to do next. This guy started shouting, then jumped on me and knocked me to the ground. He saved me from being hit by the chair that was going back down the mountain. The downside was I broke my wrist in the fall. I had to sit it out at the lodge for the rest of the week."

I chuckled. I grew up in Montreal where skiing is a popular winter sport. My brother, Jon, was a hot-dog skier as a teenager.

"Where did you grow up, Nuala?" Celia asked.

"Small-town southern Ontario."

"Where?" I asked.

"Dreary little place." She gave a wave of dismissal. "Couldn't wait to get out. We were hours away from the ski centers like Collingwood, and skiing was something I always wanted to try. It looks like ultimate freedom."

"Sports come easier when you learn them as a kid," Celia said.

"By the way, whose snowmobile is that outside?" Nuala asked.

"I've rented it for a few weeks," Celia said.

Nuala looked impressed. "Are you a snowmobiler too, Pat?"

I laughed. "I was a passenger—once."

"On a snowmobile," Celia said, "you can get into back country you can only access by canoe or kayak in the summer. But there are dangers out there—barbed wire fences and thin ice on the lakes. You need to keep your wits about you."

Farah and I cleared the table after the main course. I noticed that Nuala had taken off her high-heeled sandals under the table. Those pricey bits of leather probably weren't very comfortable.

"Do you like Braeloch?" Celia asked Nuala when we returned to the table with apple pie and ice cream.

"Very much," she replied with a smile.

"It must have been difficult to leave your friends in Lindsay," Celia said.

"I've moved around a fair bit," Nuala said. "I try to look at the upside—there's always something better ahead."

"Maybe you'll meet a nice man and settle down here," Celia said.

Nuala laughed. "Oh, I've been doing my best to avoid that."

"I like her," I said as Celia poured our nightcaps. "Nuala's bright and hardworking, and she really cares about her clients."

Celia gave a small lift to a shoulder. "Nobody has eyes that color."

"They are a remarkable shade of blue—or green. Turquoise, I guess it's called," I said. "Oh, I know. They're colored contact lenses. And her outfit tonight was over the top. But so what? She's single, and she probably makes a lot more money than her parents did. Why shouldn't she make herself look good?"

Celia took a sip from her glass. "She was out to impress. Dinner with one of the big guns from Toronto."

"That's to be expected," I said. "She wants to get ahead."

"Hmm." She looked at her watch. "Time for the evening news."

As I settled in for the broadcast, I wondered why Celia's character-judging antennae had twitched.

And why mine hadn't.

CHAPTER TWENTY

Monday morning, I found Soupy perched on the reception desk entertaining Ivy with the highlights of Saturday night at the Legion.

"I couldn't make it on Saturday," she told me. "Had to stay home with my little brother."

"Nuala in yet?" I asked.

"On the phone in her office," Soupy said.

He turned back to Ivy. "Two bikers showed up."

A shadow passed across Ivy's face. Soupy gave a slight nod. Those bikers had everyone worried.

An hour later, I went into Soupy's office and closed the door behind me.

He looked concerned. "Is something wrong? One of my accounts?"

"You're doing fine." I slid into the chair in front of his desk. "I want to understand this community better. I hope you'll fill me in on a few things."

He eyed me warily. "If I can."

"The bikers you mentioned. Was one of them wearing a leather vest with silver studs on Saturday night? Tattoos on his arms?"

He looked surprised at the question. "Yeah."

"He asked about Ruby. Those guys aren't from around here, are they?"

He shook his head.

I waited for him to tell me what he knew about them. When it appeared he wasn't about to, I continued. "Mara probably told you I've been out to Al and Ruby's place. Have these guys gotten wind of what goes on there?"

He gave a curt nod. "They've been sniffing around for the past few weeks. We think they're members of the Dead Riders, though they haven't been wearing their colors. Al's tried to scare them off with her gun."

I winced at the thought of Al and her gun. "They want in on the action?"

"Yeah."

Was this what Jamie was checking out?

"Saturday night was the first time they came out to a social event," Soupy said. "We were afraid there'd be trouble, but Dad talked them into leaving."

"Your father must be persuasive."

Soupy grinned. "He can be."

"Tell me something. Everyone knows about the grow-op and turns a blind eye to it. Why?"

His smile faded. "What does it matter?"

"For starters, it's illegal. Al and Ruby could be looking at jail time. And now there are the bikers. They mean trouble."

He sat stone-faced.

Keith Kulas would have been ranting by this time. "And it could mean trouble for this branch."

Soupy blinked in disbelief. "What?"

"Its integrity could come into question."

"How?"

"Marijuana is a multi-billion-dollar cash crop," I said. "I don't think Al and Ruby make billions, but I bet they make thousands, maybe hundreds of thousands of dollars every year. They have to deposit their money somewhere. If it's here, that will invite police scrutiny. Head office wants our branches to be squeaky-clean."

"Well, on that score, you don't have to worry," Soupy said. "They don't have an account here."

"They still may. We've been open less than a week. If their operation has attracted the bikers' attention, it's only a matter of time before the police—not Bouchard—start investigating." I paused. "Fill me in."

He hesitated. "You can't go to the cops with this."

I just looked at him. "Al and Jennifer Collins were an item when Jen lived up here. Was Jen part of the operation?"

He shook his head. "No. Jen set her sights high and won a scholarship to college. Al was heartbroken when she went down to Toronto and seldom came back."

"So she turned to Ruby?"

"They turned to each other. Ruby was going through a rough patch of her own. Her dad died in a logging accident, and Ruby and her mom tried to make a go of their farm." He paused, seeing the puzzled look on my face. "You didn't know the farm belongs to Ruby?"

I shook my head.

"Anyway, Ruby invited Al to live with her and her mother on the farm. Then—"

"Hold on," I said. "Ruby's mother was in on the grow-op?"

"It wasn't like that." He paused. "Ruby's mother—Norma Taylor—needed both girls to help out on the farm. Al and Ruby agreed, but it was a real struggle. Land around here isn't great for farming.

"Then Norma got sick with cancer. She was real sick with the chemo treatments, and Ruby told her that smoking pot would help. But she wouldn't hear of it."

"Norma was a heavy smoker—something she wouldn't give up—and she rolled her own cigarettes. One day, Ruby slipped some pot into the tobacco, and it helped Norma with the nausea. When Ruby told Norma what she'd done, she was furious at first but she gave in. And Ruby and Al started to grow their own."

"Couldn't they have applied for a government okay for medical marijuana?" Family doctors now give cancer patients prescriptions for marijuana that they take to licensed distributors. But just a few years back, patients had to apply to the Canadian government to purchase marijuana from government producers.

"Ruby figured getting approvals would take too long." He paused. "She was right. Norma died less than a year later."

"How do you know all this?"

"Everyone around here knows what Ruby did to help her mom."

"Go on."

"Folks started going to Ruby and Al when someone had cancer or arthritis pain. Stuff like that."

"Their business isn't just about medicinal marijuana," I said.

"You're right. Ruby and Al saw their chance to make some money."

"And nobody squealed?"

"They let it be known they wouldn't sell to anyone underage. People here respect that."

My mind was reeling. I clearly wasn't in Toronto anymore. "Underage meaning what?"

"Meaning they won't sell to you unless you've reached legal drinking age."

"Nineteen," I said.

He nodded.

"How do they enforce that? Ask for ID?" I was being sarcastic.

He grinned. "They're from here. They know this community."

"What about cottagers?"

"If they're long-timers, and Ruby and Al know them. Otherwise…" He smiled. "No one knows what they're talking about."

"Do Ruby and Al deal elsewhere?"

"Probably, but we don't ask. It's none of our business."

I needed to think. "Thanks for filling me in." I hesitated at the office door. "What do you think will happen...with the bikers?"

"I don't know." His brow creased. "Word's bound to get out now. And then...well..."

I nodded. Ruby and Al's business was running on borrowed time.

In my office, I printed out a client portfolio that Monty Buchanan had sent me from Toronto, but my thoughts kept returning to the bikers. Had Lyle told Jamie that a biker gang had threatened the grow-op? But what stake could the reformed boozer have in Al and Ruby's operation?

At eleven-thirty, I drove over to the Winagami and had lunch with the president of Braeloch College. I suggested that we organize a series of financial planning seminars for faculty members and students. He seemed interested. When we'd said our goodbyes, I headed for the parking lot where I found Al Barker seated in her pickup beside my Volvo. I wondered if she had her rifle with her, but when she got out of the truck her hands were empty.

"Afternoon." She leaned back on the truck.

I nodded.

"Got a favor to ask."

I waited for her to go on.

"Ruby and me want you folks to cool it. You been out to our place three times now. And this morning your friend Gavin Ridout turned up."

She probably scared the poor teacher off with her gun. "I've met Gavin once," I said. "I'd hardly call him a friend."

"If you say so, Miz Tierney. But these visits gotta stop. Ruby gave Tracy a message the other night."

"Jamie's working on something and let her get on with it," I recited.

She locked eyes with me. "Bad guys been comin' to our place. Wouldn't want you caught in the crossfire."

That said, she jumped into the truck and roared away.

It had started to snow again. I was wiping snow off my windshield when Foster pulled up beside me.

"What are you doing here?" he asked as he got out of his car.

"Business," I told him. "I've been pitching our services to Braeloch College. Any luck with tire marks at the park?"

He shook his head. "Several snowmobiles went through there on Sunday morning. All that was left were snowmobile tracks."

"And the prints on our deck?"

"No joy there, either. It was mild yesterday, and the snow on top of them bled through."

"The glass doors on the deck?"

"Nothing. Your visitor either wore gloves or was careful about what he touched."

He needed to know that Al and Ruby were helping Jamie, but I couldn't bring myself to tell him that.

He seemed to read my thoughts. "Something you want to tell me?"

I met his eyes. "No," I lied.

On the drive back to Braeloch, I wondered why Gavin had stopped by the grow-op. He spent his summers in the area so he probably knew about the operation. But Al had been surprised by his visit, so he wasn't a client.

And Gavin was a high-school teacher. Winter break was over and he should have been back in the classroom.

I parked in the lot behind the branch. I walked around to the front of the building where I found Lainey coming down the front walk.

She smiled when she saw me. "Just dropped off a folder for Paul. He forgot it when he came over last night."

Ted Stohl rounded the street corner and walked briskly toward us, a smile on his face. "Hello, ladies."

We stepped aside to let him pass. He climbed the front steps and went into the branch. Lainey watched him with a troubled look on her face.

I remembered the photo on Lyle's mantle. Lainey, Ted and Lyle had been friends when they were younger. "Must be nice for you to have Ted here again," I said. "What brought him back to Braeloch?"

She gave me a tight smile. "He found himself at loose ends when he retired from the Toronto newspaper. *The Times* was up for sale, and he bought it. Last year, Bruce turned up here. We hadn't seen him since he was a baby."

"They never came back for a visit?"

"Ted's parents were dead, and Vi's mother went down to Toronto with them." She held out her hands. "You know how it is. We were all raising families. I called Vi one time when I was in the city. I wanted to meet for lunch but she was busy."

"Bruce moved here to be near his father."

"To be near his mother. Vi's in Highlands Ridge." She gave me a sidelong look. "Bruce and Ted don't get along."

"Our kids don't always turn out the way we'd like. That can be difficult to accept." I gave her a parting smile and headed up the stairs.

Inside, Soupy's office was empty and Nuala's door was closed.

"Soupy's visiting a prospect," Ivy told me. "Bea Greeley and Ted Stohl are in Nuala's office."

An hour later, I'd finished compiling the list of businesses that we could approach. I heard voices in the hall, and Ted poked his head around my doorframe.

"Have a good session?" I asked.

"It was interesting." He sat down in the chair across from me. "*The*

Times plans to run a series on fraud next month. We'll start with a piece on handymen who take large deposits and never finish the work. Then we want to do something on investment fraud. Any suggestions on how to approach that?"

Jamie Collins was the first name that came to mind. She'd secured the landmark judgment on behalf of Betsy Cornell. But she was lying low for the moment.

"Start with IIROC. That's short for the Investment Industry Regulatory Organization of Canada. It oversees all the investment dealers in the country. Frank Cardone in Toronto is its head of regulation. He'll give you an overview of investment fraud, and he'll probably point you to other sources."

Nuala and Bea appeared at my door. "Ready, Ted?" Bea asked.

Ted nodded at me and stood up. He hadn't written down the names I'd given him.

When Ted and Bea had gone, Nuala came into my office.

"Well?" I asked.

She took the chair Ted had just vacated. "Ted questions every move I make on Bea's portfolio. What's the point of having an investment manager?"

"He's a journalist. He wants to understand what you're doing. Explain why you're putting Bea into different holdings. Considering her age, they'll be pretty conservative positions. And don't forget that Ted can steer business our way."

She didn't seem convinced, but she changed the subject. "Has Jamie turned up?"

"Not that I've heard."

"Do you think she's looking into what Lyle told her in that letter?"

I stared at her, surprised that she knew about the letter. Then I remembered Laura had talked about it when she dropped by the office.

"She might be," I said.

Ivy left early for a doctor's appointment. Nuala and I were the only ones in the building when five o'clock rolled around.

I put on my coat and stopped at her door. She was poring over spreadsheets on her desk. "Time to the call it a day," I said. "Grab your coat and I'll lock up."

She looked up, startled. "I got caught up in all of this…" She waved her hand to indicate the papers on the desk and the computer.

"You put in long hours, Nuala. Ivy says you're usually here when she leaves." I glanced down at the paperwork on her desk. "This can wait until morning. You don't have to worry about scoring more brownie points with me."

"I want to check something with Soupy. I'll wait till he gets back."

"He won't be back today. He told Ivy his prospect lives an hour from town. Let's go."

She hesitated. "Well…"

"I insist."

She sighed. "Okay." She scooped the papers into her briefcase and got her coat.

I watched her Lexus pull out of the parking lot before I headed off in the opposite direction. But the dedicated-employee number gnawed at me. I drove down Main Street, waited five minutes outside the Catholic church and returned to the branch. The Lexus was back in its parking spot and a light was on in Soupy's office. I parked farther up Main and walked to the branch.

The front door was locked. I let myself in as quietly as I could and slipped off my boots. I tiptoed into the reception area where I stashed the boots.

Nuala's front office was dark. The only light in the building came from Soupy's office, the next room down the hall. I crept as close as I dared to the door and saw Nuala crouched behind Soupy's computer. She seemed to be fiddling with the wiring at the back.

Then she stood and looked down at the computer with a smug grin. She pulled something off her hands. Latex gloves, the kind you can buy at any hardware store.

I returned to the reception area where I stood in the shadows at the back of the room and waited for her to leave.

A few minutes later, she turned off the light in the office. The building was in darkness until the hall light came on. Then that clicked off and I heard the front door close.

Beeping sounded. *The security alarm!* I had thirty seconds to deactivate it. In the darkness, I groped my way to the keypad on the hall wall, where flashing red lights provided enough illumination to see the buttons. I punched in the code. The beeping stopped and a green light came on. I exhaled in relief.

I made my way along the darkened hallway to my office at the back of building. A glance out the window told me that Nuala's Lexus was gone from the parking lot. I headed for Soupy's office and turned on the light.

I'm no techie and I couldn't see anything amiss at the back of his computer. All the wires looked intact, and the keyboard, mouse, monitor and tower were all connected. What was I missing?

In my office, I studied the arrangement of the wiring at the back of my computer. I grabbed a notepad, sketched a quick diagram of the hook-up and returned to Soupy's desk.

I studied my diagram and his computer hook-up. It looked the same...except where the keyboard plugged into the tower. The connection appeared to be a tad longer than on my PC. Not something that was easily noticed.

I disconnected the keyboard and examined the plug. I tugged on the wired end and I was left holding what appeared to be a small memory stick or adapter, maybe two inches in length. I turned it over in my hand. The keyboard could be connected to the tower without it, so what did it do?

I reconnected Soupy's keyboard to its tower and returned to my office. I deposited the adapter—or whatever it was—in my desk drawer and locked it.

CHAPTER TWENTY-ONE

I came home to an empty house and found no sign that Farah had given any thought to dinner. I assumed that she and Tommy were out with Kerry, but I decided I'd go easy on her. I needed her to look after Tommy.

I had lasagna defrosting in the microwave when Farah and Tommy came in. Tommy ran over to give me a hug.

I took him in my arms. "Have fun today?"

"You bet! I rode on Kerry's snowmobile."

I looked at Farah, and saw that she was wearing jeans and a heavy sweater instead of the skirts she usually favored. "You went out on the snowmobile, too?" I asked.

She smiled and began to laugh. "It is very scary. The ice, I think it will open. But I..."

You didn't want to let Kerry out of your sight.

"He is nice man, Kerry. He has nice house."

She was smiling when she went upstairs to change. I knew she'd be with us a little longer.

Celia got in soon after that and we sat down to dinner. We had just finished washing up when we heard hammering on the front door.

Celia went to open it. Two men in leather jackets pushed her aside and barged into the house. One of them was Nuala's dancing partner at the Legion, the guy with the tattoos and the leather vest.

"You." He jabbed a finger in my direction. "Got something' to say to you."

Celia went over to Tommy, who was working on a jigsaw puzzle at the table. She stood behind him, her hands on his shoulders.

My heart was thudding in my chest, but I lifted my chin and walked over to the biker. I looked him in the eyes. "Say it."

"We know what yer up to," his buddy, a skinny man with a

squashed nose, put in. "Yer tryin' to horn in on the dykes' business. Well, we're not havin' it."

"No, siree," Leather Vest said. "If anyone's goin' to be distributin' for Al and Ruby, it's us."

Out of the corner of my eye, I saw Celia move toward the telephone on the sideboard. The guy with the squashed nose had been watching her, too. He crossed the room in a few strides and grabbed her arm as she was about to reach for the phone.

"Leave that alone." He gave her a push that sent her stumbling across the room.

"You have no right to be here!" she cried.

"Calm down, little lady," Squashed Nose said, a leer on his face.

Leather Vest turned back to me. "We seen you out there," he said. "And we seen you and Al Barker at the Winagami today."

If he was watching the Winagami's parking lot, he must have seen me talking to Foster as well. I was about to ask whether he thought I was a police informant as well as a drug dealer, but I realized the less I said the better. Then I saw Squashed Nose look at Tommy, and my heart turned to ice.

Leather Vest put a hand on the door. "Don't make us come out here again. Someone might get hurt."

His eyes swept the ground floor of the house and lingered on Farah, who was cowering on the sofa.

"Hey!" Squashed Nose inclined his head toward Tommy. "The kid."

Leather Vest went over to Tommy. "Which one of these bro—ladies—is your mom, kid?" He put a finger under Tommy's chin and tilted his face upwards.

Tommy stared at him, his mouth open.

"None of them, eh? Then no one will care if we take you with us."

"No!" I ran over to Tommy. I put an arm around him and glared at Leather Vest. The air bristled between us.

The biker's face crinkled into an ugly smile. "C'mon, Weasel," he said to the other man and turned toward the door.

As soon as they'd left the house, Celia flew across the room and locked the door. I went to the window and watched the men climb into a gray panel van.

"Are they bad guys?"

I looked down to see Tommy peering out the window beside me, a mixture of terror and delight on his face. I ran a hand through his hair. "I think we can call them that."

"Will they come back?"

I picked him up and held him close. "I hope not."

"Hey!" Celia held out her arms. "Come here."

I moved toward her and beckoned Farah to join us. She got up from the sofa and crossed the room.

Celia put her arms around Farah and Tommy and me. "That was just bluster," she said. "We are not going to let them scare us."

We huddled together for a good minute, then I felt Farah shiver beside me. "Guy with ugly nose," she said. "I see that face at window Saturday night."

I broke away from the group. "We'd better get the police over here. There must be tire marks outside."

Foster answered on the second ring, and I told him about our visitors. And that Farah had recognized one of them.

"Paul Campbell told me they've been around here for a few weeks," I added. I didn't say what had brought them to the area.

"One vehicle?"

"Yes. A gray van."

"I'll send forensics over."

CHAPTER TWENTY-TWO

It was nearly one in the morning when the forensics team finished up. I went straight to bed, but I tossed and turned and wondered when we could expect another visit from the bikers. Would they be back for Tommy? I finally fell asleep only to be jolted awake by the alarm clock.

In the shower, a new worry surfaced. Would Farah stay with us? If she returned to Toronto, who'd look after Tommy?

But Farah seemed quite willing to hold the fort while Celia and I were at work that day. "Kerry, he come over this morning," she said at breakfast.

I nodded, grateful for our neighbor's attentions. I knew he wasn't going to get much painting done in the next little while.

Farah took Tommy upstairs to get dressed. I lingered over my coffee and watched Celia arrange the contents of her backpack at the table. There was an ugly bruise on her right arm where the biker had grabbed her.

"Does your arm hurt?" I asked.

She scowled and shook her head. "The teen group wants to put on a play later this spring. I'll run some ideas by them this afternoon."

"You're going to…?"

"I taught high school drama for a couple of years and I mounted all the school's productions. That was an all-girls' school, so this show should be much easier. The girls won't have to play male parts."

She looked thoughtful as I refilled our mugs. "I put the condoms out on Saturday."

Coffee sloshed over the side of my cup.

"I had them in a basket on the stage, and I told the kids to help themselves. Then I went over to the rectory for ten minutes. When I got back, the basket was empty."

I chuckled and wondered whether the birthrate in the Glencoe

Highlands would be down the following year.

I had another business lunch that day. When I returned to the branch, I found Gavin Ridout waiting for me. I hung up my coat and waved him into my office.

Then I went to check in with the others. I found Soupy and Nuala laughing in her office. "What's going on?" I asked.

"I've been telling Nuala about our cover of'Mustang Sally'," Soupy said. "We played it for the first time on Saturday night."

"I don't remember that," I said.

"We opened the last set with it. You and Nuala had left by then."

Back in my office, I closed the door. "Shouldn't you be in the classroom today?" I asked Gavin.

"I called in sick yesterday morning and drove back up here. There were a couple of things I needed to look into. I didn't get them all done so I called in sick again today."

"You stayed at your cottage?"

"No, my place isn't winterized. I stayed at the Winagami."

I settled behind my desk. "So what can I do for you?"

He took the chair across from me. "I want to run something by you. Is there anything investors can do to prevent financial types from stealing their money?"

I'm always taken aback by this kind of question, although it's one that people in my line of work are sometimes asked. "The best safeguard is to become an educated investor," I said. "And keep an eye on your quarterly or monthly statements. If there's activity in your account you didn't authorize, you've got a problem that needs to be addressed."

I looked at him closely. "Has something happened?"

He ran a hand through his short red hair. "Someone I know—knew—had a problem."

His use of the past tense raised a red flag. It was just a hunch but…"It's Pearl Critchley you're talking about."

"Yes. She lost about $50,000."

"And Lyle knew about it?"

"Yes. After she died, he took a close look at her financial statements. He told me about it when he stopped by my home before Christmas. The investment firm eventually repaid the money to Pearl's account, but it seemed a matter of family pride for Lyle to get to the bottom of it."

Was this why Lyle contacted Jamie? "What company was Pearl invested with?"

"Optimum Capital."

I wasn't surprised. "Did Lyle say who she worked with?"

"No, and I didn't think to ask. But since he…died, I've wondered about it."

"The money missing from Pearl's account wasn't an isolated case," I said. "A number of other clients fell short. The police made an arrest, but the stolen money hasn't been recovered. There's a cool million still out there. Did Lyle mention that?"

"No, he just told me about Pearl's loss."

"The week Lyle was killed he sent a letter to my daughter's friend and asked her for help. Exactly what kind of help we don't know, but Jamie Collins is a lawyer who's made a name for herself representing small investors."

"Jamie Collins. Would that be Jennifer Collins, the woman the police are looking for?"

"That's right. We've got to tell them about this."

I turned to the phone on my desk and punched in Foster's number. He didn't answer. "Pat Tierney here," I said when I got his voicemail. "I have something for you. Give me a call at the Braeloch branch."

"What now?" Gavin asked.

"I'll try Optimum in Lindsay."

When I reached the branch, I asked who the manager was. I was told it was Christine Ritter, and that she was out of the office for the day.

"Pat, Inspector Foster for you on line two," Ivy said over the intercom.

I thanked the Optimum receptionist and hung up. There was no point in asking who Pearl's advisor was. She wouldn't tell me. I hit the button on my phone for line two.

"What have you got?" Foster asked.

I told him about Pearl's missing money, and that Lyle had been talking to Gavin about it just before Christmas. Then I put Gavin on the line. He spoke to Foster for a few minutes, then returned the phone to me.

"Can you find out who Pearl worked with at Optimum?" Foster asked.

"They won't tell me. Client confidentiality," I said. "But you're a police officer in charge of a murder investigation. They'll speak to you. Ask for Christine Ritter, the branch manager. She'll be there in morning."

I paused for a few seconds. "Lyle might have been on to something new. Ask Christine if he contacted her recently."

"Right," Foster said and hung up.

Gavin and I stared at each other for several moments. I was the first to speak. "If you thought there was a connection between Pearl's missing money and Lyle's murder, why didn't you go to the police?"

His eyes opened wide. "I...I thought I'd run it by you first. You're a financial advisor, so you'd know how to proceed."

"Well, we've told the police. Now I'd like to know who Pearl's advisor was. Inspector Foster will find out in the morning, but I don't think he'll share that information."

The advisor's name would be on Pearl's account statements. It crossed my mind to look for them at Lyle's house, then I remembered the empty drawers in his filing cabinet.

"Did Pearl have a lawyer?" I asked Gavin.

His face brightened. "Jerry Muloney, my buddy from high school. Pearl told me he drew up her will. She liked to give business to her former students."

"He probably knows the name of her financial advisor. Would he tell you?"

He slid the phone across the desk. "Only one way to find out."

While Gavin made his call, I went out to the kitchen to stretch my legs. When I returned to my office with two bottles of Evian water, he had a grin on his face. "Ken Burrows," he said. "Burrows was Pearl's advisor. Heard of him?"

"He's the guy who's in jail. The case against him seemed airtight."

Gavin slumped in his chair. "And I thought I could help."

"You have helped. Burrows was arrested months ago, but Lyle was looking into the case recently. He must have come across something else."

I studied Gavin's face. *Does he know more than he's telling me?* "You were at Al and Ruby's place yesterday."

He looked startled. "I went over there, yes."

"Were you looking for Jamie?"

"No, I wasn't. The only thing I knew about her then was what I'd heard on the news. Is she there?"

I ignored his question. "What were you doing over there?"

He leaned back in his chair and pressed his fingers on his temples. "I brought those women some trouble."

I waited for him to say more.

"It's a bit of a story," he said slowly. "When school ended last June, I treated myself to a wine-tasting holiday in California. Ten of us spent a week at a small resort in the Napa Valley. We had wine-tasting dinners, private tours of wineries, cooking classes. Over the week, we got to know one another fairly well."

I smiled encouragingly, but I wondered where Al and Ruby came into this. I couldn't picture them discussing the merits of a Californian Sauvignon Blanc over an Italian Pinot Grigio.

"I was the only Canadian in the group, and I bragged about this part of the world. About its unspoiled beauty and about some of the colorful characters around here. And I told them about the grow-op that everyone in this area seems to have a stake in. It seemed like a good story at the time."

He closed his eyes. "And now those bikers are here."

"What makes you think something you said in California brought them here?"

He cleared his throat. "That wine holiday was for gay men. I had a fling that week, although nothing came of it. He lives in Florida. With his long-time partner, I found out later. I also learned that he sometimes walks on the wild side."

He paused for a few moments and went on. "A couple of months ago, I got a phone call from someone who asked about the grow-op."

"The guy you had the fling with?"

"I'm not sure. It didn't sound like him. When I wouldn't give any names, he threatened to out me to the school board."

"They can't fire you for being gay. That would be against our human rights charter," I said. But it was exactly the kind of discrimination I was afraid Tracy would come up against.

"No, but they can make my life a living hell. So I panicked. I've been pretty low-key about my orientation. You tend to be in a place like Lindsay. I save that part of my life for vacations."

The closet is a dark and lonely place. I felt very proud of Tracy for standing up for who she was.

"So you told this caller about the grow-op," I said.

"I told him it was near Braeloch. And...I gave him Al and Ruby's names. On Friday, I heard they were being harassed by bikers."

"It may have nothing to do with your caller."

"I don't think so."

"So you went over to Al and Ruby's place."

"To apologize, whatever. Though I can't undo what I did."

"And Al greeted you with her gun."

He smiled wryly. "They don't seem to want visitors."

I walked him to the front door. I was on my way back to my office when Nuala came into the hall. "I overheard Ivy tell you the detective was on the line," she said. "What did he want?"

"We know what Lyle was looking into before he died."

CHAPTER TWENTY-THREE

I was drifting out of a dream about bikers and ballet dancers when I heard a car start up outside my bedroom window the next morning. I turned on the bedside light. Six o'clock. Then I remembered that Celia planned to leave early to visit a sick parishioner. I snuggled under the covers for another hour of shut-eye.

Tommy was in high spirits at breakfast. He'd had a great time on the snowmobile the day before. "I'm going out with Kerry tomorrow," he said.

"Kerry, he visit art dealer in Toronto today," Farah told me. "He come back tomorrow morning."

On full alert, I scanned her face for a sign that she wouldn't stay in the house alone with Tommy. But she continued to turn the pages of her fashion magazine, apparently absorbed by the photos of models in haute couture.

I was halfway through my second piece of toast when she raised her eyes from the magazine. "I look at Kerry's house when he is out with Tommy. His mother, she have many clothes. Beautiful clothes," she added wistfully.

I was stunned by her brazenness, but I had to bite back a smile at her assumption that Wendy was Kerry's mother. "Did Kerry show you his paintings?" I asked.

"Yes." She puckered her mouth into a moue of distaste. "He do paintings on third floor. Terrible mess up there—paint cans, other stuff. And many paintings he don't finish."

"It takes time to finish a painting."

She looked at me, apparently digesting that piece of information.

At five to nine, I put on my coat and boots, and stepped out into a spring day. Sun filtered through a light cloud cover, and a mild breeze caressed my face. I loosened the scarf around my neck. Only a few patches of snow remained on the driveway and a large puddle had formed at the base of the eaves trough's downspout. The next cold snap would turn the driveway beside the house into a skating rink.

I got into the Volvo and turned the key in the ignition. The engine refused to turn over. Instead, I heard that ominous, grating sound. But I knew the battery couldn't be frozen because it was the mildest day since I'd arrived in the Glencoe Highlands.

I headed into the house to call the Volvo's roadside assistance service. When I picked up the receiver, the line was dead.

Panic rose in my throat. The car was out of commission and so was the phone. And our only neighbor was on the road to Toronto.

Farah looked at me inquiringly when I put the receiver down.

"Car won't start," I said. "Did Kerry say when he planned to leave this morning?"

"Early, he say."

"Maybe he hasn't gone yet. I'll go over there."

She opened her mouth to say something, but I beat her to it. "Stay here with Tommy."

Outside, I walked around the house and saw the telephone wire dangling in the air, cut at the point where it fed into the house. Fear oozed from my pores like sweat from a sick person. Someone had gone to considerable trouble to make sure I stayed at home.

Celia's car had started, but she'd set out early for that sick call. *Sick call?* The faces of Leather Vest and Weasel floated into my mind. I sprinted down the driveway.

The pavement on Wendy's driveway was as bare as ours. I went up to the front door and pounded on it. Nobody answered. I banged on the door again.

I looked around me. All was quiet and peaceful. A blue jay hopped along the branch of the tree beside the house. Another bird warbled in the woods between the properties. A lovely spring day in the country— except for the thudding of my heart.

I hurried back down the driveway, terror mounting with every step. The bikers had taken away my wheels and my only means of communication with the rest of the world. The three of us would be sitting ducks when they returned. They were convinced that I was working with Al and Ruby, and they were going to make me pay. They'd be back for...*Tommy!* I raced down the driveway, my lungs aching with the exertion.

At the highway, I slowed my pace and took deep breaths. No vehicles were on the road. Get a grip, I told myself. If they'd wanted to hurt us or take Tommy, they would have done it when they immobilized the Volvo and cut the phone line. Maybe they just wanted us to stay at home. But why?

Al and Ruby's weather-beaten farmhouse flashed into my mind. The grow-op had brought the bikers to the area. I broke into a run again. Jamie would be right in the line of fire. I had to tell Foster even though it would bring Al and Ruby to his attention.

I looked up and down the highway. The closest store was within walking distance but it was closed for the winter. Should I try to hitch a ride into town? I shook my head. Too dangerous. With a sinking feeling, I realized the snowmobile was my only option. Celia had locked it in the garage after the bikers' visit, so I figured it was in running order.

I looked at the bare pavement on the highway and its gravel shoulders. I wouldn't get far on the roads. I turned and looked at the lake, and my pulse began to pound in my throat. I'd have to travel over the lakes into town.

But I couldn't leave Farah and Tommy in the house. My head told me that the bikers had accomplished what they'd come to the house to do, but I couldn't shake the fear that they'd be back for Tommy. I couldn't risk anything bad happening to the boy or to Farah. Could I get them to town on the snowmobile?

Back at the house, I took the garage key from the peg beside the front door.

"Kerry is there?" Farah asked.

"No." I scooped the key to the snowmobile out of the vase on the sideboard where Celia kept it.

In the garage, I removed Molly's plastic cover. The seat looked big enough for the three of us. I inserted the key in the ignition.

I straddled the beast and tried to remember Celia's lesson. I put my thumb on a lever on the right handlebar. That was the throttle. I pressed it, and Molly roared to life. I found the brake lever beside the throttle, then grasped the handlebars. "Turn them the way you would to steer a bike," Celia had said.

I eased Molly out of the garage and across the bare driveway to the back of the house where there was still a thick blanket of snow on the ground. The lake was a vast, white expanse. I hoped it was still frozen solid.

"Get on your outdoor duds," I said to Tommy and Farah when I returned to the house. "We're all going out on the snowmobile."

"Yay!" Tommy cried.

One look at his happy face and my heart turned over. I couldn't let anything happen to this little boy.

"I do not..." Farah started to say.

I fixed my eyes on her face. "Farah, please do as I say. Put on warm clothes. Tights under your jeans."

I let Maxie out on the deck, and put bowls of chow and water on the floor for her and Cleo. Maxie's bladder wouldn't hold out until we returned, but that was beyond my control.

In my room, I changed into long underwear, jeans and a heavy sweater, and spent a minute studying Celia's map of the lake system. Then I went back downstairs, let Maxie into the house and helped Tommy into his snowsuit. When Farah joined us, I told them that the phone line was down and I didn't want to leave them in the house without a phone. I didn't say the line had been cut.

"Let's go!" Tommy said.

"We'll find something for you and Farah to do in town."

Farah glared at me. I ignored her, and grabbed the two helmets off the pegs by the door. I handed one to Farah and the other to Tommy. "Put these on."

"Pat—" Farah began.

"Helmet on your head, please."

My tone of voice must have told her I meant business because she put the helmet on her head. I pulled on my warmest tuque. There was probably a law against riding on a snowmobile without a helmet, but that was the least of my concerns.

I locked the front door, and put my key on top of the doorframe. Then I led the way to the back of the house where Molly waited.

"Are we all going to ride on it?" Tommy asked.

"Yes." I turned the key in the ignition and let the engine idle.

"Where am I going to sit?" he asked.

"I don't—" Farah said.

"Farah, you can stay in the house if you like, but Tommy and I are going into town. You'll be alone here till we get back this evening."

Farah said nothing, but she didn't go back to the house.

"Tommy, you'll sit between Farah and me. Both of you will have to hold on tight to me. Tommy, put your arms around my middle. Farah, you hold the handgrips."

I made sure their helmets were on properly and adjusted their face shields. Then we all climbed on the machine. I took a deep breath.

"Here we go. Hold on!" I pressed the throttle.

I heard Farah's shriek above the roar of the motor.

I eased up on the gas as we crossed the sloping lawn, and I slowly steered Molly down to the lake. The sight of all that snow-covered ice terrified me. Celia had said spring breakup was some time away, but that was more than a week ago when the temperature had been much lower. I felt Tommy's little arms around my waist. It wasn't just my life that was at stake.

We zoomed over the ice, down the frozen creek and onto the second lake in the chain. I'd started to think I could handle this beast after all, when it suddenly skittered on its left ski and threatened to keel over. Farah screamed. I eased up on the gas, and the machine regained its balance. I put the engine in neutral, and turned around to face my passengers.

Farah lifted her face shield. Her eyes were enormous in her pale face. She opened her mouth to speak, but I cut her off.

"I'm sorry. That was my fault," I said. "I forgot to tell you something. When I raise my arm, the two of you need to lean in the opposite direction. That way we'll stay balanced."

I raised my right arm, and watched as they leaned to the left. Then I raised my left arm, and they leaned to the right. "Good," I said. "Hold on tight now, both of you."

There were no other machines on the lakes that day, and the fishing huts stood empty. It was the middle of the week, and winter break was over.

The gas gauge was already down a notch from when we'd started. If we ran out of gas, there'd be no one around to help us.

The sun burst out from behind the clouds and beat down on the lake. Pools of water shimmered on the ice. Water sprayed my face. *Will the ice hold us?*

I squared my shoulders and gripped the handlebars tighter. *We have to get to Braeloch. And we will!* I raced across the fourth lake as fast as I dared, and steered us down the last creek that fed into Serenity Lake.

Halfway down the creek, I saw that the ice had started to recede from the shoreline. I kept to the center of the creek, but cracks appeared on the windswept ice under us. I took a deep breath, muttered a prayer and opened the throttle. We flew onto the lake.

The town of Braeloch hugged the far shore. I pointed Molly at the municipal dock. The closer we got, the bigger the buildings grew. Soon I could make out the *Coca-Cola* sign at the back of the Dominion Hotel. My spirits were soaring when, with a jolt of recognition, I saw a ribbon of black water along the lakeshore.

I eased up on the gas and we crept forward. The black ribbon wasn't very wide, maybe a few yards across, but I knew the ice in front of it wouldn't hold our weight.

I held out my right arm and turned the machine around. But there was nowhere to go with the gas gauge almost at empty. *Can I risk crossing that water? Risk sinking the machine—and my passengers?*

I remembered what Celia had said about snowmobile skipping: *The heavier the machine and the rider, the faster you need to go to get across the water.* Molly was a heavyweight, and she had three people on board. We needed to be as quick as lightning to cross that water. My neurons fired with a sense of urgency. I held out my arm again and turned the machine around again to face the town.

We raced toward the dock as fast as I could make Molly run. The sound of her engine throbbed in my bones. As we approached the water,

I held the throttle wide open. My heart in my throat, all I could think of was something else Celia had said. *If they don't make it across open water, they sink like stones.*

Droplets of water stung my face. I tightened my grip and pointed the machine toward the small beach beside the dock, and focused on going in a straight line.

We hit land with a thud and careened up the bank. I grabbed the brake lever. Molly stopped with a shudder at the edge of the gravel road that ran up to Main Street.

I removed the key from the ignition and slid off the seat. Farah was shaking like a leaf, and I put an arm around her. "We're here in Braeloch, Farah. We made it."

Tommy lifted his face shield. His eyes sparkled. "That was awesome! Wait'll I tell Kerry."

His snowsuit was waterproof, and so were the jackets Farah and I had on. But our jeans were soaking wet.

"Let's get ourselves dry," I said before Farah could complain. "And have some lunch."

I linked arms with her, grabbed Tommy's hand and propelled the three of us up to Main Street.

CHAPTER TWENTY-FOUR

The blinds were drawn on the windows of the Norris Cassidy branch and a *Closed* sign hung on the front door. I fumbled in my pockets only to find that I'd left my office keys back at the house with my car keys. And I hadn't taken my cell phone with me.

A glance at my watch told me it was eleven-fifteen. Soupy had scheduled another meeting with Veronica that morning, and after that he planned to help his dad set up a new computer. But where were Nuala and Ivy?

I left Tommy and Farah on the walkway, and sprinted around to the back of the building. The parking lot was empty. Nuala liked to drive her Lexus to work so I assumed she was with a client. When I returned to the front of the building, I saw Ted Stohl hurrying down the sidewalk across the street in the direction of *The Times* building. He gave us a wave and continued on his way.

"I'm hungry," Tommy said when he saw me.

Farah was shivering. I remembered that the young moms in the area met at the church on Wednesdays for a potluck lunch. I figured Celia would be back from her sick call, and we could join them. Celia might even have some dry clothes for us. She would definitely have a phone I could use.

We found her in the church basement with Sherry Vargas and four young women. A long table in front of the stage held a few platters of food. Card tables had been set up, and several children were seated at them eating cheese and crackers. Celia waved when she saw us.

"I need to use your phone," I told her.

She pointed to a telephone on the wall beside the stage.

"And would you have dry clothes for us?" I asked.

"As a matter of fact, I do." She took Farah's arm. "First door at the back of the hall when you finish your calls, Pat."

I punched in the phone number of the Norris Cassidy branch and got Ivy's recorded voice. I pressed the numbers of my extension and accessed my voicemail. No messages.

I called Foster, and he answered on the first ring. I gave him a rundown of my morning, and when he made no comment, I drew a deep breath and went on. "The bikers have been harassing two women who live east of Braeloch off County Road 8. Al Barker and Ruby Taylor."

There I've done it. I've brought Al and Ruby to his attention, but I had no choice. I need to get him over to their place.

"We knew those guys were in the area for the grow operation," he said.

My jaw dropped. He knew about the grow-op. "How—?"

"Our Drug Enforcement Section and our Biker Enforcement Unit have been sniffing around and comparing notes," he said. "They want to build a solid case before they move in."

"I think something will happen out there today."

There was a silence over the line before he continued. "What aren't you telling me, Ms. Tierney?"

"Those men think I'm involved in Al and Ruby's operation. That's why they came to the house the night before last. To tell me to back off."

"You kept that from us. What else did you hold back?"

I took another deep breath. "Jamie and Al Barker were close friends when they were younger. I thought Al might know—"

"Is Collins with them?" he barked.

"I think she might be there."

"You think?"

Tracy would never forgive me for giving Jamie up to the police, but I had to get Foster over to the farm. If the bikers came down on the grow-op, all three women would be in danger, Al's rifle notwithstanding.

"I'm not absolutely certain but I think she's there. And I think there'll be trouble today. Those guys wanted me to stay at home for a reason."

"I'm an hour away from Braeloch. How much further east is this place?"

I gave him directions. Then, although I knew I was pushing my luck, I asked if he'd spoken to Christine Ritter.

"I did," he said to my surprise. "I'm on my way back from Lindsay right now. All the clients who fell short at the branch worked with Ken Burrows."

That's why Ken was in jail. I was about to ask Foster if money had disappeared from client accounts in Lindsay after Ken's arrest, but he cut me off.

"Stay in town today, Ms. Tierney. Don't go out to County Road 8," he said and hung up.

More women and children had come into the hall, and more food was on the table. Children, seated on mats on the floor, listened to a woman read from a *Harry Potter* book.

Celia was at a table with Tommy. He had sandwiches and a tetra pack of apple juice in front of him. When she saw that I was off the phone, she waved me over.

"Tommy told me about your ride on Molly." Her eyes searched my face. "And that you skipped over black water."

"That was fun!" Tommy said.

I handed her Molly's key. "Molly's on the gravel road that leads up to Main Street."

"I'll get the rental place to pick her up. Looks like snowmobile season is over."

"Good lunch?" I asked Tommy.

He nodded, his mouth full.

I told Celia about my car and the telephone line. "Someone tried to make sure we stayed at home today, which made me think we shouldn't."

She frowned. "And I went on a fool's errand to Beaver Dam Road. The road's in terrible shape, full of potholes. When I came to the roadside number I'd been given, I found a cottage that was completely snowed in."

I felt the hairs stand up on the back on my neck. "No one was there?"

"Not for months."

"When did you get this call?"

"Late yesterday afternoon. A Sarah Hayes said her father was having surgery today, and asked if I'd come over at seven this morning before an ambulance took him to hospital. She gave me directions and a phone number. I called that number at the rectory and got voicemail."

"Someone wanted you out of the house early today."

Our eyes met, and she nodded. "Let's get you into dry clothes. I'll be right back, Tommy."

She led me down a corridor, and we stepped into a room full of clothing. Shirts, pants, dresses and jackets hung from clothing racks. More clothing spilled out of dozens of cardboard boxes and shopping bags. Farah had changed into a pair of gray flannel trousers, and was checking out some other items.

"The fruits of our Bundle Sunday three weeks ago," Celia said. "All clean and gently worn. Help yourself."

I found a pair of black corduroy jeans and stripped off my wet ones. The cords were on the roomy side, but they were warm and dry.

"I'll leave you to it," I said to Farah, who looked like she'd be in there for some time. "Make sure you get some lunch."

Back in the hall, I saw that Tommy had joined the group of kids on the floor. Another woman was reading to them.

I went over to Celia who had joined a table of young mothers. "The police know about Al and Ruby's business," I told her quietly.

Her eyebrows shot up, and we looked at each other for a few moments. "Do you think the bikers killed Lyle?" she whispered. "Was that what he wrote to Jamie about?"

"If it was, there are parts to the puzzle we don't know about. Like what Lyle had to do with the bikers or the grow-op."

"Have some lunch," she said.

"No, thanks. I've got to run. By the way, there's no one at our branch this morning."

"You stopped by there?"

"There was a *Closed* sign on the door, and I left my keys at home."

"Soupy and Nuala must be out with clients. But where is Ivy?"

"Exactly what I was thinking." I got up from the table. "I'd like to go out to Al and Ruby's place, and ask Jamie to stay with us. You don't mind, do you? She can sleep on the foldout sofa in the basement."

She unzipped the pouch at her waist, pulled out her car keys and handed them to me. "Take my car. Tommy and Farah can stay here this afternoon. There's a movie after lunch, then Farah can help me sort those clothes."

I pocketed the keys and smiled my thanks.

She looked around the room. Bruce was rolling a table that held a large TV set onto the stage. "The moms enjoy our Wednesday potlucks," she said. "It's a chance for them to get out and socialize."

I thought of Edna Critchley and her friends who met for coffee at Kresge's forty years before. Mothers of young children have enjoyed the company of other moms since the beginning of time. But the world had changed since Edna was a young mother. The women who met for lunch in that church basement would never leave their kids unattended.

Al came out on the veranda when I drove into the yard. She wasn't holding her rifle, and the dogs were nowhere in sight. When I got out of the car, she came down the path toward me.

"Is Jamie here?" I called out.

"No."

"Al, something strange is going on. I'm worried—"

"Jen took off in the pickup an hour ago."

"Where?"

"Outta the blue, she calls out,'I'm takin' the truck.' Then I hear the kitchen door slam." A frown creased her face. "She'd just got an email. It was still on the screen when she left."

I raised an eyebrow. "From whom?"

"My sister."

"Ivy?"

"Yeah. She wanted to meet Jen."

"Where?"

"Ivy told her to come to the back door of the Norris Cassidy branch."

Why would Ivy Barker want to meet Jamie? "The truck isn't in the parking lot behind the branch," I said. "They must've gone for a drive. Al, the bikers who've been coming around...were they here today?"

She puckered her mouth into a grimace. "No."

I told her about their visit to Black Bear Lake two nights before, and about my car and the cut telephone line that morning. "They wanted me to stay home today."

She glanced in the direction of the woods behind the house. "If they turn up here, nobody will be around. Ruby's gone to Huntsville in the van. And I'm coming into town with you. I don't want Jen drivin' around in the pickup. Cops'll spot her." She went to the passenger side of the Hyundai and opened the door. "Let's go."

"You're not worried they might...take something?" I asked before I start up the engine.

"Nothin' to take. We wound down the operation. Had problems with the generator, then those guys showed up. Ruby delivered the last of our product this morning. We're gonna clear out. Put the property up for sale."

I expected to meet Foster on the winding lane, but we reached the highway without seeing anyone. We rode along in silence. Nuala would be at the branch by now. I pictured her dressed in one of her power suits behind her big mahogany desk. Something scratched at the edge of my memory.

Al was the first to speak. "How did you get to town if your car wouldn't start?"

I gave her a brief rundown of my trip over the lakes.

She looked at me with new respect. "You drove over the lakes on a snowmobile!"

I nodded and tried to appear as if that was something I did every day. "Jamie got a letter from Lyle just before she came up here. Do you know what he told her in it?"

"Nope. The less Ruby and me know, the better it'll be for us, she said."

"It sounds like Ivy and Jamie were in touch before today. Did you find any other emails from your sister?"

"Not a single one. Jen must've deleted them. I don't know why she and Ivy were emailing."

"They're not strangers. You and Jamie are friends, and Ivy is your sister."

"Ivy was six years old when Jen left here."

As I drove down Braeloch's Main Street, I kept my eyes peeled for

Jamie and Ivy on the sidewalks. At the branch, the *Closed* sign was still on the front door and the parking lot was empty.

"Where would they go for lunch?" I asked Al.

"There's a place out on the highway. Friends of ours run it. Ruby and me took Jen there for supper a few nights back."

"How far?"

"Keep drivin' through town. It's a little ways down the road."

Five minutes later, we rounded a bend in the highway and a rambling gray building, Christmas lights still strung along its eaves, came into view. *Becky's Bistro*, its sign said. A dozen or so vehicles were parked in front of it.

"Here," Al said, and I pulled into the lot.

A statuesque black woman, a big smile on her face, came over to us as soon as we were inside. "How you doin', girl?" she said to Al, and the two women embraced.

"Jen been in today, Becks?" Al asked.

Becky shook her head. "Not yet."

"Well, put us in the snug. Might as well have us some lunch. Somethin' quick."

Becky took us through a set of swinging doors to a small room behind the main dining room. "I'll bring you the daily special. Something to drink?"

"Water for me, babe," Al said.

"Coffee," I said.

Minutes later, Becky returned with bowls of fragrant jambalaya and a basket of sourdough bread. I set upon the food like a starving woman.

I finished first, and sipped my coffee until Al was mopping her bowl with a hunk of bread. "Did the bikers kill Lyle?" I asked.

She looked at me with troubled eyes. "I don't know. But it seems like too much of a coincidence, don't it? Nothin' much ever happens around here. Then those guys show up and Lyle gets killed."

"And Jamie hasn't said what she's up to?"

"No, I told you. But she spends the entire day on the computer."

"Has she mentioned a Ken Burrows?"

"Never heard that name."

I found a $20 bill in a zippered pocket in my jacket, and I put it on the table. "Let's get back to the branch."

"Yeah." Al got out of her chair.

I followed her. She was halfway through the swinging doors, when she froze and backed into the snug.

I stepped out of her way. "What is it?"

"They're here."

"Jamie and Ivy?"

"No, the guys who've been hasslin' us."

I nudged one of the doors open a few inches and looked out. Leather Vest and the biker with the squashed nose—his name was Weasel, I remembered—were seated at a table at the back of the room. Weasel was hunched over his plate, but Leather Vest looked right at me. My heart dropped into my stomach.

I quickly closed the doors. "They saw me."

"We'll go out the back way." Al headed to the door at the back of the snug. She opened the door and we raced to the car.

"Hold on, ladies!"

Leather Vest and Weasel were barging toward us.

"Get in the car," Al said. "Quick!"

"Not so fast." Leather Vest took his right hand out of the pocket of his parka. He held a gun in it. He stepped up beside me, and Weasel went over to Al and put an arm around her shoulders.

She tried to shake him off. "Get yer hands off me!"

The restaurant's front door opened and Becky came out. "You guys haven't paid your bill." Then she looked at Al and me. "What's going on?"

Leather Vest turned to her and brandished his gun. "Get back inside and close the door. We'll settle up with you later."

Becky did as she was told, and Leather Vest pointed the gun at me. "You wouldn't listen, would you? Now we're gonna have a proper talk. A business meetin'. Turn'round."

I turned and saw something metal glint in Weasel's hand. "Get over to the gray van," Leather Vest spoke into my ear. The gun poked into the small of my back.

With one head, he unlocked the rear door of their panel van. Inside was a large wire cage. "For our dogs." He gave a nasty laugh and pushed me forward.

I scrambled into the smelly cage and knelt on a pile of filthy rags. I put a hand down beside me, and touched something hard and cold. A bone. I jerked my hand away from it and scrubbed my palm on my trousers.

Then Al was beside me. "Becky will call the cops."

I wanted to ask what good that would do us once the van left the bistro's parking lot. Instead, I reached out and rattled the cage door. It was locked.

At least they didn't have Tommy. But what did Leather Vest mean by a business meeting? Al and Ruby might have closed down their operation, but would these guys believe that? They'd got it into their heads that I was a distributor and they wanted me out of the way. Were they about to cut me—quite literally—out of the competition? A river of ice ran down my back.

The motor started and the van backed up. Then it swung around,

CHAPTER TWENTY-FIVE

I huddled beside Al in the dark, and took deep breaths to calm myself.

"Wish we could see where we're goin'," she muttered, echoing my thoughts.

We'd been on the highway about ten minutes when the van slowed down and turned right. We jounced along a road. Loose gravel bounced against the undercarriage like popcorn.

"Potholes." Al's voice rose in pitch. "Cripes, this is our lane!"

The van careened down a steep incline, and I clutched the cage wire. When I'd taken this lane, I'd hugged its shoulder in case a vehicle appeared around a curve. At the speed we were traveling, we were an accident just waiting to happen.

We finally came to a stop. Two doors banged shut, then daylight poured into our quarters. Weasel turned a key in the padlock on the cage. "Out y'get, ladies!"

I held on to the cage wire and manoeuvred myself out of the van. There were no other vehicles in the yard. If Ruby was at home, she'd have put her van in the barn.

Leather Vest poked my back with the gun. "No funny business."

When Al was out, Weasel locked the rear door. Leather Vest gave us a bow and gestured toward the path. "Up to the house, ladies. We'll be right behind you in case Ruby starts shootin'."

Al's eyes darted around the yard, taking in the tire tracks in the mud. She was wondering whether Ruby had returned. Then she led the way along the path and up the stairs to the veranda. At the front door, she paused for a few moments.

"Open the door," Leather Vest said behind us, "or d'we hafta shoot our way in?"

Al glared at him, then bent to tinker with a combination lock.

"Inside, everyone," Leather Vest said when she pushed the door open.

Fang raced down the hall and leaped at Leather Vest. Al caught the dog's collar. "Good boy, Fang," she said.

"Where's the other mutt?" Leather Vest asked.

"Ruby took Killer into town," Al said tersely.

A potbellied stove sat in the middle of the front room with a rocking chair and two armchairs pulled up in front of it. A table stood behind the stove covered with stacks of paper. The chairs around the table held more paperwork, as did the buffet and china cabinet. With one hand on Fang's collar, Al led the way down the hall to a large kitchen at the back of the house where a scarred wooden table stood in the center of the room. She pulled out a chair and sat down. Fang stood beside her, growling.

"Got any beer?" Leather Vest asked as he sat down across from her.

"Fridge," she said.

"Weasel." Leather Vest pointed the gun at the refrigerator. "Get me two while yer at it."

Weasel moved toward the fridge. Fang followed him, a low growl emanating from his throat.

"Get this mutt away from me," Weasel cried.

"Fang!" Al said. "You said you have dogs." Fang returned to her side and she grabbed his collar.

"Yeah, we got dogs," Weasel said. "Not crazy mutts like yours."

"Is there a washroom I can use?" I asked.

Al gestured to the back of the kitchen and I turned in that direction.

"Hang on, Blondie," Leather Vest said. "Weasel here will escort you to the shitter."

Weasel banged two bottles of Molson on the table, then led me to a small washroom beside the back door. He looked inside before he let me enter. "Don't take all day."

As soon as I closed the door, I yanked open the window, but I could only raise it a few inches. I pushed on the glass, but it wouldn't budge. I nearly cried in frustration. *Where the hell is Foster?*

When I returned to the kitchen, Leather Vest pointed his gun at the chair beside Al. "Take a seat, Blondie."

How I could convince them that I had nothing to do with the grow-op? My mind scrambled for ideas as I watched Weasel get himself a Molson from the fridge. He sat down on the ancient couch that faced the table.

The telephone on the kitchen wall rang. We all turned to look at it. Al made a move to get up.

"Back in yer seat, Al," Leather Vest said. "Let'er ring."

We listened to the phone ring—once, twice, three, four times. When it finally stopped, Leather Vest got off his chair and came over to me. His beer belly was just a few inches from my face.

"Too bad that you wouldn't take our advice, Blondie," he said. "Told you to get outta the picture."

"Leave her alone," Al said. "She got nothin' to do with us."

"Nothin'?" Leather Vest said. "Then why do I keep seein' you two together?"

"Her daughter's…a friend," Al said.

"Daughter?" Leather Vest said. "Pretty little thing that went off with Ruby Saturday night? Were they talkin' business or was that a quickie? Must've been business. Girl like that wouldn't go for an ugly dyke like Ruby."

Al's face reddened. She tightened her grip on Fang's collar until her knuckles were white.

"She'd have more choices than you, Al," he said.

"Fuck you!"

He smacked the side of her face with the gun.

Her hands flew to her face. Fang hurled himself at Leather Vest.

Leather Vest pointed the gun at the dog and pressed the trigger. The shot rang through house. Fang dropped to the floor, whimpered and was still. Blood seeped from his body onto the linoleum.

"No!" Al screamed. "Fang!" She hurled herself on top of the dog's lifeless form.

"You'll get back in that chair if you don't want to join him," Leather Vest snarled.

She looked up at him, her face wet with tears. "You sick bastard. You killed my dog!" Then she lunged at him.

I grabbed both her arms and pulled her back into the chair. She squirmed for a few moments, then sank back in the seat. Her head slumped on her chest.

"Sit back, both of youse." Leather Vest trained his gun on us. "I got more bullets."

I tasted bile in my mouth. They weren't making empty threats.

"Ruby and me, we shut down the operation," Al said in a flat voice, her eyes on Fang's body. "Ruby took the last of the product to Huntsville this mornin'. That's it. We're done."

"No siree," Leather Vest said. "You gals are gonna keep on just like you been doin'."

"It's all gone," Al said. "We got nothin' left."

"Then get yerself some more fuckin' plants and make'em grow. Where are yer sheds?"

Al stared at Fang.

"I asked you a question!"

Her face crumpled with grief.

"Check out the property," Leather Vest barked at Weasel. "Sheds'll be back of here in the woods. Look for a path through the snow."

He went back to the chair, turned it around and sat down. "Well, ladies," he said when Weasel had let himself out the back door, "we want in on the business. That means Blondie and her daughter's got to step aside. Now, there's a couple of ways we can do it. I can pull this trigger and Weasel can dump Blondie into one of the lakes that's breakin' up'round here. She won't surface for weeks."

I refused to let what he'd said get to me. Instead, I tried to catch Al's eye. With Weasel gone, there were two of us and just one biker— although he had a gun. Could we get hold of it?

Leather Vest grinned malevolently. "Or we can have us a guarantee. The boy."

The anger and frustration that had been building for the past hour erupted. "Don't you dare go near Tommy!"

He continued to grin. "Weasel and me, we'll take the boy on a little holiday. He'll like hangin' out with the guys fer a change. You can talk to him on the phone every day. Stay in line and he'll be fine."

Prickles of sweat skittered down my back.

"You guys'll regret this," Al said, holding a hand on the side of her face.

Leather Vest laughed. "Sure we will!"

The back door opened and Weasel burst into the kitchen. "Al wasn't bullshittin'. Two sheds back there in a clearing are picked clean. Not a leaf in'em."

Leather Vest stood, grabbed his chair with one hand and plunked it down beside Al. "Here's the way it's gonna be, sister." He sat on the chair and leaned over until his face was inches from Al's. "You and Ruby get yerselves a new stash of plants, and get'em quick. If you know what's good fer youse."

Al studied the ceiling. A muscle twitched on the side of her face.

"Got that?" Leather Vest shouted.

She turned her head and gave him a small nod.

"Good." He got to his feet and handed Weasel the gun. "You stay here with the ladies. I'm goin' to Black Bear Lake for the boy."

Weasel took the gun, pointed it at me and grinned. Then he flopped down on the couch and retrieved his bottle of beer, his gun still aimed at me.

At the back door, Leather Vest paused. "On yer best behavior, ladies. Weasel can be a mite trigger-happy."

Despair flooded my heart. Leather Vest wouldn't find Tommy at the house, but it would only be a matter of time before he tracked him down. I had to warn Celia, get Tommy out of the area.

Outside, the van started up and roared down the lane.

"Another brew, Weasel?" Al asked.

He studied the beer in his bottle and nodded. "Don' mind if I do." He lifted the bottle to his mouth and sucked back the rest of the Molson.

Al winked at me. At least, I thought she did. Weasel put down the bottle and belched.

She went over to the refrigerator and took out a bottle. While the door was open, she ducked down to open the freezer compartment at the bottom. From where I sat, I saw her whisk something out and hold it behind her back.

She walked over to Weasel on the couch. "Here y'go." She held out a bottle in her left hand.

He reached for it. As his fingers wrapped around the bottle, Al raised her right arm. A frozen leg of lamb came down on the top of his head with a thumping sound. Weasel slumped on the couch. She gave him another whack, and his head lolled to one side, his mouth open.

I grabbed the gun that had dropped out of Weasel's hand. It was heavier than I'd expected.

I saw that Al was about to swing the leg of lamb again. I grabbed her arm. "Stop!"

She glared at me.

"Do you want to kill him?"

"Yes!" she hissed. "For what they did to Fang."

"Leave him for the police."

She stared at me for a few seconds, then her body relaxed. I let go of her arm and nudged Weasel's motionless form with the toe of my boot. "He may be dead already."

"Brain-dead? Yeah." She flung the leg of lamb back into the freezer. "It'd take more than a bop on the head to top a tough nut like Weasel. Keep that gun on him."

"You take the gun," I said. "I've got to call my friend who's minding Tommy."

She held out her hand. "Boy's not at the house?"

"No, thank God." I gave her the gun.

I went to the phone on the kitchen wall and dialed the rectory. The line was busy, so I left a message telling Celia that Leather Vest had gone to Black Bear Lake for Tommy.

"Do you have another vehicle in the barn?" I asked Al.

She shook her head. "Jen took the pickup and Ruby's got the van." She bit her lower lip. "I gotta check the sheds."

"Weasel said there was nothing in them."

"Weasel's a few sandwiches short of a picnic. Probably missed somethin'." She thrust the gun into my hand. "Watch him real close." She hurried out the back door.

With one eye on Weasel, I tried Foster's cell phone number. When he didn't answer, I left a message.

I stared at the telephone receiver in my hand. I considered asking Tracy to drive up after work and take Tommy back to the city. But where would he stay? Leather Vest could easily find our address. I thought of Tommy's grandmother but quickly dismissed that idea. Norah Seaton had a heart condition. She'd have a bad turn if she knew Tommy was in danger.

Weasel was still out cold. I hit redial, but the rectory line remained busy. I slammed the receiver into its cradle in frustration. Who else could I try?

I flopped back into the chair, the gun trained on Weasel. "I hope the cavalry arrives soon," I muttered.

A few minutes later, Al burst through the back door holding a red plastic gasoline container.

"Trees back there should be okay," she said. "Still lots of snow in the woods."

I looked out the window and saw a plume of smoke rising from the back of the property. "You've set fire to the sheds."

"Don't want to leave no, what do they call it on those cop shows, material evidence. Anyway, I didn't do it." She pointed at Weasel. "He did it before his buddy lit out. Didn't know what he was up to, did we? That's our story."

She opened a closet door, grabbed a rag and carefully wiped the gasoline can. "Don't want to leave no fingerprints." Holding the container with the rag, she placed it beside the door. She wiped her hands and tossed the rag into the closet.

She stared down sadly at Fang. "Ruby'll take it hard. Fang was her favorite."

I watched as she rolled a big piece of plastic around the dog. "I know you don't want the police out here," I said, "but we've got no choice. As soon as Weasel comes to…"

She held up a hand. A vehicle was coming up the lane. She dashed into the front room.

"The cops," she called out.

Car doors slammed outside.

Al came into the kitchen with the rifle. "Bouchard and the cop from Orillia." She opened the closet door, and stashed the rifle inside with the mops and brooms.

I stayed at the table with the gun pointed at Weasel. He'd fallen on his side and was snoring. Through the kitchen window, I saw Bouchard and Foster sniff the air and look in the direction of the smoke. Bouchard unclipped his walkie-talkie, scowled and put it back on his belt. He pointed Foster to the kitchen door and sprinted toward the back of the property.

Foster didn't bother to knock. He opened the door and came right in. His glance took in Weasel slumped on the sofa, the gun in my hand and the gasoline container. He bent over Weasel and felt his pulse.

"We need to get the volunteer fire brigade and an ambulance out here." He looked from Al to me. "You've had lots of excitement in the last little while. We were here ninety minutes ago and no one was home."

I pointed at Weasel who seemed to be waking up. "His buddy's gone for my son. They want to take Tommy and…"

"They killed my dog." Al pointed to the mound of plastic on the floor. "Shot him dead."

"Quiet!" Foster said. "I'll hear from both of you in a minute."

Bouchard burst in. "I'll call the boys, but that fire's really goin'. I don't think they'll get here in time. And it's only a couple of sheds."

Foster scowled at him. "Call the firefighters and an ambulance. Phone's on the wall." He took a wallet from Weasel's jacket pocket and flipped through it. "Driver's license under the name of Reginald Skidmore. See if we've got anything on him."

Bouchard went over to the phone. Foster pulled a chair up beside me. "Give me the gun."

I handed it to him, and Al joined us at the table.

He put the gun into a paper bag, and dropped it in his briefcase. "What happened?"

"A leg of lamb?" he said when we'd finished, leaving out the part about Jamie taking off in the pickup. "Like that Alfred Hitchcock television show?"

"That show was based on a story by Roald Dahl," I said. "And nobody got killed in our version."

"You can only hope." He glanced at Weasel. "You knocked this man senseless. Self-defense, you say. But did you call us? No, you just sat here with a gun pointed at him. You don't know what injuries he may have."

"I called you," I said. "I just left a message on your cell."

"Did you call the Braeloch detachment? Cells don't work in parts of this area." He turned to Al. "Or maybe you didn't want the police out here."

I wanted to scream. Tommy was in danger, and he was going on about whether we'd called the police.

"Your story doesn't include the fire," he continued. "Was that before or after the leg-of-lamb business?"

"Before," Al said. "Weasel went out for a stroll when the other guy was here. Came back with that gas can. How were we supposed to know he's a firebug?"

Foster looked at me. "Was that what happened?"

I looked at Al, then at Foster and gulped. "Yes."

"Hmmph," he said. "As soon as the ambulance arrives, the two of you will come into Braeloch to give your statements."

I glared at him. I may even have bared my teeth a little. "I just told you that a biker is out there looking for my son. I've got to find a safe place for him to stay."

"Do you have a vehicle here?" he asked Al.

She glanced quickly at Bouchard and shook her head. "Ruby took it into Huntsville to do some shoppin'."

Foster turned back to me. "We'll drive you to the detachment. Pick up the phone and arrange something for the kiddie."

The ambulance arrived fifteen minutes later. Weasel flailed his arms about as the paramedics hauled him onto a stretcher. "Hey!" he shouted. "Whatsis all about?"

The paramedics strapped him down. His eyes were still closed, but he continued to squirm and mutter as they wheeled him out of the house.

"Sergeant Bouchard will drive the two of you to your car, Ms. Tierney," Foster said at the kitchen door. "Then you'll follow him into Braeloch for your statements." The screen door slammed shut behind him.

Al locked up the house, and we got into the back of the cruiser.

"Was Lyle Critchley involved in your business?" I asked before Bouchard got in.

She gave her head a curt shake. "Lyle had nothing to do with our operation. You asked before if the bikers killed him. If they did, it had nothing to do with us. Maybe they had some other reason to."

Bouchard opened his door, and she clammed up. We rode in silence until he pulled into the parking lot at Becky's Bistro. Then static erupted from his walkie-talkie. He cut the motor and unclipped the instrument.

"Bouchard here…How bad?…Where?…I'm on my way."

He turned to us. "Accident on 36. You two drive over to the detachment. They're expecting you."

He went back to his walkie-talkie, and we got out of the cruiser.

"I need to call Ruby," Al said. "That biker will go back to our place when he doesn't find your boy at the lake." She turned toward the bistro door.

I grabbed her sleeve. "Let's get out of here before Bouchard changes his mind and hauls us off to the station."

We got into the Hyundai, and I put the key in the ignition. "We'll stop by the church," I said. "You can make your call, and I'll tell my friend that Leather Vest is looking for Tommy."

CHAPTER TWENTY-SIX

The door to the church basement was locked so we went over to the rectory. I rapped the knocker, and Bruce came to the door. He and Al exchanged nods.

"Is Sister Celia here?" I asked.

He held the door open for us and pointed to the office, where Celia was seated behind the desk. She had the telephone receiver tucked into her neck and was writing in a notepad. She looked up and waved the pen at us.

"Just a moment, please," she said into the phone.

She smiled at us. "Got your phone message. Farah and Tommy are in the kitchen. Be with you in a jiffy."

We followed Bruce to the kitchen where Tommy was on the sofa watching a fantasy adventure on television. Farah sat at the kitchen table with a newspaper spread out in front of her. Al pulled out a chair beside her. I went over to Tommy.

He looked up at me. "Are we going home now?"

"Not yet." I bent down to give him a hug.

"Why not?" he asked.

"There is nothing to do here," Farah chimed in.

Celia came into the kitchen with the pen stuck behind her ear, and I introduced Al. "Al needs to use your phone," I added.

Celia pointed to the telephone on the kitchen wall. While Al made her call, I related the events of the past few hours.

"Leg of lamb?" Farah asked at one point.

"Go on with the story," Celia said.

"That's about it," I said. "Foster arrived and the medics took Weasel to the hospital."

Al joined us at the table. "Got hold of Ruby on her cell. She was still in Huntsville. She'll stay there tonight with a friend."

"We can't go back to Black Bear Lake tonight," I said to Celia and Farah.

Tommy ran over to me. I folded him into my arms and he started to cry. "I don't want the bad man to get me."

"Shh." I pulled him closer. "He won't get you. I promise."

I set him down on a chair, and gripped his shoulders as I bent down to face him. "You've got to be a brave boy. I have to help a friend of Tracy's now." I looked over my shoulder. "Sister Celia and Farah will take care of you."

"Hey, what about me?" Bruce said.

"And Bruce. He'll look out for you, too," I said. "Okay?"

Tommy sniffed, then nodded.

Al rose from the chair. "I need to find Jen before the cops do. She and Ivy should be at your branch by now."

"We'll start there," I said.

She nodded and headed for the front door.

Celia clicked the lock on the kitchen door and pulled down the shade on its solitary window. "Don't worry." She placed her hand on Tommy's shoulder. "We'll hold the fort here, won't we, kiddo?"

Tommy looked up at her and then at me. "Sure."

"Careful," Bruce said. "That guy's a nasty piece of work."

I nodded and hurried to catch up with Al.

The *Closed* sign was still on the door of the branch. I drove around the street corner, and saw that the parking lot at the back of the building was empty.

"Ivy told Jamie to come to the back door," I said. "Did she tell her to park behind the building?"

"Nothin' about parking. Just come to the back door."

"Then Jamie wouldn't know about our parking lot. Let's see if she left the truck in the municipal lot."

Bingo! The blue Ford pickup was parked behind Stedman's in the public lot.

"They gotta be at the branch," Al said. "It's just past four and Ivy don't finish till five."

"Then why is the *Closed* sign on the door?"

Al opened the passenger door. "I'll bring the truck around to the back."

"I'll go in and take Jamie out the back door."

I left the Hyundai in the municipal lot and walked over to the branch. As I approached the front door, I saw a sliver of light though the closed blinds of Nuala's front office windows.

I tried the door and the handle turned. The lights were off in the reception area and hallways. Through the gloom, I could see that Nuala's office door was closed.

"Hello," I called out.

I turned to shut the front door and felt something hard poke into the small of my back.

Nuala stood behind me, a gun in her hand.

She waved me into the reception area with it. Then she clicked the door lock into place.

"I went to a lot of trouble to give you the day off, Pat. Why couldn't you stay at home? Now I've got two people to get rid of."

Fear sliced through me.

She pointed the gun at me. "Into my office. Move it."

The Tiffany lamp on the desk sent out a halo of soft light, but the far reaches of the room were in shadow. A woman with spiky black hair was seated in front of the desk, her back to us. She was bound to the chair with duct tape.

"Jamie!" I said.

She twisted her head around. Her green eyes opened wide with surprise when she saw me. Her mouth was gagged with a rag. Fear replaced the recognition in her eyes as she focused on the gun in Nuala's hand.

"You two need no introduction," Nuala said.

We were alone in the building and the cleaners weren't scheduled for that evening. No one would come to the branch until morning. Except Al. She'd bang on the back door. When no one answered, she'd go around to the front door. She'd find a way in…*No, get the police, Al!*

Nuala waved the gun in the direction of my office. "You have something of mine, Pat, that I want back. Let's go."

I shuffled toward my office. I had to buy time for Al.

"Get the lead out of your feet," Nuala said behind me.

Thoughts tumbled through my mind like pieces of a kaleidoscope and a new pattern emerged. At dinner on Sunday, Nuala had told us she'd stayed at the Legion until the end of the evening. But she hadn't heard Soupy's band play "Mustang Sally." She'd left before the party ended, probably right after us. She tried to run us off the road.

A lot of things started to add up.

I turned to her. "After Inspector Foster left the branch yesterday, I told you we knew what Lyle was looking into before he died. That got your attention. You came over to the house last night and drained my car battery."

"Leaving the headlights on all night will do it," she said. "You should remember to lock your car. Keep moving."

"Now what?" I said when I was behind my desk.

"Open it."

"I don't have my keys."

She grinned and fished a key ring out of her jacket pocket. I recognized the office keys that Ivy kept in her desk.

She tossed them to me. "Quit stalling."

I opened the drawer and fished out the memory stick or whatever it was. I held it up in front of me. "What's so special about this memory stick?"

"It's no ordinary memory stick."

Buy some time for Al.

I held the device in front of my face. "The keyboard connects to this, which connects to…" I snapped the fingers of my left hand. "Of course! This memorizes a password."

"That and more," Nuala gloated. "It's a keystroke logger. It records whatever the user types into the computer—passwords, account numbers, reports, you name it."

"You're not afraid someone will spot your logger?"

She smiled. "Who looks at the back of a computer?"

"Wouldn't a techie clue in?"

"I remove the logger, there's no trace."

Her scheme was coming together for me. "You plug this into your computer to get the information you need. Then you tap into accounts and move money out."

She gave me a big smile.

"Police examined the work and home computers of all the Optimum employees in Lindsay. Wouldn't they have come across that activity on one of your computers?"

"I suppose they would have if I'd used my own computer. But I didn't." She smirked. "I used Ken's. And when I downloaded the logger data, I did it at an Internet café, not on one of my computers."

"Clever." I had to keep her talking. "How did you manage the overseas accounts?"

"You're a smart woman, Pat. You should be able to figure that out."

"You have access to Soupy's information in the personnel files." I paused. "You can use it to open an account in his name and move your stolen funds into it. Just like you did with Ken Burrows."

"Go on."

She was enjoying this. "Then you create other accounts and move the money around online until it gets to wherever you keep your nest egg. Have I got it right?"

She raised her free hand to give me a mock salute. "Bravo! Now give me the logger."

I closed my fist over the device and shook my head.

Bang! I jumped when Nuala fired a shot at the floor inches from my feet.

"That was a warning." She motioned with her left hand. "Don't be foolish. Hand it over."

I heard the door at the back of the building close, followed by the sound of heavy boots on the staircase. *Al!*

"Pat! Ivy!" Al called out. "Turn on some lights in here."

Nuala turned toward the door. "What the—"

"Here! It's all yours!" I threw the logger at her.

She swung around to me, then jumped back as she fumbled her attempt to catch it.

I sprang at her and grabbed her right arm. I forced it up as high as I could. The gun exploded, sending a bullet into the ceiling. Bits of plaster and dust fell on us.

We toppled to the floor. I clasped the wrist of her gun hand as we rolled over, but she squeezed off another shot that hit the office wall.

"Yee haw!" Al rushed in and stomped on Nuala's arm. Nuala yelped and loosened her grip on the gun. Al snatched the weapon and flung it into a corner.

I disentangled myself from Nuala. Al straddled her and pinned her arms over her head.

"Get off me!" Nuala cried. She flailed about and kicked her legs.

"Got any duct tape?" Al yelled over her shoulder.

"Coming right up."

I hurried over to Nuala's office where Jamie was squirming in her chair. She gasped and coughed when I pulled the rag from her mouth.

"You okay?" I asked.

She coughed again and nodded.

I grabbed a roll of duct tape and a pair of scissors from Nuala's desk. "Al's here, and we've got Nuala on the floor. We'll be back for you, but we have to tie her up first."

"Go!" Jamie croaked.

In my office, Nuala was still struggling beneath Al.

"I'll get her feet." I knelt and grabbed one of Nuala's slender ankles.

She bent her other leg and aimed her stiletto heel at my face. I leaned back, but she was persistent. She swiped her leg at my face again.

I ducked and reached for the shoe. I grabbed it by the heel and yanked it off. Then it was an easy matter to get hold of her ankle.

She continued to thrash and swear. I knelt, holding her ankles. *What can we do now? Neither of us can let go of her.*

"Sit on her legs and throw me that roll of tape," Al said.

I pulled off Nuala's other shoe and planted myself on her legs. With her thrashing under me, it was like riding a bucking bronco. I threw the roll of tape to Al and slid the scissors across the floor.

"Don't you dare!" Nuala cried.

Al's back was to me so I couldn't see how she did it. But she managed to tape Nuala's wrists together. She cut another long strip of tape and gave it to me. "Truss'er up real good."

Nuala rolled from side to side, but I managed to stay in the saddle. I bound her ankles together. Then I wound another strip of tape around her calves.

"Heave ho!" Al flung a screaming Nuala over her shoulder and deposited her in my desk chair.

I quickly moved to tape her to the chair.

"You'll be in jail for a long time," I said as I bound tape around her. "For the murder of Lyle Critchley and the theft of $1 million."

Nuala glared at me like a malevolent cat. "Stupid bitch!" she spat. "You still haven't got it right."

Al picked up the roll of tape. "Shut yer trap or I'll do it for you."

"If you think I—"

Al cut off a strip of tape.

"Hang on, Al," I said. "Let her continue."

Nuala lifted her chin and appraised us coolly like celebrity condescending to meet the press. "You think I killed that old man but I didn't. I never even met him."

Of course she'd say that. "Then who killed him?" I asked.

"How would I know?" Fire flashed from her eyes. "All I know is what I heard on the evening news."

"Why did you get Jamie to come here today?"

She turned her face away.

I nodded at Al. "Tape her up. The police will get her to talk."

She slapped the strip of tape over Nuala's mouth.

I retrieved the keystroke logger and picked the gun off the floor. My hand was shaking. I dropped the logger in my shirt pocket and stuck the gun in my handbag. We left Nuala squirming in her bindings and went to free Jamie.

"At least Foster can't say we knocked Nuala senseless," I said.

"Wouldn't have been the end of the world if we had," Al muttered.

Jamie rubbed her wrists after Al and I cut her loose. "You arrived in the nick of time." She put her arms around our shoulders.

Then she stared at Al. "What happened to your face?"

Al touched her face where a bruise had started to blossom. "Just a bruise. I'll tell you about it later." She gave Jamie a hug.

Then it was my turn. "I've finally caught up with you," I said.

Jamie returned my embrace. "I know Tracy's been out of her mind with worry, but I had no choice."

"We have to get the police over here," I said. "Is there anything you can tell Inspector Foster, Jamie?"

"I didn't learn as much as I'd hoped, but I'll tell him what I know."

I patted the shirt pocket with the keystroke logger. "I might be able to fill in some blanks."

She looked at me quizzically.

"I'll explain later," I said. "Go on."

Jamie retrieved her handbag, which had been flung into a corner of the office, and pulled out a cell phone. "Nuala knew I was on to her and she got me here with an email from Ivy."

She started to punch in a number. "I'll tell you about it, but there's something I have to do first." She held the phone to her ear, "Tracy…Yes, I'm okay…"

Al and I stepped out of the office so she'd have some privacy.

"We still have to give the police our statements about the bikers," I said. "And we need to tell them what happened here with Nuala."

"You bet." Al turned to look at Jamie on the phone, then back at me. "After what she put Jen through, if there's anything I can say that will put Nuala behind bars, I sure as hell will."

I went over to Ivy's desk and punched Foster's number into the phone.

CHAPTER TWENTY-SEVEN

The next two calls I made were to Toronto. I left a voicemail for Keith Kulas and told him what had just happened at the branch. My third call was to Norris Cassidy's compliance department, the office that ensures that company employees follow all regulatory requirements to the letter. I connected with a deputy compliance officer, and I asked her to go over all the accounts that had been opened at the Braeloch branch.

Five minutes later, Foster arrived with two uniformed officers. As usual, he didn't look happy.

"You were told to proceed to the detachment when you left the police cruiser," he said when I opened the front door.

"If we had, there'd be another murder to investigate." I led the way to the office where Al and Jamie stood guard over Nuala.

"We finally catch up with you, Ms. Collins," Foster said. "And I understand we nearly didn't."

Jamie looked him in the eyes, but said nothing.

At a signal from Foster, the uniformed officers cut Nuala loose, handcuffed her and took her away.

I handed Foster Nuala's gun and the keystroke logger.

"What's this?" he asked as he turned the logger over in his hand.

"What Nuala hoped would make her very rich," I said.

He cleared his throat. "Right, then. Over to the detachment, the three of you."

We gave our separate statements. Al and I finished around the same time, and we sat in the reception area.

"Jamie could be a while." The words were no sooner out of my mouth when I began to shake. I pulled on my parka, thinking that would do the trick, but it didn't.

"Delayed shock reaction," Al said.

She went over to the machines on the other side of the room and returned with a paper cup and a handful of sugar packets. She dumped three of them in the cup, stirred the contents and handed the cup to me. "Sweet tea. Drink up."

The beverage tasted like something that would remove the enamel from my teeth. But I managed to drink it and the shaking gradually subsided.

I called the rectory on Al's cell and told Celia what had just gone down at the branch.

"Good Lord!" she said. "That gun could have gone off in your face."

I closed my eyes and held my breath for a few moments. "What are you up to?"

"We've just had soup and sandwiches, and Tommy is about to fall asleep in his chair. I'll put him in Father Brisebois's bed."

"I'll wait here for Jamie. I want to talk to her."

"We'll stay in the rectory tonight," Celia said. "I'll take the sofa in the office. You and Farah can bunk in with Tommy. Father's bed is big enough for three."

I left Al at the police detachment and walked down Main Street to scout out some snacks. I was about to pay for a big bag of potato chips and two cans of Coke when Kerry walked into the convenience store.

"You're working late," he said to me.

He took a bag of milk from the refrigerator at the back of the store and joined me at the cashier's counter. "You okay?" he asked. "You look beat."

We left the store, and I told him about my day as we walked down the street.

"Never rains but it pours," he said.

He looked so sympathetic that I blurted out, "And we can't go home tonight."

"Hey, there's plenty of room at our place. Three guest bedrooms. I can put all of you up."

Not a good idea.

He put a hand on my arm. "I'm serious, Pat. Get the others and come over."

I pulled my arm away but gave him a smile. "Thanks, Kerry. We'll be fine at the rectory."

It was after eight when Foster escorted Jamie to the reception area. "Tomorrow morning, Ms. Collins," he said. "Nine o'clock sharp."

He fixed his eyes on Al and me. "And let me know if either of you is even thinking of leaving the area."

"I'll be needed here for a while," I said. "Until we get a new branch manager."

Al put an arm around Jamie's shoulders as we left the building. "Let's get some supper at the Chinaman's place. How about it, Pat?"

"Sounds good." I wanted to hear Jamie's story.

We ordered green tea and the Dinner for Three—the vegetarian option—at the Tiger Lily Café. The pretty teenage waitress brought a pot of green tea to the table, and Al filled our cups. With her hands cradling her cup, Jamie launched into her story. She began with the car accident that killed her sister and broke her parents' hearts.

"Then two weeks ago I got a letter from the old geezer. I couldn't believe my eyes." She shook her head. "Four pages, handwritten. He wanted my help."

"Written by hand!" I said.

Jamie and Al looked at me, clearly puzzled.

"I wondered why the police didn't find a copy of the letter on Lyle's computer," I said. "But a man of his generation would write any personal correspondence by hand."

"That's right," Jamie said.

"He wanted you to find out who had bilked client accounts at the Lindsay branch."

She nodded. "He knew I'd been legal counsel for Betsy Cornell."

"Betsy Cornell lost a lot of her savings when a financial advisor put her into high-risk investments," I said to Al. "Jamie got a good deal of her money back. After that, she led the victims' committee in the Edward Lloyd case, a slimeball advisor who'd swindled more than a hundred investors out of $30 million in a Ponzi scheme."

Those creeps made me ashamed of my profession.

"I didn't know you was such a hotshot lawyer, Jen!" Al's face glowed with admiration.

Jamie looked embarrassed. "Yeah, Lyle's letter mentioned those cases but I shredded it as soon as I read it. Lyle, of all people, asking me for help. Then I started to think about what he'd written. If I ignored him, it wouldn't bring Carly back. And I might be able to stop another fraud artist from harming more small investors."

"There was a conviction in the Lindsay case," I said. "What made Lyle think the wrong person had been charged?"

"His letter rambled a bit, but he said that what happened at Optimum in Lindsay might repeat itself in Braeloch."

"Did the letter mention Nuala?"

"No names." She paused for a few moments. "Optimum reimbursed the victims, but Lyle couldn't believe that it should let anything happen to its clients' money, short of a robber with a gun walking through the door. And he was cantankerous enough to think the police had messed up the arrest. He talked about a fall guy."

"You got all that out of one reading of that letter?" I said.

Jamie smiled. "I've got a pretty good memory."

"Did you talk to Lyle on the phone before you drove up here?" I asked.

"It never occurred to me to call him," she said. "I assumed I'd find him at home. Old folks around here are homebodies."

The waitress placed bowls of egg-drop soup and a plate of spring rolls on the table. Al and I turned our attention to the food, but Jamie kept talking.

"I took Tracy's car and got up here around one o'clock that Thursday," she said. "I went straight to Lyle's place. There were no vehicles outside, but I went to the house and knocked in case his car was in the garage. No one came to the door."

She sipped a spoonful of soup and went on. "I spent the afternoon with Al and Ruby and went back to Lyle's place before it got dark. No vehicle around, and no one answered the door. So I drove into town and got a room at the Dominion Hotel. I planned to go back to Lyle's first thing in the morning."

Our waitress unloaded a tray with platters of chow mein, honey-garlic tofu, fried rice, steamed vegetables and three dinner plates. Al ladled the food onto plates. Jamie pushed her bowl of soup aside.

When our plates were empty, Jamie and I leaned back in the booth. Al pointed to the food left on the platters, but we shook our heads. She slid the remaining contents of the platters onto her plate without ceremony.

"I heard about the fire on the TV news that night," Jamie continued. "They hadn't identified the body, but I knew it had to be Lyle."

Al put down her fork and looked at me. "Jen called us, and I came to get her at seven the next morning. We left your daughter's car in the parking lot."

"Why didn't you tell the police about Lyle's letter?" I asked Jamie.

"When I heard that Lyle had been killed, I figured his suspicions were correct. I needed to find out who'd been skimming money from those accounts. When I found the fraudster, I'd have Lyle's killer. I decided to get on to it before the police started asking a lot of questions. With the history between Lyle and my family, I'd be a suspect. The police would tie me up for days."

She paused for a few moments as emotions flickered across her face. "The next night, I heard on the news that the police were looking for me. Somebody saw me at Lyle's place." She ran a hand through her short black hair. "My hair was burgundy then, so I was easy to spot."

"The fire that killed Lyle broke out around nine," I said. "You went out to his place before it got dark. Then you drove into town and checked in at the hotel. You were out of there long before Lyle was killed."

Jamie gave me a small smile. "That didn't give me an alibi. I had a sandwich in the hotel dining room, and I went up to my room and read. Nobody knew I never left the hotel."

"You should've spent the evening in the bar," Al said.

"So you started to check things out on your computer," I said.

"On *my* computer." Al raised her cup to signal the waitress to bring more tea. "Jen left hers back in Toronto."

"I thought I'd just be up here for the day." Jamie glanced at her watch. "Now, two weeks later..."

The waitress brought us a fresh pot of tea and fortune cookies. Jamie waited until the girl had refilled our cups. "I started with the premise that Ken Burrows, despite the evidence, was not the thief. I did background checks on the other employees at the Lindsay branch. I have a friend at Optimum in human resources who's been a big help. I found that Nuala worked for three different firms in five years. There were thefts at each firm, someone was arrested and Nuala moved on."

"She was at it for some time," I said.

Jamie nodded.

"But you had no proof," I continued. "This was all circumstantial."

"Right. You could argue that the moves showed that Nuala was an ambitious woman who was trying to move up in the world. But she continued to go to small-town offices, not corporate headquarters in big cities. So I kept digging."

She tossed back her tea and set the cup on the table. "I contacted the two firms where Nuala worked before she went to Optimum. And on Monday, Ruby drove me down to Lindsay so I could talk to Christine Ritter, the branch manager. But it's so frustrating. I still have no hard evidence against Nuala and I still don't know how she managed to pull everything off."

I smiled. "I think I can help you." I told them about Nuala's keystroke logger scheme.

"Ingenious," Jamie said when I'd finished.

"She stuck to small-town offices because there'd be fewer eyes on her. Fewer techies around who might have spotted the logger."

"What did Lyle know?" Al put in.

"He didn't tell me in the letter," Jamie said. "But Christine said he'd been by recently to ask about the Burrows case—and about his sister's money."

"So when Lyle started askin' questions..." Al said.

"She somehow got wind of it and decided she had to get rid of him." Jamie opened a fortune cookie and smiled."'All your hard work will pay off,' it says."

"Nuala's a tiny little thing," I said. "I can't see her taking on Lyle."

"It didn't take brawn to kill Lyle," Jamie said. "She splashed gasoline around the garage, and when he drove in she lit a match. Whoosh! That's all it took."

But I still had questions. "Was Nuala going to kill everyone who caught on to her?"

Jamie held out her hands, palms up. "People like Nuala are incredibly arrogant. They think they're smarter than everyone else and can get away with just about anything. That's their fatal flaw."

Al tapped the table with a spoon. "You said Nuala sent you a message on Ivy's email."

Jamie nodded. "Put one over on me. I'd been in touch with Ivy. Asked her some questions about Nuala, who must have had access to the emails of everyone at the branch. The message from Ivy today said she had something to show me. And that she'd be alone at the branch for an hour or two."

I broke open a cookie. "You are almost there," it said. Almost? The events of the day flashed through my mind. The trip across the lakes on the snowmobile, the bikers and meeting up with Nuala. I felt drained. What more did the day hold?

"You'll be okay out at the farm?" I asked them.

Al gave me a wicked grin. "We'll be right as rain. We got the rifle."

CHAPTER TWENTY-EIGHT

At the rectory, I found Farah and Celia on the kitchen sofa watching *The Highlands Tonight*.

"Anything on about Nuala?" I asked.

"Not a thing." Celia turned down the volume. "The lovely Mara Nowak wasn't on the ball tonight."

I took her car keys out of my pocket. "I pulled your Hyundai up to the end of the driveway. If the bikers see it, they'll know Tommy and I are here."

She turned to Bruce who was standing beside me. "Would you put my car in the garage?"

He nodded, and I handed him the keys.

"Where's Tommy?" I asked.

"In Father's bed," Celia said. "My guess is he's fast asleep. If he heard you come in, he'd be down for a good-night hug."

I sighed. "I'll spend some time with him when everything's cleared up."

"What did Jamie have to say?" Celia asked.

I pulled up a chair and told her what Jamie said in the restaurant. Bruce slipped back into the kitchen and took another straight-backed chair.

Celia stared at me. "I can't believe Nuala would...But there was something about her that wasn't right. She wouldn't tell us where she grew up. And I couldn't figure out—"

She was interrupted by sound of the front door knocker.

She scrambled to her feet. "Come with me, Bruce."

They hurried out of the kitchen. I was close behind them, and Farah was right behind me.

"You think those guys—?" Farah said.

"Who is it?" Celia called out at the door.

"Kerry Gallant, your neighbor at Black Bear Lake."

Celia motioned for Bruce to open the door. Farah had a big smile on her face.

"What are you doing here, Kerry?" I asked when he stepped into the hall.

He pulled off his tuque. "Wanted to see how you people are doing." He turned to Celia. "Pat told me about the trouble she had today."

"We're doing quite well," Celia said.

"Wendy called when I got back," Kerry said. "She wants you to stay at the house."

Farah's face lit up.

"We're fine here," I said.

"But, Wendy—"

"We're here for the night, Kerry," I said. "Tommy's already in bed."

"You've gone out of your way to rescue us," Celia said, "so the least we can do is offer you a cup of tea."

He grinned. "Sounds good to me."

"Are the people in the parish giving you a hard time?" Kerry asked when Celia had replenished the teapot and we were seated around the kitchen table.

"Because I'm a woman in the pulpit?" she asked.

Pounding sounded on the front door again. Celia and I looked at each other.

"I have to see who's there." She inclined her head toward the hall. "Could be a parishioner who needs my help. Bruce, come with me please."

The rest of us followed them.

"Who's that?" Celia called out at the door.

"Kerry Gallant here?" a male voice said.

I froze. *Leather Vest!*

Kerry edged past me to the door. "Nothing to worry about."

"Who is it?" Celia asked.

"A friend," Kerry said. "Do you mind if I—?"

Celia nodded. "Go ahead."

"No!" I lunged for the door, but Kerry held me back with one arm and opened it. Leather Vest and a man with gray hair drawn back into a ponytail stepped in. Kerry scowled at them.

"What are you doing here?" Celia cried.

"Hey, man," Leather Vest said to Kerry. "Been callin' you for hours. Saw yer Jeep out front here. Caught a case of religion?"

Celia placed a hand on Bruce's arm as the men came inside. "Kerry," she said, "I don't care for these friends of yours. Tell them to leave."

"Leave?" Leather Vest bellowed. "We're not going anywhere just yet, are we, Kerry?"

"Kerry?" Farah said.

Kerry shook his head in anger. "You idiots!"

"We're the ones out there drumming up business while you—" Then Leather Vest saw me. "Blondie here and that other dyke Al nearly killed Weasel today. He's in the hospital."

Ponytail crossed the hallway in a couple of strides and pinned my arms behind my back. "You're the bitch been causin' all the trouble."

Farah gasped.

"Take your hands off her!" Celia cried.

"You heard the Sister. Let Mrs. Tierney go," Kerry ordered.

"I don't think so," Leather Vest said.

I struggled to shake Ponytail off, but he was too powerful. The sadist twisted the skin on my wrists. I wanted to scream—or cry. But I was determined not to give him the satisfaction.

"Kerry! Bruce! Stop him!" Celia said.

Bruce moved toward me. Leather Vest pulled a handgun from his jacket and cracked it against Bruce's skull. Bruce slumped to the floor.

Celia rushed to Bruce's side.

Leather Vest pointed the gun at me. "It's got outta hand. Cops'll make Weasel talk."

Kerry held up a hand. "Chill, guys. There's nothing he can tell them."

Ponytail pulled me toward the door. "She's goin' with us."

"Mrs. T!" a voice called from the top of the stairs. Tommy stood there, rubbing his eyes.

"Tommy, get back to bed." I yanked myself free of Ponytail, ran up the stairs and folded the boy into my arms.

He peered over my shoulder, then looked back at me, his eyes wide. "The bad guys got in. And Kerry—"

"Join the party, little man," Leather Vest said.

"Tommy's going back to bed," I said.

"Get the kid down here. Now!" Leather Vest waved his gun at us.

I felt Tommy shaking as I carried him down the stairs. "Everything will be okay," I whispered.

He blinked his tear-filled eyes and nodded.

"Let's go into the kitchen, shall we?" Kerry said.

"I'm staying here with Bruce," Celia said.

"You'd better come with us, Sister." Kerry waited until she got to her feet and pointed to the hall.

I sat down with Tommy on the kitchen sofa. A subdued Farah sat on the other side him. Kerry, Ponytail and the gun-wielding Leather Vest took chairs in front of us.

"What am I going to do with all of you?" Kerry said. "My cover's been blown."

"Cover?" I said. "You make it sound as if you're a secret agent. You're just a cheap crook."

He drew himself up. "I'm an artist. My work hangs in Bay Street offices."

I snorted. "Thanks to Wendy Wilcox."

"Wendy introduced me to the financial types who were dying to purchase what I offered."

"And not just your paintings."

"Correct."

"I can't believe someone of Wendy's standing is part of this."

"She isn't. Wendy knows nothing about my other work."

Leather Vest had grown impatient. "We got unfinished business with those dykes on the farm. Let's get movin'."

"Yeah," Ponytail chimed in.

Kerry studied us. "Does anyone have a suggestion about what I should do?"

"We won't tell anyone," Farah cried.

I gave her a sharp look.

"Tommy's grandmother would pay handsomely for his safe return," Kerry said. "Yes, Pat, Wendy told me who Tommy is."

I held the boy close.

Leather Vest turned to Kerry. "She's gotta go, man."

"Give me that." Kerry clamped a hand on the gun that was now pointed at him. It went off, the sound of the gunshot deafening in the room.

I stifled a scream and turned Tommy's face to my chest.

Kerry toppled to the floor, the front of his shirt red with blood.

"Lord have mercy!" Celia knelt beside Kerry. She whipped off her sweater and pressed it against his chest.

Leather Vest stared at them. "I…I didn't mean…"

"Jesus!" Ponytail slapped Leather Vest's arm and the gun fell to the floor. "Shit's gonna fly."

"Kerry needs an ambulance," Celia said.

I eased Tommy onto Farah's lap. "Cover his eyes," I whispered to her.

Leather Vest gave Ponytail an angry shove. Ponytail lunged back at him, sending them both sprawling to the floor.

I sprang from the sofa and scooped up the gun.

"Freeze!" I yelled. I had both hands on the gun and pointed it at the bikers, just as I'd seen cops do on TV shows. The bikers looked up at me in surprise.

"Get up!" I motioned with the gun. "Very slowly."

They eased themselves up, glared at each other, then at me.

"Now what, Blondie?" Leather Vest growled.

"Hands up, real slow," I said.

They did as I directed, their eyes fixed on me.

Ponytail laughed. "Do you know how hokey you sound? Freeze? Hands up?" He laughed again. "I bet you never fired a gun in your life." His eyes narrowed. "You don't have the nerve."

I swallowed hard. "Try me," I said with as much bravado as I could muster.

Ponytail lunged at me. I pointed the gun lower and pulled the trigger. He cried out in pain and crumpled to the floor, clutching his right leg. Blood oozed through his fingers.

I staggered from the recoil but regained my balance as Leather Vest dropped his arms and seemed poised to jump at me.

I swung the gun up and pointed it at him. He slowly raised his arms.

"Tommy." I kept my eyes and the gun trained on Leather Vest. "You okay?"

"Y-y-yes."

"Get me a doctor for Chrissake," Ponytail moaned.

"Kerry needs an ambulance," Celia said. "Right now."

"Farah, call 911." Then I turned to Leather Vest. "If you've got any other weapons on you, slide them over."

Leather Vest glowered, but fished out a knife, dropped it to the floor and kicked it toward me.

"Now him." I motioned the gun toward Ponytail.

Leather Vest bent over Ponytail and held up a switchblade.

"On the floor," I said.

He placed it on the floor and slid it to me.

I waited for Farah to return from the phone.

"Farah, get some towels," I said. "Hurry."

When she returned, I pointed at Kerry. "Toss some to Celia. And throw a few to the boys."

"For your buddy," I said as Leather Vest caught the towels. "Try to stop the bleeding till the ambulance gets here."

Bruce staggered into the kitchen, with a hand held to his head.

"Sit down beside Farah, Bruce," I said.

Sirens sounded outside. I looked over at Kerry and Celia. "He's hanging on," Celia said.

Foster burst into the kitchen. He surveyed the room and shook his head. He came up to me with his hand held out for the gun.

I gave it to him. "Excuse me," I said. "I've got a little boy who needs me."

"This one doesn't look good," a medic said as he wheeled Kerry into the hall on a stretcher.

Foster nodded at me and turned back to the others. Two officers took Leather Vest out the back door, and the medics got Ponytail onto a stretcher.

I went over to Tommy and wrapped my arms around him. He started to cry.

"Hush," I whispered. "It's all right."

But was it? Would he be traumatized by what he'd seen?

"The bad men are gone?" he asked.

"Yes," I said softly. "They're gone."

CHAPTER TWENTY-NINE

Celia traveled with Kerry and Bruce in the ambulance. Farah, Tommy and I got in the cruiser and were taken to the police detachment. I wondered when the day would end.

By the time I'd given the police my second statement of the evening, I was beyond tired. Farah and Tommy had fallen asleep in the waiting room. We all needed hot baths and beds, but the rectory was no longer an option—it was sealed off as a crime scene. And I didn't want to return to Black Bear Lake. I had no idea how many bikers were still out there.

I sat down beside Tommy and lowered my head into my hands.

"Ms. Tierney, are you all right?"

I looked up.

Foster, concern written on his face, stood over me. "Anything I can do?"

Tears spilled from my eyes. "I'm wiped, and I don't know where we can spend the night."

He sat beside me, and I told him my concerns about the house at the lake. And that I was worried about Maxie and Cleo.

Then I remembered Kerry and Bruce, and asked how they were doing.

"You're a real mother hen looking after your chicks," Foster said.

I smiled. "Mother bear, please." I couldn't picture myself flapping around a chicken coop.

"Mother bear, then." Foster stood up. "Give me a few minutes."

I thought of Kerry plowing our driveway the week before, dancing with Wendy at the Legion, nibbling my ear on the dance floor. He was so full of life, even though he was a crook.

Beside me, Tommy stirred and opened his eyes. "Can we go home now, Mrs. T?"

"To Black Bear Lake?"

He shook his head.

"To Toronto?"

He nodded.

"Sorry, sweetie, but we can't just yet."

His face fell. "Why not?"

"Well, it's late and—"

"We need your help," Foster said to Tommy. "We want to make sure we've got all the bad guys. You wouldn't want them still out there, would you?"

"N-n-no." Tommy eyed him warily. "But how will you know you've got them all?"

"Young man, I give you my word. We're working on it right now, but we need you and Ms. Tierney to give us a hand. Will you help us?" Foster extended a hand. "Deal?"

Tommy shook his hand. "Deal."

"Good." Foster turned to me. "Ms. Tierney, two officers will go out to Black Bear Lake and look in on your pets. Feed them, whatever."

I gave a nod of thanks and told him where they could find a key. "How is Bruce?" I asked.

"He'll stay in the hospital tonight and should be released in the morning. Sister Celia is on her way over here."

"And Kerry?" I was afraid to hear his answer.

"Kerry Gallant lost a lot of blood and is in serious condition." He paused. "I phoned the Dominion Hotel and they have two rooms available, each with a double bed. I've reserved them for you, but I'm afraid we can't pay for them."

"Thank you. Norris Cassidy can foot the bill."

Farah wouldn't be happy with the arrangement, but I decided that she and Celia could share a bed. Tommy would cuddle up with me. I'd be with him if he had nightmares.

"Shall we, then?" Foster motioned us to the door.

"Let's go," I said.

I was asleep as soon as my head hit the pillow, but I found myself wide awake at three in the morning. Still dressed in his clothes, Tommy was snuggled up beside me, sleeping soundly.

My mind combed over the previous day's events. Jamie had said a small woman could have set Lyle's garage on fire. But how did Nuala know that Lyle was away from home and when he'd return?

I fell back into a fitful sleep, and was roused by the hotel's wake-up call at seven. Pulling the covers over Tommy, I eased myself out of bed and called Tracy. Jamie had filled her in on what happened at the branch the day before.

"You and Jamie could have been killed!" she cried.

"It's over, honey. We're fine." I didn't tell her what went on later at the rectory.

"When will Jamie come home?" she asked.

"Pretty soon, I'd say. She'll spend some time with the police today, but she should be back in Toronto on the weekend."

Around eight, Tommy and I joined Celia and Farah in the hotel dining room.

"I just called the hospital." Celia poured coffee from the carafe on the table. "Kerry is stable."

I put an arm around Tommy. "Kerry's going to be all right," I said to him.

I asked Celia if I could borrow her car again. "I have to go out to the house."

"Do you think that's wise?" she asked.

"I'll take a chance."

"Be careful." She handed me her keys. "It's in the rectory's garage."

I couldn't see Wendy's house from the highway, but sadness washed over me as I passed her driveway. Kerry and Wendy were an unconventional couple, but they seemed to care for each other. He may have been the great love of her life.

I got out of the car in front of our house and took a deep breath before I approached the door. I glanced at the long driveway before I entered the house. Then I locked the door behind me.

Maxie and Cleo greeted me in the hall. They'd apparently become friends in our absence. I let Maxie out on the deck while I went upstairs, changed into a pantsuit, and packed clothes for Tommy and Farah. I wanted to get out of the house as quickly as I could, but I put more food into Maxie and Cleo's bowls, and watched while they ate.

Then I attached the leash to Maxie's collar. Her tail waved in anticipation of a walk.

"You're in charge here," I told Cleo.

On the way back to town, I stopped at Tim Hortons for a box of donuts. I returned the Hyundai to the rectory garage. And I dropped off Maxie and the clothes in the church basement where Celia had set up shop until the forensics team finished in the rectory.

When I arrived at the branch, I found Soupy and Ivy at the reception desk. "Tell us what happened, Pat," Soupy said.

I put the *Closed* sign on the front door and locked the door behind me. "Brew some coffee," I said to Ivy. "I'll call Toronto, then we'll talk."

Keith picked up on the first ring. "What in the hell is going on up there? I send you to fly the corporate colors and what happens? A client is murdered and there's a hostage-taking at the branch. And you're nowhere to be found."

I told him there'd been a problem at the house and I'd spent the night in a hotel.

"And there was no telephone at this rustic establishment?"

I said it had been late when I'd checked in. I didn't remind him that the wonder woman he'd hired to run the branch had nearly added me to her hit list. There was no reasoning with Keith when he was on a rant.

Then he seemed to calm down a bit. "Compliance is looking at your client accounts. They say there are no pending orders, but they're checking them out. I want you to do the same. Go over all those accounts with a fine-tooth comb. Not just Nuala's, Paul's as well. Every single account that has been opened at the branch."

I told him I'd do what he asked.

He cleared his throat. "You'll have to stay up there a while longer, Pat. You'll run the branch until we find someone else—or close it down."

I didn't have a choice. For Soupy and Ivy's sake, I wanted to see that the branch got off to the best possible start. But what about Tommy? When he said he wanted to go home, he didn't mean the house at Black Bear Lake.

I told Keith I'd get back to him later in the day.

Ivy had coffee and the donuts on the coffee table in the reception area. I was about to sit down when I saw ELK TV's van pull up in front of the building. Mara got out and hurried up the walk. I opened the door.

"Ms. Tierney, I'd like to talk to you about what happened yesterday. Nuala Larkin—"

"I'm sorry, but we have work to do in here." I shut the door and locked it.

"Mara just wants to—" Soupy started to say.

I held up a hand and returned to the sofa.

Soupy helped himself to a Boston cream. "You don't want to talk to the media," he said. "But you'll tell us what happened?"

I gave them a rundown of what happened at the branch the previous afternoon.

"Oh, my God!" Ivy said when I'd finished. "That's why Nuala told me to go home. She said the computers would be down for repairs."

Soupy shook his head. "She was bilking client accounts. Unbelievable. All her talk about transparency and accountability."

"One of the people she took money from at Optimum was Lyle's sister," I said.

He looked thoughtful. "When Lyle stopped by here he went over to Nuala's office door and looked at the nameplate."

"Lyle was on to Nuala," I said. "He must have approached her about Pearl's account."

"Nuala killed Lyle?" Ivy asked.

"It looks that way," I said, "but we'll see what the police turn up. In the meantime, head office asked me to check all the accounts that have been opened at this branch."

Soupy's face clouded. "Do they think—?"

I put a hand on his arm. "Don't take it personally. All client accounts are being vetted. We have to protect our clients, you know that."

He sighed.

"We're down one advisor here," I continued. "I'll stay on until things get back to normal."

"You're the acting manager?" Soupy asked.

"That's right." *And too bad if you don't like it.*

I looked at them brightly. "Now let's get to work."

Ivy started to gather up the coffee mugs. I asked her to call the telephone company and have them reconnect the landline at Black Bear Lake. I wrote down my Volvo's licence plate number, and told her to have Sam's Service Station bring the car into town and replace the battery. And check to see if there was anything else wrong with it.

Ivy had just returned to her desk when there was a knock on the front door. I looked out the picture window and saw Foster outside.

I brought him into my office and closed the door.

"Ms. Collins briefed us on her research this morning," he said as he took the client's chair. "Two white-collar-crime investigators are going over it with her. That, plus your statements and that device you turned over to us yesterday should put Nuala Larkin away for some time."

I sat down behind my desk. "Nuala—?"

"She hasn't admitted that she took clients' money at Optimum or anywhere else. Yet."

He looked at some papers in the folder he held. "And she's adamant that she didn't kill Critchley. She said she was at a restaurant in Lindsay that evening, and seven other people were with her."

It took me a few moments to digest what he'd said. "She didn't murder Lyle?"

"We'll check her story," he said.'Talk to the people she said were with her that night."

I waited to hear what he'd say next. I didn't think he had come to the branch to update me about Lyle's murder.

"There's been a raid on the Dead Riders' Toronto clubhouse. There won't be any bikers headed this way in the next little while. And with Gallant under arrest, there's likely to be an internal power struggle. You'll be off their radar."

"We'll be safe out at the lake?" I asked.

"Safe from that biker gang."

I breathed a sigh of relief.

He cleared his throat. "I'd like speak to Paul Campbell now. I want to go over Critchley's visit to this branch with him again."

That meant he had no other leads.

I took him to Soupy's office. I was headed for Ivy's desk when Ted and Bea walked into the building.

"Is my money still here?" Bea cried when she saw me. "When I heard the news about Nuala on the radio this morning, I got Ted to drive me right over."

I took them into my office, and called up Bea's account on the computer. I told her I'd go over it carefully in the next few hours.

"You don't know whether my money's all there, do you?" she said.

I was pretty sure her account was fine. I didn't think Nuala would have touched it until I returned to Toronto. Even then, she'd have second thoughts with Ted hovering in the background.

But Bea had a right to know exactly where she stood. "Not until I look at it carefully," I said. "I'll call you as soon as I do."

"I should never have trusted that woman," she said. "My money has to last me the rest of my days. My mother was nearly a hundred when she died so I've got a ways to go. I don't want to be a burden on my daughter."

Ted put an arm around her. "If anything's been taken by a Norris Cassidy employee, I'm sure the company will reimburse you. Right, Pat?"

"That's right." I noted how tired he looked. The lines around his eyes seemed to have deepened since the last time I'd seen him. "I'll give you a call later today, Mrs. Greeley."

She didn't look happy.

"Did this have something to do with Lyle's death?" Ted asked. "Was Lyle one of Nuala's clients?"

Ted ran a newspaper. "Is this for publication?" I asked.

He threw me a smile. "We have a short item that says Nuala Larkin is in custody following an incident at the Norris Cassidy branch. I'd like to add to it if I can. We go to press at noon tomorrow."

I didn't see any harm in giving him some background. "Nuala worked at Optimum in Lindsay where money went missing from client accounts last year. The police are looking into whether she was involved."

"And Lyle? Was she investing his money?"

"He wasn't one of her clients, but his sister, Pearl, lost some money at Optimum."

Ted raised an eyebrow. "She did?"

Too late, I realized I shouldn't have told him that.

"When Lyle discovered something funny had happened to Pearl's account," he said, "he must have confronted Nuala."

"We don't know that." I rose from my seat. "I'll get back to you as soon as I can, Mrs. Greeley."

I walked them to the door, and found Lainey Campbell at the reception desk. "I came over to find out what went on here yesterday," she said. "Ivy tells me that Nuala had a gun."

"Goodness!" Bea cried. "She could have killed somebody."

"Nuala Larkin would have killed anyone who got in her way," Ted said. "And Lyle confronted her about Pearl's money."

Bea gasped. "Nuala killed Lyle!"

The color drained from Lainey's face. "Nuala wasn't the only one who wanted Lyle out of the way."

"Nuala is in custody and the police will get to the bottom of it," I said. "In the meantime, we have work to do here."

Soupy came out of his office with Foster. The detective nodded at us and hurried off.

"Hey, Mom," Soupy said. "Everything okay?"

Lainey stepped around him and went into his office.

I opened the front door for Bea and Ted. "I'll call you, Mrs. Greeley."

I reached Celia at the rectory. "You're back in your office," I said.

"Got the green light from the police twenty minutes ago. And Bruce is back from the hospital. He just went upstairs."

I told her we could return to the lake that evening. She said she'd like to head out early with Farah and Tommy, who were growing more restless by the minute.

"Leave whenever you want," I said. "My Volvo is at the service station. It should be ready late this afternoon."

I had just started on Bea's account when Soupy rapped on my door. He looked worried.

"Come to my office, Pat. It's Mom."

I got up from my desk and followed him down the hall. Lainey was seated in front of his desk crying softly into her hands.

"She won't tell me what's wrong," he said.

Lainey lifted a tear-stained face. "I don't know what to do."

I pulled up a chair beside her. "About what, Mrs. Campbell?"

She opened her mouth to speak, then turned her head away. "I'd better get back home. Got bakin' to do."

"Mom—"

Lainey got up and walked out of the office.

Soupy followed her to the front door where she whirled around to face him. "Stay inside, Paul. You'll catch a cold without your coat on."

I watched from the window as she hurried down the sidewalk. Ted crossed the street to speak to her, but she walked right past him and got into her car. He stared after her, looking upset. More than upset, angry.

"What's going on?" Soupy asked behind me. "I've never seen Mom break down like that. She's always on top of things."

Ted glanced at our building. He scowled when he saw us at the window. Then he crossed the street and got into a maroon van.

"Strange," Soupy said.

"D'you know Ted well?"

"Mom and Dad hung out with him when they were young, but he went down to Toronto a long time ago. Before I was born. He came back here two years ago, and I just got back myself. But he seemed like a good guy." He pointed to Ted's van, which was pulling away from the curb. "Something's happened."

The client accounts—all twenty-three of them—were squeaky-clean. I'd just started on the last one when the compliance office gave me a thumbs-up from Toronto.

At two-ten, I called Bea and told her that all was well. I was leaning back in my chair, relieved that our clients had suffered no harm, when Jamie walked into my office.

"I'm on my way back to the city," she said.

"Tracy will be happy about that." I paused. "I'll be in Braeloch until a new manager can take over. I wonder—"

She reached across the desk and placed a hand on mine. "Tracy and I will stay at your house while you're here. If that's okay with you."

I smiled my gratitude. "Thank you, dear. Have you heard anything more about Nuala?"

"It looks like she didn't kill Lyle. Seven people told the police she was in a restaurant with them when Lyle's garage went up in flames."

"But she's been charged—?"

Her eyes sparkled. "With fraud and embezzlement. She'll never work as a financial advisor again."

I got out of my chair and gave her a hug. "Drive safely."

When I was alone again, I mulled over what I knew about Ted. He grew up in the area, worked briefly at *The Times*, then spent decades in Toronto. Returned to Braeloch when he bought *The Times*. His wife, Vi, was a resident in the town's nursing home. Bruce was their only child, and he and Ted didn't get along.

I knew firsthand that parents and children don't always see eye to eye. But Bruce needed a place to live. Wouldn't a father help him?

I got out of the chair and told myself that I didn't know the full story. Bruce would certainly be a challenge for most parents.

I thought of what Lainey had said to Ted that morning. *Nuala wasn't the only one who wanted Lyle out of the way.*

I flipped through the Glencoe Highlands phone directory and found a Burt Campbell listed on Highway 36. I dialed the number and hung up when Lainey's recorded voice came on.

I grabbed my coat and went into Soupy's office. He looked up from this computer screen. "Calling it a day?"

I bit back a tart reply. "Your mom said she was going home, but she's not answering her phone."

He picked up the telephone receiver and hit a button on the phone. "Today's Mom's baking day," he said as it rang. A frown on his face, he replaced the receiver in its cradle. "She's always at home on Thursdays. I was surprised to see her here today."

"You might want to check on her."

He hit another button. "Soupy here, Rena. Is Dad around?"

A few moments later, he thanked Rena and hung up. "Dad's out on a job. I want to check on Mom, just to be sure. Would you...come with me?"

I nodded. "Let's go."

He pulled his parka off the coat rack, and we went out the back door.

CHAPTER THIRTY

Soupy twitched and sighed behind the wheel of his Porsche as we headed down Highway 36. Something was gnawing at him, and I had a hunch that it wasn't his mother and Ted.

"What's up?" I finally said. "Out with it."

"I want to say…need to say…I apologize."

I looked at him, puzzled. "For what?"

"The night of the big snowfall last week. Tuesday night."

"Yes?"

"I drained Hank Corcoran's battery. Went over to his place and turned on his headlights."

"It's Hank you owe the apology to," I said. "A neighbor plowed us out. Why did you do that?"

"On your first day at the branch, you told us that the Corcorans plowed your driveway. Later, Nuala asked if I knew who they were. I sure did. Their son, Hal, was our drummer a few years ago. Nuala said we were in for a big whack of snow that night and maybe we should arrange that you didn't get plowed out in the morning. You'd miss the launch."

"And I'd be in the doghouse with head office."

"Right."

"And they'd yank me back to Toronto lickety-split."

"Right."

"Hindsight being twenty-twenty, I can see why Nuala wanted me out of here—to avoid any oversight. But why did you go along with it?"

"She said you'd get all the credit for the clients we brought in in the next little while, and anything else we did to build the business. I thought we'd score more points without you."

"So she suckered you," I said. Just like she did everyone else, including me.

"You got it. I'm sorry, Pat. Can we turn the page on this?"

"We'll forget it happened." I paused. "Now let's see what's up with your mom and Ted."

A few miles farther down the road, he turned into a lane that led to a white clapboard house and a red barn. A maroon van was parked in front of the house.

"Ted's van," Soupy said.

He led the way to the side of the house and peered through a window beside the door. "Mom and Ted are at the kitchen table. They seem to be arguing. C'mon."

"Lainey, I beg you, don't—" Ted fell silent when we entered.

"Mom, Ted, what's going on?" Soupy asked.

Lainey was about to speak, but Ted held up his hand to silence her. "Your mother and I have something we need to discuss. It's none of your concern." He glared at me. "Or yours."

"I want them to stay," Lainey said. "Sit down, please."

Ted pulled his chair back from the table. "Then I'll be going."

"You stay put, Ted Stohl," Lainey said. "You're not going to run away again. I won't have it."

He scowled, but eased back into the chair.

Soupy sat beside his mother. I took the chair next to Ted.

"Ted and I are going over old times," Lainey said.

I shifted uneasily in the chair. "If this is a family matter, perhaps I should—"

"Please stay," she said. "It is a family matter. A matter that concerns the Stohl and the Critchley families."

She had my attention.

Lainey patted her son's arm. "We're talkin' about something that happened a long time ago."

Ted opened his mouth to say something. Instead he drew a deep breath and slowly exhaled.

"Forty-two years ago last December, Ted and Vi's son, Bruce, was born," Lainey said. "Vi called him her Christmas gift from God."

Ted closed his eyes. The combativeness had ebbed, and was replaced by sadness and resignation. A tear ran down his cheek.

"A few months later," Lainey went on, "around the beginning of April, Ted went down to Toronto for a few days for *The Times*. The paper ran the articles he wrote, but I can't remember what they were about."

Ted mumbled something. All I could make out was "conference."

"The day after Ted left Braeloch, Edna Critchley's baby was taken from his carriage outside of Kresge's. It was a terrible thing and everyone was talking about it. Nothing like that had ever happened around here before."

She paused for a few moments. "Ted got back home late that Friday evening. Vi was asleep, so was the baby. It wasn't till the next morning that Vi told him."

"Told him what?" Soupy said.

"Crib death," Lainey went on. "Vi told him that Bruce hadn't woken up the morning he left town."

I sucked in my breath.

Ted closed his eyes and clenched his hands on the table.

"The Critchleys' baby is taken from his carriage," Soupy said. "And Ted's son is found dead in his crib. You mean—?"

Lainey looked at her son. "After Lyle's funeral last week, I went upstairs with Bruce. He changed his shirt in his room, and I saw the port-wine birthmark on the back of his neck and down his back. The same birthmark Lyle and Edna's baby had, though it's darker now. They darken after infancy."

Soupy's eyes nearly bulged out of his face. "Bruce is the Critchleys' son?"

Ted ran a hand over his forehead. "As soon as I saw the baby, I knew he wasn't our kid. They both had blue eyes and that fair, fuzzy hair, but he wasn't our kid."

"Man, I can't believe this!" Soupy said.

"Vi was out of her mind with grief," Ted said. "The only thing she could think of was to get her baby back. We lived in one of the second-floor flats across the street from Kresge's. From our living room window, Vi saw the baby carriages on the sidewalk."

"One of those babies was mine." Lainey turned to Soupy. "Charlie. When Edna's son went missing, I thought,'That could have been my Charlie!'"

"Charlie's my older brother," Soupy said to me.

"Vi took our carriage across the street," Ted said in a flat voice. "When no one was around, she put Edna's baby in it. She wouldn't have taken Charlie, not with his dark hair. She took Edna's son because he was fair, like our boy. And she knew that Edna was bottle-feeding him, just like she was."

His face collapsed. "I've been over this so many times in my head. If only she'd called me when Bruce died. If I'd been there for her, it wouldn't have happened."

"You should have taken the baby back to Edna and Lyle as soon as you found out." Lainey's eyes bored into him. "Do you know how much Edna suffered? All those years, she had no idea what happened to her child. She wondered if he was still alive. And it turned Lyle into a mean old drunk."

He bowed his head. "I had to protect Vi. She would have gone to jail, and that would have driven her over the edge. I couldn't let that happen." He looked up at us. "She was a good mother. She loved that baby. Both those babies."

Lainey threw him a scornful look. "So you ran away."

He looked longingly at her. Pleading for forgiveness, I thought. "We couldn't stay here. Edna and Lyle would've recognized their child as soon as they saw him. I'd been applying for jobs at the Toronto newspapers and I'd been offered one the month before. But Vi refused to leave Braeloch so I turned it down. Now I told her we had no choice. We had to get away. Luckily, the editor at *The World* still wanted me."

"What happened to your son's…body?" I asked.

"The ground was still frozen." Ted looked down at his hands. "But the ice on the lake at my cabin was breaking up. I weighted him down with stones and put him in the lake."

"In the lake!" Lainey cried. "He didn't get a proper burial."

"The body was never found?" I asked.

"No." Ted croaked the word out.

"The turtles and fish would have eaten him in no time," Soupy said.

We sat in silence for several moments. How could Ted and Vi get away with kidnapping a child?

"Healthy babies' blood types weren't recorded back then," Lainey said. "We filled out a government form with our names, our address and where our baby was born, and a few weeks later a birth certificate arrived in the mail. When the baby got his shots, the family doc wrote them down in a little booklet. Vi would have given her booklet to her new doctor in Toronto."

She looked at Ted. "Did Dr. Sloan send Bruce's medical records to Toronto?"

"The Toronto doctor didn't ask for them," he said.

"So Lyle Critchley Junior grew up as Bruce Stohl," Lainey continued, "with a birth certificate to prove it."

"Lyle found out who Bruce was and he confronted you, Ted." I felt a flicker of fear as soon as the words were out of my mouth.

He jerked upright in his chair. "It's not what you think."

"Lyle must've seen Bruce's birthmark, with the two of them working at the church," Lainey said. "Maybe when Bruce mowed the lawn last summer."

Ted gave us a smile that didn't reach his eyes. "Wasn't summer. It was just a few weeks ago, after Father Brisebois went into hospital. Bruce took a shower in the rectory and came downstairs without his shirt."

His shoulders collapsed. "I should've left Vi in that nursing home in Toronto." His voice was mixed with bitterness and regret. "Bruce only came to Braeloch to be near her."

"When did Lyle speak to you?" I asked.

"Came to the house one evening."

"What happened?" I had to keep him talking.

"I denied everything, of course. Then Lyle said he was going to the police and they'd have a DNA test done."

"But he didn't." Of course he didn't. If Lyle had told the police, Ted would have been their prime murder suspect.

"My guess is he hadn't got used to the idea that Bruce was his son. Those two rubbed each other the wrong way. Like chalk and cheese."

"But it was only a matter of time till he told the police," I said. "And Bruce."

His Adam's apple rose and fell. "I knew from Maria Dawson, our copy editor at *The Times*, that Lyle went to an AA meeting in Lindsay every Thursday afternoon. He drove down with her husband Ross. After the meeting, Lyle and Ross usually had a bite to eat before they drove back home. Maria could work late Thursday nights when we put most of the paper to bed. But Thursday two weeks ago, Maria came down with the flu. I sent her home at noon, said I'd finish up what I could that evening and put the front page together in the morning."

"You and Maria were the only ones who worked late on Thursdays?" I asked.

"Right."

"A perfect opportunity," I said.

"Damn right it was!" His eyes blazed. "I drove out to Highway 123 with two cans of gasoline, parked behind the old Anglican church that closed down last year. It's a few properties up the road from the Critchley place and there's a bike path behind the lots. A cold front had moved in, but earlier that week we'd had a thaw with lots of rain. The asphalt on the path was clear of snow, and so was Lyle's driveway. There was even a strip of bare asphalt behind the garage where I waited for him."

Ted met my eyes. Now he was a penitent seeking absolution. "I just wanted to scare Lyle enough so he'd back off. I splashed gasoline on the garage and opened the door. It wasn't locked. When he pulled into the driveway, I set fire to the building. But he drove right into the garage. There was a great whoosh of flames and the entire building was ablaze. I didn't think it would go up so fast."

He held a hand over his face.

I feared his mood swings—anger, defiance, remorse and back again—would erupt into violence. He was unraveling.

"You didn't try to get him out?" Lainey asked.

"I couldn't. The garage was an inferno. The heat was ferocious."

I pictured the building alive with flames. I hoped the smoke had gotten to Lyle quickly.

"It wasn't enough to take his child and ruin his life." Lainey's voice was filled with fury. "You had to kill him, too. And brutally."

"It's not what I intended," Ted said in a hoarse whisper. "I didn't expect him to drive into the garage."

"Then why did you open the door?" Lainey asked. "Then you closed it on him. The door was down when the firefighters arrived."

Ted closed his eyes. "I wanted him to drive in but I panicked. I didn't want him to come out and find me. When his back was turned, I pulled down the door."

She stared at him for a few moments, her mouth partly open. "You locked him in there."

"No. I just pulled down the door."

"You might as well have locked him in," Soupy said. "The metal handle on the door was probably too hot for him to hold."

"You started the fire *after* Lyle was inside the garage," I put in. "If he'd seen flames, he wouldn't have driven in. You meant to trap him in there."

"No, you're wrong. I never planned..."

"It was cold-blooded and calculated," I said.

The angry Ted was back. "Yes, I did plan it that way." His voice rang out. He pounded both fists on the table. "He threatened me. He was going to ruin my good name."

He stood up. "And what are you going to do about it?"

Soupy was about to go over to him, but Lainey held him back.

"You want to tell the police?" Ted said. "You think they'll believe you? It would be my word against yours. My word! The word of the editor and publisher of *The Highlands Times*. You have no proof, no witnesses."

He was at the door. "Go ahead. Call them. I dare you." He slammed the door behind him.

I pulled out my chair away from the table and motioned for Soupy to get up. "Call the police," I said to Lainey.

She reached across the table and gripped my wrist. "Let him go."

Something in her eyes made me sink back into my chair. We heard the van start up outside and drive off. I turned to Lainey. "The police need to know about this."

"Tomorrow. I'll tell them what he said and let them handle it." She shrugged. "What could we have done here? Tackle Ted and tie him up like a hog?"

"Yeah, Mom, that's what we should have done," Soupy said.

"Let's go to the detachment now," I said.

Soupy rose from his chair. "C'mon, Mom, I'll follow your car. Pat can ride with you."

Lainey crossed her arms over her chest. "No. I'll go with your father tomorrow."

"Mom..."

"You think Ted will run off," she said, "but that's not very likely. Everything he's got is here. The newspaper and his home. And Bruce."

She stared at me. "And he's not dangerous. The only person that man's a danger to is himself."

She was wrong. The farther Ted was from the Glencoe Highlands, the safer we'd be. He was a violent man.

The expression on her face told me that nothing I could say would change her mind about going to the police. I hadn't taken my cell when I went out to the house that morning. I looked longingly at the phone on the wall.

"Don't even think of using that phone." Lainey swung around to Soupy. "And don't you give her your cell."

Soupy put a hand in his jacket pocket.

"I said no!" she said.

"It's okay, Mom." He tossed me his car keys. "Take the Porsche, Pat. I'll stay here with Mom in case Ted comes back."

She turned to Soupy. "He wouldn't hurt me, really he wouldn't."

Soupy and I didn't say a word.

"That's not the Ted I knew." She raised her hands to her face.

She was weeping as I closed the door behind me.

CHAPTER THIRTY-ONE

My sense of foreboding grew with every mile on the drive back to town. Ted had killed a man to safeguard his secret. Now three more people knew about Bruce. And that Ted had killed Lyle.

The house at Black Bear Lake was at the end of a long driveway. Perched on the edge of a frozen lake. With no neighbors around. Would Ted pay a visit?

I could move my little household to the Winagami for the night. *No, damn it! I'm not going to be turfed out of my home again.* I clutched the steering wheel and turned into Braeloch. I drove straight to the police detachment.

The woman at the reception desk smiled at me. "What can we do for you this afternoon, Ms. Tierney?"

I asked for Inspector Foster and was told that he had returned to headquarters in Orillia.

"Sergeant Bouchard is out on a call, but I'll try to reach him," the woman said.

I didn't trust Bouchard, but I had no choice. "I need to speak to him as soon as possible. When do you expect him back?"

"It could take a while, but I'll give him a message. What's the problem?"

"Tell him I know who killed Lyle Critchley. Can you try Inspector Foster as well?"

"I'll do my best."

The woman kept smiling. She didn't take me seriously.

"I'll check back with you in fifteen minutes," I said.

There were no pay phones in the reception area. I was about to head over to the branch to use the phone, but the rectory was closer and Celia might still be there. I drove down the street and saw a light on in the rectory kitchen. The back door was unlocked.

I made a beeline for the phone on the kitchen wall and punched in Foster's cell number. "I have to talk to you," I said when he answered.

"What happened?" He must have heard the fear in my voice.

"Ted Stohl—" Out of the corner of my eye, I saw Bruce in the hall and I couldn't continue. "I need to talk to you in person."

"Tel Stohl, who runs the newspaper," Foster said. "What happened to him?"

"Can you come to Braeloch?" I glanced at Bruce. "I think there might be…trouble."

"Trouble? You attract trouble, Ms. Tierney," he thundered over the line. "Tell me what is going on."

Bruce stood listening to my end of the conversation.

"It's…awkward at the moment. It's about—" I turned my back to Bruce, hoping he was out of earshot. I lowered my voice as much as I could. "Lyle Critchley."

"Is someone with you now?"

"Yes."

"Is that person a threat?"

I looked back at Bruce. "No, but I need to talk to you in person. Now." I enunciated each syllable, praying that Foster would twig to the gravity of the matter. "Can you come to Braeloch?"

He sighed. "I'll be at the detachment in an hour. Where are you now?"

"The Catholic church rectory."

"Go over to the detachment. I'll try to reach Sergeant Bouchard."

"What's happened to my father?" Bruce asked as soon as I was off the phone.

"Nothing's happened to him. Where's Sister Celia?"

"She went back to your place with Farah and Tommy. Who were you talking to just now?"

I didn't answer. Instead, I punched more numbers into the phone.

"Keep the doors locked," I told Celia when she answered the phone at Black Bear Lake. "Don't open up for anyone. I'll be at the police detachment for a bit."

"What's going on, Pat?" she asked. "I thought the bikers had been rounded up."

"It's not the bikers." I looked at Bruce. "Can't talk right now."

"What don't you want me to hear?" he asked when I put down the receiver. "And why are you going to the police? It's something to do with Dad."

I hesitated, and that was all the affirmation he needed.

He disappeared down the hall and returned wearing his parka and tuque. "I'm going over to *The Times* building."

"Bruce, why don't you—?"

He went out the kitchen door. I grabbed my handbag and followed him. Ted was a dangerous man, and I didn't want Bruce to get in his way.

He was about to sprint ahead, but I grabbed his arm. "Bruce, don't!"

He jerked his arm free. "I'm going. Dad must be in serious trouble if you called the police." He paused. "It's bad, isn't it?"

I nodded. "But there's nothing you can do."

"How do you know? I'm a disappointment to Dad, but maybe there is something I can do."

Deep down, Bruce was still a young boy who wanted to connect with the man who'd raised him.

"And don't tell me to leave it to someone else," he said. "I'm sick of people saying that."

I couldn't stop him, but I thought I might be able to keep him from harm if I stuck with him. Just how, I didn't know, but the mama bear in me told me to try.

"Okay, but I'm going with you. We'll take Soupy's car."

At *The Times*, Bruce led the way to the newsroom on the second floor where a middle-aged woman was seated at a computer.

"Is Dad around, Maria?" Bruce asked.

"I haven't seen Ted all afternoon," she said, "and we have a lot of work to do."

I followed Bruce outside and placed a hand on his arm. "Come out to the house with me. Sister Celia will have dinner on."

He pulled his arm away. "Dad must be at home. I'll check there."

I knew I couldn't dissuade him. "All right." I opened the passenger door for him. "Let's go."

Pine Avenue curved up the hill behind Braeloch. The higher it went, the swankier the homes became. The street ended at a park that overlooked the town, and we pulled up in front of the last house. It was an elaborate affair of stone and glass and stained wood, fronted by a multi-level deck.

Ted's van was not in the driveway.

"Bruce—"

He scrambled out of the car and up a ramp to the main door on the second level. I was right behind him. He stopped at a pair of French doors. He raised a hand to rap on the glass, then changed his mind and turned the handle on the door. I followed him into a large room with a wall of floor-to-ceiling windows that looked out on the lights of Braeloch. A stone fireplace took up most of the back wall. The room was dimly lit, and much of it was in shadow.

Bruce walked across the room. "Dad?"

I hung back as he went through the house, but his calls received no reply.

"I'll check the basement." He clumped down a flight of stairs. "Dad?"

Maybe a minute went by before he hurried back up. "There's a gun-storage cabinet down there where Dad locks up his hunting rifles. It's open and one of them is gone. So is a box of ammunition."

I had to warn Celia and the Campbells that an armed Ted might be headed their way. I also needed to notify Foster and Bouchard.

"Bruce, would you wait outside?" I asked. "I need to use the phone."

With my gloves on, I lifted the receiver of a telephone on an end table and made my calls.

Bruce was staring sadly at the park when I joined him on the deck.

"The police want us to wait here. There's a pileup on Highway 123 because of black ice. It may be a while before they arrive." I paused. "You understand that I had to call them."

He looked down at his boots. "Tell me what he's done."

I didn't know how to tell him about Lyle, so I didn't. "Your dad isn't himself right now. He has a lot of people worried."

He looked up at me. "I know where he went."

"Tell me."

"Only if you drive me there."

"You know I can't."

He stared at me for a moment, then turned and walked down the ramp.

I knew I should wait for Foster or Bouchard, but I didn't want to let Bruce out of my sight. I hustled after him and grabbed his arm. "Okay, let's go."

We got into the Porsche and I turned the key in the ignition. "Where is it?"

He gave me a weak smile. "North on Highway 36. The Fortress of Solitude."

"When I was a kid, I loved Superman comic books," Bruce said when we'd put Braeloch behind us. "Dad was my hero and he worked at a newspaper, just like Superman did."

"Like Clark Kent at *The Daily Planet*."

"Yeah, like that. Anyway, Dad would come up to this cabin he had every so often."

The cabin on the lake where Ted put his child's body. "Is there a lake at this cabin?" I asked.

"Porcupine Lake. Dad built the cabin before I was born. Said it was his place to get away from it all."

"So you thought of it as his Fortress of Solitude, just like Superman's."

Out of the corner of my eye, I saw him smile.

"Turn north here," he said as we approached an intersection.

"You and your mother never went up to the cabin?" I asked when I'd made the turn.

"Mom never did, but twice, when I was a teenager, Dad took me up for a week of hunting. It would make a man out of me, he said." He paused. "It wasn't my thing. He didn't understand."

"Accommodation was pretty rough, I imagine."

"Yeah. Couple of cots, a table, two chairs."

"No running water, no electricity by the sound of it."

"We cooked canned stuff on one of those camping stoves, you know, with the propane canisters. And Dad had kerosene lanterns for light."

"Not much fun."

He turned to glare at me. "You think you know, but you don't." He turned his attention back to the road. "The mornings were beautiful. We'd hike to the other side of the lake looking for game. Sometimes there was mist on the water…"

Black Bear Lake was on our left, and the driveway to our house was just around the curve in the road. I slowed as we approached it, checked for vehicles on the highway and made a left-hand turn.

"Hey," Bruce said. "Where are you going?"

"Won't be a minute. This is where Celia and I are staying."

I let myself into the house with my key. Celia stood on the other side of the door brandishing a cast-iron frying pan.

"It's you!" she cried. "You had us terrified. Why didn't you call?"

"No phone. I'm here to get my cell."

I found it fully charged on the dresser in my bedroom. I asked Celia to call Foster, and tell him that Bruce and I were headed north on 36. And that I'd call him when we reached Ted's cabin.

I grabbed my waterproof boots and returned to the car.

We rode along in silence for the next twenty minutes. The sun had just gone down when Bruce pointed to something ahead of us. "The lane coming up on the right side of the road."

I turned into the lane—a single set of muddy tire tracks through the woods. I parked in a small clearing just off the highway. I didn't think the Porsche was built for off-road treks.

"We'll have to walk from here, and it's pretty muddy," I said. "You know, Bruce, we don't have to do this. It'll be dark soon. Let's call the police."

"I'm going."

He got out of the car and started to follow the tracks. I dug out my cell and called Foster.

"It's me." I figured by then I needed no introduction. I told him approximately where we were.

"There must be a roadside number where you turned in," Foster said.

I got out of the car and walked over to the highway where I found a small sign with a five-digit number. I gave it to Foster.

"Stay at the car," he said. "Don't go near the cabin."

I found a high-beam flashlight in the Porsche's glove compartment. I stepped into my waterproof boots and hurried to catch up with Bruce.

Ten minutes later, we reached a cabin at the edge of a frozen lake. Darkness had fallen, but under the full moon I could make out the silhouette of Ted's van. The building was bathed in shadows. Its roof sagged under the weight of snow or time, probably both.

The cabin was smaller than I'd imagined, probably no larger than a modest living room.

I heard a chugging sound that I guessed was made by a gas-powered generator. It seemed that Ted had put in a few amenities since Bruce's last visit.

I shone the flashlight on the building. A gas canister sat on the small porch beside a barbecue. I could see a propane tank beneath the tarp.

A light came on in the cabin window.

"He's here." Bruce plowed forward.

The door swung inward. A man stepped out on the porch with a rifle in his left hand and an oil lamp in his right. "Who's out there?" It was Ted's voice. "Show yourself. I'll shoot if I have to." He set the lamp down beside him and raised the rifle to his shoulder.

"It's me, Dad."

"Who's that with you? You with the flashlight, show yourself."

I took a few steps forward and shone the light under my chin. "Pat Tierney."

"Go away, both of you." He swung the rifle up in the air and fired. "That's your warning. Now go."

Bruce moved forward. "I can help, Dad. Whatever's wrong, I'm here for you. I'm your son."

"You're no son of mine." Ted's voice was as cold as ice.

Bruce stopped a few feet away from him. "What?"

"I said you're no son of mine. Ask her."

I stood frozen, unable to say anything. Bruce took a step toward Ted. Ted fired again, this time into the snow next to Bruce. "Get back!"

"Tell me what's wrong. Let me help," Bruce said.

I switched off the flashlight and inched forward.

"That crazy idea of Vi's," Ted said. "I bought into it because I wanted a son, but I got you."

Bruce raised his head in defiance. "I'm a good son. You just never let me show you."

"It's too late, boy. It's time to end the lies." Ted braced the rifle against his shoulder and aimed at Bruce.

"No!" Bruce lunged sideways.

I switched on the flashlight and aimed the beam straight into Ted's eyes. He stumbled and knocked over the lamp beside his foot. Glass broke, lamp oil spilled on wooden floor of the porch and a tongue of flame licked at the rivulet of fuel.

Bruce jumped onto the porch. He and Ted both gripped the rifle. They spun as each tried to wrest it from the other's hands.

A shot ricocheted off the barbecue and punctured a hole in the gas can. Gasoline streamed out of the container and met the fiery rivulet from the lamp oil. There was a whoosh, and flames began to crawl along the cabin walls and roof. Fire enveloped the propane tank and it exploded.

I dropped the flashlight on the ground and rushed forward. Flames were devouring the wood and it wouldn't be long before the cabin came crashing down.

Bruce and Ted toppled through the open doorway, neither giving up his grip on the rifle. They fell on the floor, and Bruce was on top, his eyes locked with Ted's.

I ran in after them and grabbed Bruce by the shoulders. "We've got to get out of here!"

Bruce released his grip to brush me away. Ted shoved and kicked from beneath, sending Bruce and me sprawling toward the door. The rifle clattered to the floor. Bruce and I staggered to our feet and began to cough from the smoke. Flames greedily worked their way along the walls. Above us, the roof was a checkerboard of fire.

Ted seized the rifle and got to his feet. "Now I've got you!"

As he raised the gun to fire, a fiery piece of ceiling fell on him. He screamed, and his shot went wild.

I yanked Bruce's collar and dragged him out of the cabin. We fell on the snow and landed on our backs. As I got to my feet, I saw Ted flail away at his burning clothing. I helped Bruce up. Screams came from inside the blazing cabin.

"Dad!" Bruce took a step toward the house, then threw up his hands to shield his face from the heat.

The screams had stopped. I picked up the flashlight and touched Bruce's shoulder. "He's gone."

I put an arm around Bruce and steered him toward the highway. At the edge of the clearing, he turned to look at the burning cabin. He fell to his knees and let out a wail.

"That's it." I looked across the desk at Inspector Foster after I'd given my statement at the Braeloch detachment.

"You sure you have nothing to add? That's quite a story."

Not only had I described what had happened at the cabin, but I'd also related what Ted had told us that afternoon. "What more is there to say? Bruce can corroborate what happened at the cabin, but he doesn't know about Lyle's murder or his...parentage. You need to speak to Lainey Campbell."

I paused. "Will you tell Bruce about his parents?"

Foster leaned back in his chair. "First I'll hear what he has to tell me."

He picked up the telephone receiver. "Please send Mr. Stohl in."

Lainey and Soupy walked into the detachment while I waited for Bruce. They spoke to the woman at the front desk, then took chairs across from me.

"The cops told us Ted was dead, but nothing more," Soupy said.

I gave them a short version of the struggle and fire at the cabin.

"How horrible." Lainey took a tissue from her purse and dabbed her eyes. "That's not the Ted I knew."

"If you'd called the police he might still be alive," I said.

"I like to believe the best about people, even if...evidence...shows otherwise."

"What did you think he'd do?" I asked.

"The right thing," she said softly. "I hoped he would go to the police. Confession is good for the soul, they say. But he was a proud man. I guess he couldn't admit to himself that he'd done wrong."

Soupy patted her shoulder. "What about Bruce?" he asked.

Lainey gave him a stern look. "Bruce, poor soul, had nothing to do with it. He was a baby when he was taken from his parents."

"He's got be told who is his real parents are."

"I don't think so, son. Bruce is devoted to Vi, always has been. He and Lyle never got along. He even threw a rock into Lyle's grave." She closed her eyes. "His own father."

I had to step in. "Bruce has the right to know who his parents were. But not right now. Maybe in a day or two."

I excused myself and went to the other side of the room to call Celia. We agreed that Bruce shouldn't be alone for the next little while. She said she'd have the pullout couch in the basement ready for him.

Foster brought Bruce back to the reception area. I asked Foster if I could have a word with him.

"Did you tell Bruce that Vi took the Critchleys' baby?" I asked when we were in his office.

"No, I didn't," he said. "I'll look up that missing child case tomorrow. If we can find some hair samples at the Critchley place, we'll see if there's a DNA match. Hopefully we'll be able to close the case."

"Can we tell Bruce that Lyle and Edna were his parents? He'll want to know why you've asked him to give a hair sample."

"Tell him anything you like. But it won't bring the Critchleys back for him. Or Stohl, for that matter."

He locked eyes with me for a few moments, then gave a slight nod to his head.

I realized I was still without my car, and the service station would be closed for the night. "Any chance of a lift out to Black Bear Lake?"

Foster sighed. "One of the officers will take you."

He came out to the reception area with me. "Mrs. Campbell, I'll speak to you now," he said.

Lainey gave Bruce a hug, and followed Foster.

Bruce watched them leave the room. Then he looked up at me with mournful eyes.

"Bruce," I said, "it's time for us to go."

CHAPTER THIRTY-TWO

Ivy's voice came over the intercom the next morning as Soupy and I divided up Nuala's client accounts. "Mr. Kulas is here to see you, Pat."

Keith out here in the boonies? I didn't like the sound of that.

"Pat!" Keith said, when I met him in the reception area. He had a smile on his face, but he didn't look happy. He nodded briefly at Soupy, who'd followed me out of my office. "We need to talk, Pat. In your office."

I had a feeling that this wasn't going to be fun.

"Nuala Larkin's stunt yesterday is bad for our business," he said as I closed the door. "Clients and prospects will be spooked as soon as word of that and her other...activities gets out."

I didn't tell him it already had.

Keith sat down in my chair. I dropped into the chair facing the desk.

He rested his elbows on the desktop and leaned forward. "We've got a problem here, Pat, and you're the girl to fix it. You'll stamp out any fires that start up and you'll focus on building this business." He cleared his throat but didn't meet my eyes. "By the way, there's a vice-president's title in it for you when the branch gets up and running."

Vice-president! Adrenaline hit my bloodstream. The bastard knew I wanted that title. And that I'd do whatever he wanted to get it.

Keith addressed the Tom Thomson print behind my head. "You'll be based here in Braeloch and run this branch. You'll also oversee all our operations from Lindsay in the south all the way up to North Bay. You'll be our vice-president, north-central Ontario."

Reality came into focus. *What about my clients in Toronto? Those are relationships I've nurtured for years. My home? The kids?*

Keith's pale blue eyes shifted and fixed on mine. "So it's settled. You can stay out at Black Bear Lake while you look for a place of your own. You'll have it until the beginning of July, but it's booked for the summer."

I pulled myself together and looked Keith in the eyes. "I need to think this over. And talk to my daughters."

"Take the weekend. But I'll need an answer on Monday."

If my answer was no, there'd be no vice-president's title for me. And my career at Norris Cassidy would sink like a stone.

"I'll let you get back to work." He stood up and flashed me a smile. "Norris Cassidy is counting on you, Pat."

So confident I'd take his offer, I thought as I watched him leave the office. I got up, closed the door and slammed my fist against it.

A minute later, there was a knock and Soupy came into the office, looking wary. "So?" he asked. "What's up?"

I took my coat off the rack. "We talked about the branch and how it's doing. I've got an errand to run."

Five minutes out of town, I turned the Volvo into the parking lot at the public beach. I walked down to the water's edge where the snow had receded. Leaving the sandy beach area, I wandered along the rocky shore of Serenity Lake until I came to a small point of land that stretched out into the water. I sat down on a log and looked out at the ribbon of black water along the shore. Beyond it, the lake was covered in snow and ice.

If I accepted Keith's offer, I'd have to leave Tracy and Laura in Toronto. They wouldn't be happy about that, but they were moving on with their lives. But Tommy?

I had another option. I could leave Norris Cassidy and start my own business. The company maintained that it owned its clients and reassigned them whenever an advisor left the fold. I would have to give up people I'd worked with for years. I'd need to rent an office suite and build up my business again. On the other hand, I'd be my own boss. I wouldn't be jerked around by people like Keith.

I stood up. I didn't know what to do, and I had to talk to someone. I returned to the Volvo.

I was about to get in when a vehicle honked. Al and Ruby's Ford pickup, with a U-Haul trailer hitched behind it, pulled into the parking lot.

Al rolled down the window of the passenger door and waved me over.

"Glad we caught you before we headed out." She extended her hand. Killer growled in his seat between the two women.

"This is goodbye?" I said as I shook Al's hand.

"We figured it was time to move on," Ruby chimed in.

"Ruby put up the farm for sale," Al said. "We're movin' out to B.C."

I smiled. The province of British Columbia is known for its cannabis culture. Except for medicinal purposes, marijuana use is illegal there, as it is throughout the rest of Canada. But news reports had recently called it the province's leading cash crop, worth billions of dollars.

"Good luck to you," I said.

"You too, Pat," Al said.

She rolled up her window and waved. Ruby honked again. Then they disappeared down the road.

The kitchen light was on in the rectory. I opened the back door and found Celia and Bruce seated at the table.

Bruce glanced at me and turned back to Celia. "What are you saying? That I'm—"

She touched his arm.

He jerked away and stood up. "Mind your own fucking business." He looked at me. "Both of you. Get out of my fucking life!"

He grabbed his parka from the hook beside the door. The kitchen door slammed behind him as he left the rectory.

"You told him about his parents," I said.

"He had to be told. He needs to sort out his feelings about Ted and Lyle. Right now, he's overwhelmed by Ted's death."

I looked out the window. Bruce was gone. "You're not afraid...?"

"Let him walk off some steam," Celia said. "He's angry. Anger is a reaction to grief. He's just lost the only life he's known."

I stared at her. Bruce was a troubled man who'd been given information that would shatter anyone's world. I didn't think he could handle it.

"Bruce is a grown man. We need to respect that," she said. "He'll be back, probably with questions. I'll tell him what he wants to know, but I won't dump a lot of information on him."

I hoped she was right. I took a chair and turned my thoughts back to my problem. "My CEO paid a visit to the branch this morning," I said, and told her about Keith's plans for the branch.

"That's a big decision for you," she said when I'd finished.

"I don't know what to do."

"Sleep on it. Then drive to Toronto tomorrow and talk to the girls." She looked down at her hands that were clasped together on the table. "If you stay in Braeloch, I won't be around."

"Why? What's happened?"

"Remember the condoms I handed out to the teen group?"

"Ah...yes?"

"Word of that got around. All the way to the bishop."

"That means...?"

"I'm out of here."

"Dammit! I'll miss you."

"I'll go into the office tomorrow to tie up some loose ends, but I won't hold a service on Sunday. I'll meet Father Luke Rankin when he arrives on Monday, then I'll be off."

"Father Luke...?"

"A retired priest. I don't think he'll hand out condoms."

"What will you do?"

"A few days of R and R at our order's retreat house, then I'll wait for my next assignment." She placed a hand on mine. "Hey, I wasn't going to be around here forever. Father Brisebois will be back in a few weeks."

She smiled. "If you don't mind, I'll take Cleo with me."

"By all means." *One less thing to worry about.*

She pushed her chair back and stood up. "I'll go over to the Dominion Hotel. Bruce doesn't need to drown his sorrows."

"I'll come with you."

We walked down Main Street to the hotel. "Will Bruce stay on at the rectory when you're gone?" I asked.

"I hope Father Luke will let him stay. I'll talk to him about it. But when Father Brisebois comes back..." She shrugged.

"I imagine that Bruce will come into a fair bit of money when Ted's estate is settled," I said. "He could probably live in Ted's house right now."

"I don't think he'd do that."

"Well, he should be able to buy a home of his own down the road."

Bruce wasn't in the hotel bar or dining room.

"Has Bruce Stohl been in today?" I asked the young man I'd spoken to about Jamie.

"Yeah," he said. "He was here for a few minutes and left."

"Say where he was going?"

"Nope." He turned back to the tray of glasses he was sorting.

"Where else would he go?" I asked Celia outside the hotel. "Ted's place?"

"No. He wouldn't go there."

The neon lights of Joe's Diner caught my attention. "One more place to check. Then we'd better try Ted's."

At first glance through the window, the restaurant appeared to be empty. Then I saw two figures in a booth at the back of the room. I recognized Bruce's shaggy head. Soupy was seated across from him.

Celia caught my arm as I moved toward the door. "Let them be. It'll do Bruce good to talk to Soupy."

She took my arm and steered me toward the rectory.

CHAPTER THIRTY-THREE

I was up at seven the next morning. I roused Farah and Tommy, and we were on the road by eight-thirty. Twenty minutes later, Farah and Tommy had both nodded off, leaving me with my thoughts. By the time we headed down the Don Valley Parkway into the heart of Toronto, I'd mapped out what I planned to say to the girls.

I dropped Farah off at her apartment building, and drove Tommy to his grandmother's home. When I'd called her the night before, Norah Seaton had immediately agreed to take the boy until Sunday. She sounded like she hadn't seen him in a year.

Tracy, Laura and Jamie were at the house when I arrived. "What's this about, Mom?" Laura wanted to know. "I've got things to do today."

"Lunch first," I said. "I'm taking us to Milo's."

After we'd placed our orders at my favorite Toronto bistro, I leaned back in my chair. *How to begin?*

"I've been offered a job in Braeloch."

They looked at me speechless for a few moments.

Laura was the first to speak. "If you think I'm going up there—"

"Hear me out, Laura. You need to finish your school year here." I told them that Keith had asked me to run the branch and head operations in the company's north-central region. I couldn't resist mentioning that a vice-presidency was in the offing.

I turned to Tracy and Jamie. "Would you two stay at the house for the next few months?"

I held my breath while Tracy looked at Jamie. Jamie put an arm around her and nodded. "No problem, Pat. We'd be happy to."

I let out my breath. They'd keep Laura in line.

Our food arrived, but nobody started to eat. Laura looked glumly at her clubhouse sandwich. "The next few months, you said. And then what?"

I speared a piece of avocado in my California salad. "I'll have to see how it works out in Braeloch."

"And if it does?" Laura wanted to know.

"I'll put the house up for sale in July or August. You'll be off to Guelph at the end of the summer."

"The house?" She looked crestfallen.

Tracy didn't look happy either.

"We'll see what happens," I said. "Summer is months away. Now eat up, everyone."

Tracy picked up her fork. "What about Tommy?"

"Tommy's a resilient little guy. He'll cope with a new school, even this late in the year."

"And Norah?" Tracy asked.

I hadn't thought that one through yet. When Tommy came to live with us after his mother's death, I'd promised Norah that she would see her grandson regularly. If Tommy moved up north with me, he wouldn't be able to visit her every weekend.

"I'll talk to Norah," I said. "I'll see her this afternoon."

"My family's being torn apart," Laura said.

It was on the tip of my tongue to remind her of her plans to move in with Kyle. But the woebegone expression on her face made me bite back my words. At eighteen, Laura was still a child in many ways. *My baby!*

I reached across the table and took her hand. "It's early days, honey. We'll see what happens."

"That house is the only home I've ever known," she said. "I thought it would always be there. And you'd always be in it."

My heart twisted, and I gave her hand a squeeze. "Eat your lunch. You said you have things to do today."

Norah Seaton lived in a handsome red brick house in Rosedale, not far from Keith's home. The murder of Tommy's mother a few months earlier had sapped her already frail health. At first, she'd wanted Tommy to live with her but she soon realized that an active young boy was too much for her. I'd convinced her that he'd be happier in my home with other young people. How was I going to explain that I planned move up north and take Tommy with me?

Norah was seated in her favorite armchair with Gigi, her miniature white poodle, on her lap. The elderly woman's face was drawn and dark circles were etched under her eyes. But her white hair was stylishly coiffed, and she was smartly turned out in a blue tweed skirt and a blue cardigan. Tommy lay sprawled on the carpet watching a video on the wide-screen TV.

He looked up when I entered the room and flashed me a grin. Norah smiled at me, then her eyes rested on Tommy.

"His mother…" she said when I sat down beside her.

I took her hands in mine. It had only been months since her daughter's death. But does a mother ever get over the loss of her child?

We both sat there for a few moments looking at Tommy. He was the son of my late husband, Michael. I'd brought him into my home, and he'd become a son to me, too.

I told Norah about Keith's proposal. Her face became more drawn as I went on. "I'll have to see how it shakes out," I hastened to add. "But even if it doesn't work out, I'll need to be there until a new manager can take over."

"You'll leave your daughters here in the city?"

Make me feel guilty. "Tracy has a place of her own now. And Laura is in her last year of high school. She plans to go to the University of Guelph next year."

"And Tommy?"

I looked her in the eyes. "He can start at Braeloch Elementary School on Monday."

Norah didn't argue or reproach. She just sat there, her shoulders slumped, her eyes on Tommy, a defeated look on her face.

I tried to explain that if I didn't take the position in Braeloch, my career at Norris Cassidy would be over.

"Do what you have to do, dear," was all she said.

I told her I'd come by for Tommy after lunch the next day, and I let myself out of the house.

I stopped for groceries and wine on the way home. I'd promised the girls a bang-up dinner. Laura had told me to make it early because she had a party to go to. I threw myself into preparing coq au vin and mushroom risotto for Jamie, and tried to keep my attention on the tasks at hand. I'd made my decision.

But my mind was in overdrive. Tracy had a home with Jamie but they were in Toronto. And chances were that Laura would return to Toronto every other weekend. I wanted to be part of my girls' lives.

I liked the Glencoe Highlands. In less than two weeks, I'd come to know the area and many of its people. And with Tommy in school in Braeloch, I'd meet other parents.

Tommy! I thought of Norah and how sad she'd looked that afternoon. Tears welled in my eyes.

Tracy and Jamie came in at five-thirty and Laura turned up at a quarter to six. At six, I served hot hors d'oeuvres in front of the fireplace. Twenty minutes later we were seated at the dining room table. Jamie poured from the bottle of Châteauneuf du Pape that she and Tracy had brought.

"So what's your agenda here?" Laura asked when our plates were full. "You're going to try to convince us to go up north with you."

"Not at all," I said. "You have your education to complete, and Tracy has just started her law career. I've had a few more thoughts this afternoon. I'll run them by you after dinner."

While we ate, Tracy filled us in on a high-profile case her law firm had taken. She was still talking about it while Laura cleared the table, and I served coffee and crème brulé.

When I returned to the table with a bottle of Dom Pérignon, three pairs of eyes looked at me expectantly.

"I've given some more thought to Keith's proposal," I said. "It's a big decision."

Laura snorted.

"Laura, please," I said.

She rolled her eyes.

"I've decided not to take it. I want to stay in Toronto, close to the two of you." I smiled at Jamie. "And you, Jamie. Laura, you'll probably be back from Guelph some weekends. And Tommy needs to be here. It would break Norah's heart if she couldn't see him at least once a week."

"What about your job, Mom?" Tracy asked.

"That's a problem. My future at Norris Cassidy will be uncertain at best if I turn this down. So I've decided to go out on my own. I'll give financial advice at an hourly rate but I won't sell investment products. Clients can get those through brokers."

"And you won't have to sell the house!" Laura cried.

Tracy reached across the table and squeezed my hand.

"Good for you, Pat," Jamie said. "That takes courage."

"Yes." It had taken courage to come to this decision. But I knew I could do it. The house was paid for, and Michael and I had set money aside for the girls' education that Laura could draw on. Tommy had money that his mother had left him, and he'd inherit more when his grandmother died. I would live simply and build my business.

I smiled at them. "I'll be in Braeloch for a few months, but Tommy needs to finish his school year here. The three of you will have to look after him and Maxie while I'm away. Agreed?"

"No problem," Tracy said.

"Fine with me," Jamie added.

Laura slouched in her chair. "I guess." She heaved a dramatic sigh. "Okay."

"Tommy can spend his weekends with Norah so you'll be free to spend time with your friends, Laura," I said. "I'll try to get back here some weekends myself."

I passed champagne glasses around the table. Laura popped the cork, and Jamie filled the glasses from the bottle of Dom Pérignon.

"On Monday, I'll give notice that I'll be gone at the end of June, or earlier if my replacement can step in. And then..." I shrugged. "I'll see. I may take the summer off."

I raised my glass. "To our family."

We clinked glasses.

"And to new beginnings."

~ * ~

If you enjoyed this book, please consider writing a short review and posting it on Amazon, Goodreads and/or Barnes and Noble. Reviews are very helpful to other readers and are greatly appreciated by authors, especially me. When you post a review, drop me an email and let me know and I may feature part of it on my blog/site. Thank you. ~ Rosemary

http://www.rosemarymccracken.com/Contact.html

About the Author

Born and raised in Montreal, Rosemary McCracken has worked on newspapers across Canada as a reporter, arts writer and reviewer, editorial writer and editor. She is now a freelance journalist, specializing in personal finance and the financial services industry. She advocates greater protection for investors.

Rosemary's short fiction has been published by Room of One's Own Press, Kaleidoscope Books and Sisters in Crime Canada. *Safe Harbor*, her first suspense thriller, was shortlisted for Britain's Debut Dagger award in 2010, and released by Imajin Books in 2012. *Black Water* is the second book in the Pat Tierney series.

Rosemary lives with her husband in Toronto, and does much of her fiction writing at her stone cottage in Ontario's Haliburton Highlands.

IMAJIN BOOKS

Quality fiction beyond your wildest dreams

For your next eBook or paperback purchase, please visit:

www.imajinbooks.com

www.twitter.com/imajinbooks

www.facebook.com/imajinbooks

19433555R00121

Made in the USA
Charleston, SC
23 May 2013